For The Love Of FA$T Money

a novel

Wendell Shannon

Go Daddy Productions, Inc.

Baltimore * Maryland
Printed in U.S.A.

This is a work of fiction. Names, characters, places, and incidents are the products of the author's imagination or are used fictitiously. Any resemblance to actual events, locales, or person, living or dead, is entirely coincidental.

2004 Go Daddy Productions, Inc. Paperback Edition

Library of Congress Cataloging-in-Publication Data

2004109767

For the Love of Fast Money: a novel / Wendell Shannon

ISBN 0-9753938-0-4

GDP, Inc. website address: www.go-daddyproductions.com

Photos by Isaac Jones of Isaac Jones Photography (MD)

Cover Designs by Tonya Blackstone of Slammin Graphix

In Memoriam of W.S. Scott: Your departure from

This earth was never meant to happen.

This is written in apology for you becoming

A casualty in the Game we foolishly played.

This book is dedicated to my daughters,

LaDana Nicole Lucky

And

LaKierra Shanae Shannon

I Love You Both!

ACKNOWLEDGMENTS

For as long as I can remember, I have always dreamed of becoming an Alvin Ailey dancer or a writer. Attending Baltimore's School for the Arts was my plan. Unable to fulfill my first dream, I pursued and have now fulfilled my second by completing this first novel.

Our ancestors worked hard to survive the constant threats of execution. Our existence is due to your obedience to one key Commandment: "Be fruitful and multiply." Your unstoppable determination still gives us Life today. To my dad: R.I.P.

My love is my family. Margaret, my mother, your love is my *Gift in Life*. Willie (Butch), Clinton (*Patricia), Marilyn, Barbara (Bobbie Ann), Raymond, Rosailyn, Carolyn, Danny, Beverlyn, Brenda (*Marcus). A special dedication goes out to my baby boys Wendell and Shakeem. My beautiful grandbabies: Janae & Da'Naeja; Manley, Gary, Damara (Dee) Knox, Kweli Kebu Elgin, my niece Cassandra James in N. Carolina, and my many nieces and nephews. Can't forget the Shannon aunts and uncles, especially Uncle Jimmy, Captonia and Lil' Jimmy. I'm shouting out Theresa, Deshon, & Angelo and my adopted sister, Cassie (Cat). Jimbo, thanks for the years of love. Rosailyn, this one's for you! James McKelvin and Kanika McKerson—this is only the beginning!!! Keddrian & Herman congratulations on your new arrival.

*Mad love to Greg **"Wimp"** Washington*: You definitely carried me when you saved my life! You gave me another chance to make a difference. It is still you and I against all odds and I'm paving the way for you. Give me just a second partner. Within these pages lies our future: **One Love Between Two**.

A holy dedication goes to two heav'n sent Angels. My sister, **Beatrice Walker**, and **Darlene Elizabeth Lide** who both keep proving what *Love* is despite their departure. Darlene, you told me I could do it. I believed you and did! Keep being my guardian angels.

Westsiders' *R.I.P.* Tarik ***"lil Todd"*** Walker, Antwan ***"J.J."*** Lucky, Anthony ***"Tony"*** Madison, Lillian ***"Angel"*** Madison, Charles ***"Charlsie"*** Thomas, Melvin ***"Peppy"*** Sweat, Jr., Authur **"Cookie Man"** Ball, Anthony ***"Big Head Tony"*** Spence, Barbara Ann Canon, Tavon Jacobs, Michael Smith, Richard ***"Burt"*** Blake, Ricardo & Ray ***"Eggy"*** Bennett, Kevin ***"Huggy"*** Jones, Tony Kessler, Angelo **"Bey-Bey"** Howard, Bernadette Evans, Katie **"Ms. Katie"** Jones, Tonya Burton, ***"Cateye"*** Reggie, Albert Tate, Vernon ***"Black Vernon"*** Johnson, Derrick ***"Curly Head"*** Strickland, Geraldine Bonner, Roland Parker, Eric Bryant, Carlton **"Brother"** Robinson, Reggie Smith, **"Meecha"** Bowie, Julia Brown, Richard Hazel, Terry Davis, ***"Boo"*** Brown, Raycol Harris, Ricky ***"Muhammad"*** Wright, lil' Dwight Gilmore, DeAngelo ***"Lo"*** Ricks, and Breonco ***"Lil' Philly"*** Chase. Each one of you are gone but not forgotten.

Earl, Antwan, Dante' and Victoria Lyle: This shout-out is for your unselfish support—it came just when I needed it the most.

One Love *to those who placed me on their shoulders and carried me through*: Kevin Glasscho, Juan Wilson, James Pace, Antoine Lowery, David Clark, Charles Anderson, Dwight Gilmore, Michael Gray, Shelton Ball, Eric Johnson, Michael Evans, John Hayes, Joe & Rudy Edison, Marcellus Chambers, Emerson Baxter, Allen Finke, Derrick Taylor, Ronnie Hunt, Tyrone Rogers (R.I.P.), Terry Smith, Daniel Laurey, Wayne Brewton, Hercules Wms., Michael Coffee, Amin Abdullah, Frances Byrd, Peter Allen, Dexter Coy, Kurt & Karl Brooks, Jeffrey Fowlkes, Ronnie B., Hakim Wise, Carl Marine, Jean Naar, Tony & Greg Horne. *A special thanks goes out to* all my brothers--too many to name--who kept me free.

Real people with real hearts who reached me when ideas and determination was all I had left: Ms. Sarah (R.I.P), Betty & Janet Lucky, Ms. Mary, Conchetta, & Jolanda Comegys, Ms. Delores & Valerie Young-Wells, Tawanda Manigault, Jason & Alsinda Lide, Thalia Shannon & India Brown, Roslyn **"Peppi"** Smith, Sparkle S., Victoria *"Skinny Vickie"* Harris, Vicki Kane, Queen E. Stoops, Shannon Price, Patricia Simmons, Carolyn Gunn, and Betty Taylor. Crumpler, thanks for everything. A special thank-you goes out to all my sisters--too many to name--who grew inside of me.

A special thanks to my front cover crew: Marcy Crump (*www.theflywire.com*), Kenneth Hill, Marease **"Hakim"** Lucky, and Duane Alexander.

Great people who did great things: Anthony Leonard and my Downtown Southern Blues family, Ms. Clara Anthony & Richard Holland (Sepia, Sand & Sable Bookstore), Donald Comegys, Michael Ellerbe, and Charlene Baldwin from the Joseph H. Brown Jr. Funeral Home, P.A.

As you read you will see why real props goes to the real story-tellers of the streets like the Ojay's (CBS Records) for their song "For the love of money." Thanks to Jay-Z from the Roc-A-Fella Records family for bringing our real lives into a new truth.

Chapter 1

FAST MONEY

"I'm a hustler, Baby. /
I just want you to know. /
It ain't where I've been. /
But where I'm about to go!"

Jay-Z, "I'm a Hustler"
The Dynasty

It was her perfume. The place was jumping and I was crazy busy running the Platinum Party my partners and I had at Blue Crest North. It was like a Genesis Party, but ours was for hustlers, major players in the game. Money was coming from the door, pictures, and most of all, the bar. I had to be at four places at once.

As I was zooming from place to place, I caught a whiff of this scent and it stopped me in my tracks. It did something to me, stimulated my animal impulses and I was driven to find it. I took a deep breath, but the scent was fading. I looked around in a panic and saw her moving away. I moved a few steps closer and was bombarded with the most intensely pleasant, appealing and attracting fragrance.

I reached out to touch her, to turn her around but it was almost like she was expecting me. She turned around and smiled.

Johnny Gill said it best, "My! My! My!" She was a beauty that could outshine the sun. Her skin was golden brown and so smooth it looked like it would melt in your mouth. Her eyebrows were freshly done and shaped just right to accent her hair, which looked like silk, and every strand fell perfectly in place. I swear, she had those outstanding Kelly Price lips with the same type of shine from lip-gloss. Looking at that liner highlighting the curves of her lips set me on fire.

Lips like hers were the real reason two people joined at the mouth. I wanted to share a passionate kiss with a woman I didn't even know. I had no idea where she'd been or come from, but if I could get her to kiss me a thousand times it would never be enough.

Apparently her smile was not for me, because just as quickly she turned and continued walking away. I started after her but before I could take a step, I felt a hand on my shoulder. I turned my head and saw Black Face. He nodded and tilted his head slightly towards the bar.

"Damn! Not right now," I thought. *I headed in the direction of the bar with Black Face in tow. As we approached, he stopped me.*

"Man, I needed to get you away from her, and fast," he said.

"Why are you blockin' man?" I asked.

"Cause before you go up in there, you need to know the whole story." *He made a cross with his fingers and put it in front of me for emphasis and kept on speaking.*

"Wherever she is, trouble is right there too. I can tell you some stories about that chick. I don't want you hooking up with her."

"What kinds of stories can a woman that fine have?" I asked, catching a glimpse of her across the room.

It seemed like about ten men surrounded her and I could understand why. Black Face stepped to the left, blocking my view. The music volume kicked up a notch and the crowd went wild. Black Face moved in closer.

"Precious is not in the game man, but she makes it her business to know who is and to be with the ones who can give her the money and excitement. She gets them, rides their fame and fortune and moves on, knocking the brotha down on her way out the door," he said. "She learned from the best; Pretty schooled her in the game of hustling hustlers. They treated it like an art form and a science. Pretty taught Precious to play on the natural distrust between two men and to get them to compete with each other for her. In that game, there is nothing but war, and she gets the money that falls out in the process."

I leaned to look at her again, wondering how much Black Face was exaggerating. I have been dealing with Pretty and I know she's very sharp because she minds her own business, but she doesn't seem to cross hustlers that way. Maybe he had a point, but I wasn't agreeing just yet.

I trusted Black Face with my life, mostly because he had earned it. He'd saved me twice from prison and once from death in the wild streets of West Baltimore. Now he sounded like he was trying to save me from Precious.

But she was so beautiful. She turned my imagination on. That shapely woman excited me instinctively and forced my hidden intentions to show behind the smoke.

Black Face tapped me on the shoulder. "Are you listening to me man?" he asked and then shook his head as if he was getting a bit frustrated with my obsession for this woman he thinks is poison. "That's how one beef started over her. You remember Fat Peppy? Man she was the reason for his downfall. Precious was in love with money. Fat Peppy thought otherwise. She lured Peppy just like she did so many other men. Sex was her game, but he wasn't seeing that. It was right before his eyes. As he made the money, Precious would take it. Pussy is a powerful weapon. Anytime you have something that another man wants, like Precious did with him, you gain total control. And Precious was definitely in control!"

A woman passing by blew smoke in our direction and Black Face stopped talking only long enough to turn his head and wave the smoke away from his face. I wondered what he hoped to accomplish since the whole place was smoky. People were smoking just about everything from one corner of the club to the next--cigarettes, cigars and blunts. But the club was jumping and no one seemed to have a beef with anyone else. Things were really going smoothly. That's all that mattered tonight besides me meeting her. Black Face turned back to me and picked up right where he left off.

"Peppy couldn't resist her smell," he said. *That was certainly something I could relate to. A whiff of her was intoxicating.*

"He didn't believe that her shit stank! All Peppy thought about was those form fitting skirts she wore. It made him look twice when she wanted his undivided attention. All his friends knew how he melted as soon as she came around the block.

"Fat Peppy found her hard to resist when she would pout innocently and ask: 'Please? Could you do it for me, just this one time, Boo?'" *His poor imitation of a woman's voice made me laugh a little. I even pushed him off somewhat. That didn't stop him though, he just kept telling his story.*

"Peppy couldn't see the trouble he was in. He knew she had done this to other men before, but he thought those men were fools."

I couldn't argue with him because Peppy and I have the same idea. That thought ran through my mind briefly as I tried to turn the volume in my head up on the music and down on the sound of Black Face's story, without moving from the bar.

"She played him with sex," Black Face continued, "but all she wanted was his money. She had him so whipped! All he could think about was those pretty thongs that showed outside of her outfits. All she had to do was chew on her fingernails, suck on one of her fingers, whisper in his ear and call him Boo; he would get weak at the knees and do whatever."

He leaned close to my ear so he wouldn't have to shout. I was hoping he was getting closer to making his final points.

"But the street rumors are really about her sex, Fast Money. I heard her pussy taste like sweet honeydew and that it grabs a dope-dealer's dick as tight as a new leather glove one size too small. My boys said her *head* is so vicious a man's toes wouldn't just curl but would damn near break!" *I laughed out loud at that, but I knew the seriousness of what he was saying.* He got a lot louder and said, "Word is if she threw her pussy up in the air the damn thing would fly!"

"Okay. Okay. I got the point!"

Listening to Black Face I was beginning to think about how men got addicted to her. To a sane man, this woman would be someone to avoid, but I didn't think anything like that could happen to me. Knowing what she was, I was sure I couldn't get played.

I saw my man working the front door signaling to me because a young girl was trying to sneak in with fake ID. I excused myself from Black Face and walked over. All I had a chance to say was "No" to the underage teenager before he started again. He followed me across the floor, talking all the way.

"Fat Peppy had a good woman named Sista, but She wasn't good enough for his street image. She had been carrying him for years before he finally got his big break. She made sure he had cash and supported their relationship by working two jobs. But when he started making big money on the streets, Sista was no longer his only woman. He must have thought Precious was 'the one,' because he chose her. I guess he wanted to be able to say how he went out on a dose of Precious," Black Face said before becoming silent.

"DAMN!" Black Face shouted.

I glanced back and saw him pulling at his sleeve and a woman apologizing for bumping his arm with her cigarette. I kept on moving and thought I'd lose him. A few seconds later, he was back in my ear continuing with his story as if he never lost a beat.

"Check this out Money, Fat Peppy was hustling with some dudes from Hilton and Baltimore Streets. Almost everyday he worked the sub shop corner, where area crews met to get paper. He had homeboys like Byrd and Cateye, who were partners in his posse. They were responsible for bringing him into the area. Hooking up with them kept him out of a turf war.

"On this particular day, he and his crew were getting paid. Business was jumping; the three of them pulled in almost $3,500 in two hours. Precious decided that Fat Peppy needed a break from the streets and told him to meet her on the corner so he could get a quickie in the truck she was driving. Of course, money was her motive for meeting him on the street like that. The black tinted windows on her Cadillac hid them perfectly.

"Byrd and Cateye continued selling while he got his groove on. There was nothing they wouldn't do for Fat Peppy, nothing. He pumped them up in the business, and they were loyal, but he was fucking up. He was taking care of business, just the wrong kind at that particular moment."

I kept moving but Black Face knew he had my ear. The place was packed, wall-to-wall people, drinking, smoking and dancing. The air was thick and the room lights were so dim that on the dance floor, the cigarettes and other smoking paraphernalia people held over their heads glowed and swirled like fireflies as their bodies bounced to the music. Everybody was dressed to impress with every major designer represented. But bodies were so close people could no longer admire the clothes going by unless they brushed up against them.

I looked towards the door and my guy was signaling me again. I made a quick move in that direction, but Black Face was not done and he kept talking.

"In the midst of a $500 transaction going down, at least two masked guys began putting down some thunderous gunfire. It was so loud, Byrd and Cateye could not tell which direction it was coming from. So far it had been a quiet productive day--no one had tried to rob them, they hadn't had a bad exchange with anyone--so they had no idea who was shooting or why. But any gunshot is trouble, so they booked.

"They thought Peppy was out of harm's way in the truck with Precious, but they ran that way to be sure anyway. They were moving so fast they passed the truck. It didn't look damaged, so they assumed Peppy was okay although he didn't respond to them immediately. As they waited to see what was happening and for him to check on them, they realized one or both of them could have been killed and nobody would have known why. He put good pussy before his crew."

I shook my head. "Fat Peppy was whipped," I thought. At the door, Black Face waited while I grabbed some of the door money. He picked up again, so I had him follow me upstairs to the office where I could count more of the money we were bringing in. He continued talking as we made our way up the steps.

"Byrd wanted to straighten that shit. He wanted to go back down to the corner and take care of the situation. He and Cateye were shocked by Peppy's reaction.

"Peppy looked at Byrd like Baltimore City rats do trespassers in their alleys after sundown. Then he got loud and said, 'Man, I ain't stupid. Ain't nothing that good out here, no money or nothing--to make me wanna run to trouble. I told you before this is a thinkin' man's game. You gotta let opportunity find you, not traps. Going after them would be a trap. And I *ain't* trying to get us killed by just giving our lives away. It's trouble and we know it, so let's just take the loss. Besides, if it ain't right we just have to go back home down Westside.'"

"He conveniently left out how he wasn't there for his men. He should have been telling himself the same thing about Precious. She was a trap and his crew knew it. Not only should Fat Peppy have gone back down Westside, he should have gone home to Sista, the woman he really needed. Precious wasn't right for him or his business and that was only one of the signs. Now he needed to hear his own prophetic speech since he didn't understand the deep shit he had gotten himself into messing with her."

Ordinarily, I wouldn't have listened to this much talk from anyone on a night like this one. I was too busy for this buzzing in my ear, but deep inside I knew I needed this information, just like I knew I wasn't like Fat Peppy. I knew I could taste the treat and not get addicted to it, I thought. Although I kept counting the money and didn't respond, he knew I heard him 'cause I hadn't cut him off or sent him away.

"Fat Peppy didn't have to go out like he did," Black Face said. "That sucker bought her a house and couldn't go to it unless he called first. Picture that, Fast Money."

"What?" I said in shock before stopping half way up the steps to look back at Black Face.

"Imagine buying a broad that you supposed to be dealing with a house and you can't have keys—and you have to call before and let her know you're coming. Now, dat's stupid, but he did it anyway."

"I feel you because I wouldn't have either," I told him.

"Fat Peppy could have gone to almost anyone for information and advice on Precious. He could have asked her second husband, Dollar Bill, or the play toy after him, Caine. Her first husband, Petey, would have been no help because he had been killed and the word is that she set him up. According to the streets, she was the only one who knew where his safe house was and after his hit, cash and kilos were left. Petey didn't listen either.

"Dollar Bill married Precious not long after Petey was murdered. Now, he made her a real ghetto superstar by covering her in jewels, fancy clothes and expensive cars. It seemed like Dollar wanted to show Precious he could give her the life she had with Petey. But Petey was a hard act to follow. Dollar hustled extra hard and took a lot of risks to make big money for himself and his new wife.

"Dollar was known as the 'I'll give my woman anything' type of husband. He paid good money for her and provided for her, and she had to be totally for him. At shows he had her there in the finest wear. On his trips, some vacations and other business, she was right there. You know the funny thing about them two, Fast Money?"

"What's that?"

"Dollar was once involved with Precious' sister."

"He was either a helluva player or a damn fool," I said in response.

"That didn't matter to either one of them. Whatever was required of her, she played her part well. In return, Dollar supplied all she needed. Precious added the finishing touches to his image as a dealer. She helped attract more people, by word of mouth, to his business. You know how women talk in hair salons. She did that for her man because she knew those women listening would run straight to tell their men in the game what she relayed. She was always bragging. Her husband this; her husband that! The best way to advertise business and success in the streets was through the beauty salons. So Precious did her part, in bed and out, until he got knocked off!

"What took a long time to build fell apart in no time when the Feds came crashing in on Dollar Bill. Oh, yea. He's in federal prison serving a *life sentence* for operating a continual criminal enterprise under sections 848(a) and 848(b) of the criminal code. He became known as a kingpin, and Precious' status on the streets was elevated because of it.

"The houses he had were in her name. She no longer needed her jailbird husband for a secure place to stay. He'd already given her those. She was in possession of more clothes than she could ever wear. As a matter of fact, she called his family to come get his clothes and other personal things she couldn't use because the items took up too much closet space. Ice could be no colder than the way she sent his ass packing!

"But she kept the jewelry and the three cars. One, a 600 Mercedes Benz, had just been purchased with cash money. She didn't need him. She could easily find another hustler to help drive her white and cream twin turbo Porsche with the 20"Anzio rims and the Lincoln Navigator SUV."

I closed the door behind us as we stepped inside the office. Black Face grabbed a chair and made himself comfortable as I sat behind the desk. I had no time to count it all. I simply separated the hundreds, fifties and twenties and put it in the safe. It would be easier to hear him now and perhaps he would be able to finish more quickly. I had resigned myself to hearing this whole story and it was a good thing. Black Face didn't miss a beat.

"Word was Dollar needed his wife to get him a top-notch lawyer who could make big money deals behind the scenes. He was looking for a dirty judge, one who was willing to make deals to get paid. He needed his wife for access to the money he had stacked up for bail and attorneys if something like this would happen. He told her where the emergency cash was and what it was for. Aside from Dollar, she was the only person who knew. He had no other way of getting to it besides trusting her to do the right thing. That's where he made his big mistake.

"She told him finding a lawyer was his problem. After his arrest and conviction she had a simple message. 'You shouldn't have gotten locked up in the first place! You're supposed to be my husband. Yet, you are leaving me out here all alone! I'm keeping all the money. I have to take care of myself now. You deal with that jail shit! That's your fucking problem, not mine!' "

Now he really had my attention. This was getting deep.

"Precious wasn't for that collect call, sending packages, or the waiting in long ass jail lines for visits shit. And with control of all the money it didn't take her long to cancel his ass out of existence. He was dismissed. Gone! He did get one more thing from her - divorce papers. She really didn't care about him. It was all about the money. He just never knew it until it was too late.

"Everybody knew or had heard about their marriage, even Fat Peppy. He knew. That didn't matter. People hated her for that 'cruddy' shit, especially Bill. He was a good man, but that didn't seem to count. What made everybody so mad was how she acted like their luv never happened.

"Man, I'm telling you, it only took a minute for her to bait Caine in. That dude was known for all the cocaine he was able to sell. It was on again for her; the money, cars and the lifestyle were all one package. Caine ended up pretty much like Dollar Bill. Bill had a long run, while Caine, on the other hand, blew up too fast trying to satisfy her. He tried to do his thing to finance the life she was known for, but her phones were tapped. He had no idea what he was into with her and she didn't tell him. Word has it she knew her phones were probably tapped from all the other big time dudes she had been dealing with. He ended up facing state and federal charges for interstate drug trafficking, possession with the intent to distribute heroin and cocaine, a handgun violation, and, *to add insult to injury*, the IRS wanted his money."

"The I.R.S. would have fun with Precious," I thought, "if they knew about her?" She had all of what Petey left when he died, what Dollar Bill wanted her to have if anything happened to him, and what Caine left by force. She had everything authorities were looking for!"

"Dat's what I'm trying to tell you, Fast Money."

I was impressed, which I am sure was not what Black Face had in mind when he started telling me this shit. I smiled. There was a knock on the door and a barmaid stuck her head in.

"Fast Money, they need you at the bar for a minute," she said and was gone.

"I'll be right back," I told Black Face. "Wait here for me."

I needed a few moments to clear my head and digest what he had been sharing with me. He didn't seem to be about to run out of tales to stories about this woman. I was getting a headache from what was going on inside my head. One side was saying, "stay away" and the other said: "You are too smart to get caught like the other guys."

Somewhere inside I could hear my mom's voice saying, like she did when I first got into the life, "Boy, you are special, but you are not special enough to stand in quicksand and not get buried." Of course, I have spent everyday since then trying to prove that statement wrong, and so far, so good. I saw how it could apply to Precious, but that just made her more desirable. On the way back to the office, I looked around for Precious. It was early morning now and the crowd was starting to thin a little. After a quick look, I figured she was gone for the night, but I looked through the crowd again anyway and was rewarded for my instinct. She was dancing near her table. It was full of untouched drinks. I noticed my man Rock and Outlaw held her table area. I didn't know they knew Precious.

She didn't notice me, even though I was near and I had a chance to get a good long look at her. I sized her up and could tell she was worth my investment, even with all I had been told. I was definitely going to have her. I stood there imagining her vibrating like a battery-operated toy. For the right price, I would eventually have her working her body on top of mine like she did on the dance floor.

Dolce & Gabbana made the short skirt set Precious had on. Her expensive outfit showed all body. She had abs like Janet Jackson's and some tattoos that would fit perfectly in a Lycra tennis outfit designed by Serena. The one on her tummy was a black panther with four claws digging in her skin. Each red mark represented blood from imaginary flesh wounds. On her titty was a juicy read heart that reads: ***MY HEART BELONGS TO The Almighty Dollar, Dollar Bill Y'all****.*

Glittering from her nails were studs costing at least forty dollars to remove and replace. How can she not be seen as a precious jewel in every man's eye with all that material beauty? Her done up feet were excellent for showing off her Louis Vuitton footwear.

As I stood there watching her, I imagined running my fingers all over her bare body. I wanted to taste her sweet smelling body oils. I wanted her and she wasn't even mine. I knew if I ever had the chance to enter her flesh I would go deep and travel far and get lost in her pleasures. Precious was exciting as shit!

She is a woman every man's son would luv to have. Satan himself fashioned her after reading my mind. He gave life to my fantasies in order to tempt me to the dark side. She even had this devilish look that made her more exotic.

My head was spinning again. I was falling under her intoxicating spell and we hadn't even met. Despite everything Black Face had told me to this point, I was still fantasizing about this woman, still considering taking a chance with her, knowing it would never be about me but only about the money.

I went back to the office and Black Face continued his story without missing a beat.

"You see what I'm saying Money, that broad didn't even wait to see what would and could happen to those brotha's before writing them off and moving on. And Caine, that damn fool, he went down again trying to satisfy her demands. When he got back to the streets, he began hustling again to finance Precious' lavish lifestyle, despite the fact that she probably had more bank than he did at the time. For his efforts, the Feds revoked his bond and took him back into custody.

"Someone who cared brought all this information about Precious to Fat Peppy's attention. He had been warned that even though Dollar and Caine managed to survive the challenges of the dangerous streets every day. Each one of them fell victim to a common enemy. A common enemy that lived right under their roof; yet, they didn't realize it!

"Her looks attracted his attention, but she caught him with the sex. After giving him a 'tester' that snatched him off his feet, Peppy kept coming back. Everyone could see he was whipped and how he was going down. He financed his own downfall with each dollar he gave her, and he gave her a lot. There was to be no return on his investment in her and yet Peppy couldn't see it.

"Fast Money," he said, waiting until I made complete eye contact with him, "I need you to see it man. I've had your back too many times, and saved it, to loose you to this one without a fight. Are you hearing me?"

"I hear you man. I understand," I snapped. *And I did understand and was hearing every word, but I wasn't listening. All I had seen and smelled had touched a place deep inside me and I knew I wasn't going to rest until I had satisfied my curiosity. At the same time I had to be realistic. I already had a plan. It would be fun. That's it and that's all.* I heard my mother's words again, but to shut them out I said, "So what happened to Fat Peppy? So far, it just seems like he had a few lapses in judgment."

"I wish that was all man," said Black Face, who stood and began pacing the room. "It was sort of ironic what happened to him. For starters, most of his loved ones left him because he continued to ignore the facts and they couldn't keep worrying about him since he was making no effort to save himself. After a while he started taking really stupid chances. Before it all ended, Peppy knew there would be trouble. He wore Dollar Bill's jewelry and drove his cars. He just didn't care.

"Rumor had it that Pretty dropped the dime on the situation to Dollar. She had a history with Dollar that started down the projects. Nobody really knew the details, but Pretty told the Kingpin what was going on—and he made the call on Fat Peppy's life. Precious had crossed Dollar, but it was Fat Peppy who had to pay. All of Dollar's loyal homeboys made it their business to hunt down Peppy. I was looking for him, too. In the end, it was Dollar's cream twin turbo Porsche that became Fat Peppy's casket after being shot by a lone gunman. Within days of Peppy's death, Precious was out searching for who she'd work her pussy hustle on next. And Pretty was right there beside her."

Black Face stood up and went to the door. Before he opened it he said, "Fast Money, I love you homey. Don't be the next Fat Peppy. She's going to catch you under her spell. I know what you are up to; I can see it in your eyes. Just remember, what you don't see is what you always get."

After he was gone, I just sat there for a few moments. The music was still playing, but it was quieter and slower. The party was breaking up. I took a moment to really ponder all I had just heard about this woman and how she would sacrifice men for money to finance her comfort. That woman was poison; I knew it. Her big butt and tricky smile told it all. She was a hustler chaser and she made choices. But he should have realized I was a hustler. I took chances and I wanted her to know it wasn't about where I'd been. Her interest would be more of where I was about to go! I'm blowing up. One day she would choose me. That made us a match.

She was a challenge, a sweet challenge I was dying to taste. Of course, based on what Black Face just said, she was a challenge I could die from tasting. Despite all that, I just had to have her. I had heard him, but I had to see for myself. I just had to remember to never let the chase catch me, no matter how unbelievably good it became.

Not too many women captured my attention the way Precious did. I mean, I thought about her more times than I care to admit. I had met that special someone and I started to experience excitement just thinking about her. My thoughts were so strong. I immediately started to plan what I would say to her--if we ever met again. She was beautiful and for however long, I just wanted to be with her. Even though Baltimore is a small town, I didn't know if I would ever get another chance to see her. But, if what Black Face said was true, she already knew who I was and with my growing reputation, she would be putting herself in position to meet me . . .

Chapter 2

PRECIOUS

"Gotta get dat' paper, dawg /
gotta touch dat' /
love dat' paper, dawg."

Jay-Z,"Paper Chase"
Hard Knock Life Vol. 2

"Damn," I thought, as I turned away from Fast Money like I wasn't really smiling at him. I wasn't trying to be anywhere near Black Face. He's so close with his boys that you would think he was an identical twin. Black Face was the same way when he was a part of my ex-husband's crew. He was working for Dollar Bill before he got knocked off with the feds and for all practical purposes, still is. He won't let go of the past. He was the only one looking out for Bill. Black Face was sending money orders, clothes and making periodic visits. He hates me though. Still, Black gets on my nerves like he did back then. To me, what was in the past is still there. Having a present relationship with Dollar Bill and Black Face is too much. That's why I walked away as soon as he was arrested.

I looked back and saw Fast Money head towards the bar with Black Face on his heels. I followed their path to the bar with my eyes and saw them settle in for conversation.

"Shit," I said aloud. The brother standing next to me turned around and looked at me. "That wasn't for you, Sweetie," I shouted over the noise of the crowd and the music so he'd understand. "He got some nerve. He's probably talking about me because I wouldn't get with his ass." The guy just shook his head and walked away without a word. I walked over to lean against the wall.

Smoke was thick in the room and while the smell doesn't bother me, I don't smoke. But it was too thick to see into the room and I wanted to know what Black Face was up to, so as soon as I spotted a place to sit down, I moved to a table and sat so I could watch the bar.

I hipped the waitress to my standing order for the evening—club soda with a twist of lime and lots of ice before I told her to charge for an apple martini when anyone else was buying and to keep the change. Before she could walk away, two guys sat down at the table with me.

"Aren't you Precious?" said the first hustler to sit down. *I gave him a good look and liked what I saw.* "Hey, Baby. I'm Rock and this is Outlaw," he said as he extended his hand.

He was wearing the right clothes—a Versace outfit with a jazzy look and the perfect shoes to match—but his diamond jewelry gave away his true status. His jewelry was not only fly, but also expensive. I glanced at his partner, who smiled at me. He was neat and clean with some Atlanta style of clothes on. Tonight was not theirs—at least not with me. I had my eyes on someone already.

"Who's asking?" I said, smiling without real interest in either of them. *I had to rethink that real quickly. They would do for now, so I could watch Black Face and Fast Money without too many distractions. For a front, I would keep them around to cover so it won't look like I'm here alone. Maybe this will get Fast Money's attention.*

I kept my eye on him and saw him look my way a few times. Then he headed towards the door with Black Face on his heels, talking a mile a minute. I wished I knew what he was saying, but I was sure it was about me. And if I was right, then what he was saying also was not good. What really pissed me off about that was how most people just felt like they could assume they knew me. Without asking me a thing, they just seemed to think it was okay to talk about me like they knew everything that had happened to me and how I felt. I have a history of messing with big hustlers, and they just hate on that. I can't help how attracted hustlers are to me.

They laced me with diamonds, cars, and their dreams, and what I'm worth. It's an image thing for them on the streets. I don't need a relationship. It's about me getting dat' paper because I love and gotta have it! That's why our situations were arrangements. You never knew how long they would last.

The thing is, if Black Face or anybody would just talk to me, I would tell them everything they want to know—somewhat! I'm not telling anybody all of my business. But at this point, I bet no one would even believe me. So what if I do chase the root of all evil. I chase it just like everybody else. Different means to get money, but the same end. Whatdahell!

Man, my waitress was getting phat, because even though Outlaw and Rock were still sitting at the table talking at me, men from around the room were sending me drinks. There must have been at least eight untouched glasses on the table and one $350 bottle of Cristal some guy had sent with his name and number on a hundred dollar bill. It was a waste because I don't even drink that stuff. I told Stacey, my waitress, to resell it when she was ready. Anyway, Outlaw was going on about how fine I was and how happy it made him feel being in my company, the standard weak rap. Black Face and Fast Money had been upstairs in the office for a good while, so I decided to come up with another plan for meeting Fast Money.

I danced a few times with Outlaw and his partner. Being here tonight wasn't a total waste because I saw him watching me when he came back downstairs. Just for him, I made my phat ass jiggle. I pointed my body in his direction. I thought he'd come out on the dance floor, but that didn't happen. For a few minutes he just watched. Tonight was really over. So, I decided to leave without too much notice.

I finally made it home. Standing in the foyer of the house I once shared with Dollar Bill, I wondered, as I did every time I came home, why I didn't move to a new place. Despite the men who have shared my company since Dollar was here with me, I am still haunted by our memories in this house. I remember when we moved in. I wanted this house because it had so many rooms with big windows to let in the sunshine. I would talk non-stop about a day when we would fill those rooms with children when he had time to listen. He was so busy gett'n that money. Dollar Bill was always on the move. That's the part of the game I don't like.

My nose filled with lilac. The scent from the bushes blooming beside the door gets caught in the entranceway when the door is closed. Dollar used to say the smell reminded him of me and he wanted to smell it when he came home whether I was there waiting or not.

I closed my eyes and remembered how much fun we had decorating. Traveling to Arizona to get special order ceramic tile for the foyer, that are hand painted with our design and shopping for color coordinated Corian tabletop colors for the kitchen and stained cabinets made this house a home. Oh, and I can't forget about the arguments we had about whether to use African art or that Ikea contemporary crap. I reached out and touched Shaka, the six-foot tall statue by the steps, smiling at how the evidence showed who won that forty-five hundred dollar argument.

I shook my head to clear those thoughts away. When will I get tired of going through this every time I come home and move away? I glanced into the living room, more out of habit than really looking for anything, as I started up the steps, taking my shoes off as I went. The phone rang. It quickly stopped. By the time I reached the top, I was naked. I dropped my smoky clothes in the dry cleaning bin outside the bedroom door and the rest in the laundry chute in the wall. I love that thing. It was the best idea the people who built this house had. I hate hauling laundry.

The phone rang again. The caller ID let me know I didn't want to talk to this tired hustler named Squeaky Kyle from off of Hilton Street. With no money, he was still chasing the dream. He had some nerve trying to out-and-out use me to get on. Finally, one rumor about me was true. I do put my men on, if they can't do it on their own.

After taking a quick shower, I slid under the blankets of my king size bed, nestling deep in the midst of the seven pillows that stay there. Just as my body heat warmed the sheets and my head found the sweet spot in the pillow my phone rang again. I glanced at the clock-- 4:15 a.m.–and grabbed the phone. "Hello," I said.

"Gurl, was that party tough or what?" said the voice on the phone. "I saw you there but I didn't get over to holla' at you before you left."

"Who is this?"

"What you mean, who is this? How do you not know who the hell this is!"

"Well, for starters, I was asleep and it is four-something in the morning. Of course, that should probably tell me who this is, since only a few people would have enough damn nerve to call me this early to talk about that platinum party. I didn't see you there Pretty, anyway!"

"Well, it's about time you got it right," she snapped. "And I'm not surprised that you didn't see me. You were so busy trying to avoid those two hustlers you were sitting with and all those drinks on your table. They got it! We spend it! Gurl, you are still the same. I always told you to play them before they play you."

I laughed too. "My waitress got paid on that bar. She was so phat, she even offered me a cut as I was leaving. Plus, she was too funny. But those nuts at my table, they weren't getting' any play. They were cover for me. I was trying to meet Fast Money."

"Good choice. He is on his way. His business is blowin' up and he's looking for folks to help him expand. You know that's who I'm with from time-to-time. He's not at the top of his game yet, but so far, nothing has been stoppin' his rise to the top. Sometimes going to New York with him tells it all—you know what I mean?"

I propped up my pillows and settled in for a conversation. "That's what I heard too. Did you see him tonight? He looked good and he was running the show in there."

"Yeah, I know. Gurl, I'm telling you—he's the shit right now. Plus, he pays well. So what did he say to you?" Pretty asked.

"Well, I am sure he was going to say something, but Black Face showed up. You know how he is! He tied him up for the rest of the night, talking into his ear."

"Well, you know how Black Face is loyal to Dollar Bill."

"I know, but this seemed different somehow. Like it was not just about blocking my shot for Dollar, but like they were friends or something."

"They might be. So you never spoke to him at all?" Pretty asked.

"I watched him watching this ass--gurl, but he didn't get a chance to say anything. I left, although I could tell he wanted to. I would've been up on him, but that damn Black Face."

"You want me to introduce you?"

"Naw, I don't want to do it like that."

"So how are you going to meet him?"

"I don't know yet. I'm not gonna be like Stella—trying to get my groove back. I'm gonna get my groove on and he'll be my toy. I gotta get that paper he's making. That's why I'll find a way to catch him in my web!"

"Trick, I know your ass will find a way. You always do!" she said with a sneaky laugh. "I would've introduced your hot ass if I would've known. You know I got you, Precious."

"There will be a next time, Pretty. Ain't nothing change. I still practice *W.I.F.M.* Every time I see one of those hustlers the first thing I think of is W*hat's In it For Me*! I gotta get more money, power and dat' shit they call respect."

"You ain't shit, but you still my gurl!"

"Gurl, bye! I'm going back to sleep," I said before hanging up.

Police Blotter

Woman dies in shooting at Westside night club

A 28-year old West Baltimore woman died of a single gunshot wound suffered when two groups began firing weapons. Several witnesses said the single mother of two young children had just left a party at the *Blue Crest North* with friends around 3:55am when loud gunfire erupted in the parking lot. She was hit in the face and died upon arrival at Shock Trauma, officials said.

Several late model cars sped from the scene. Investigating officers have no motive and no suspects. Anyone with information is asked to call Homicide Division.

Chapter 3

FAST MONEY

"What do you say…
Me and your Chloe glasses /
go somewhere private so we
can discuss fashion?"

Jay-Z, "I'm a Hustler"
The Dynasty

I was hosting another platinum party, but it was extra special. This one was for my birthday. As people rolled into the Baltimore Grand, it was clear they all knew what was required: what you had on had to be top-of-the-line, fit right and be expensive. You couldn't be seen in the clothes you wore at the last event or even anything that looked similar to it.

This was a night of East Coast style even New York fashion shows couldn't compete with. All around was Roc-A-Wear, Mark Jacobs, Armani, Chanel, Sean John, Chloe, Christian Dior, Fendi, Prada, Gucci, DKNY, Dolce & Gabbana, Versace and more. In one-way or another, these millionaires had clothed everybody inside.

There was nothing low-key about this party. The vibe was

just like Odell's parties when his club on North Avenue was jumping. That was a while ago, but anyone who has ever been there remembers the slogan: "You'll know if you belong!"

That was true of this party, too. Only the hardest hustlers who survived another day in the life were in the club. Like celebrities showing up at exclusive Hollywood events, folks arrived in stretch limousines, Bentleys, Rolls-Royces, and in the finest sports cars money can buy. This was big shit and it was my night.

Dealers in the loop attended these affairs and it showed. East coast all-stars from every major, money-making city showed what cash and dope dreams were made of. Bling was everywhere. Watches made by Rolex, Cartier, and Movados were flashing on every wrist. And the diamonds, reflecting off the special track lighting we put up, made the ceiling look like the night sky, sparkling everywhere.

Those weren't the only stars inside that night. New York hip-hop artists from different record labels moved through the crowd showing all of what glitters isn't gold. Instead it was platinum! This kind of jewelry had been featured in Don Diva magazines I read all the time. One day I'll make the front cover for Baltimore.

Jay, Kim, and X showed up with their entourage. The D.C. crowd was in the house, showing money, as were players from New Jersey and Philly. Everybody thought they should be in the spotlight position, trying to see and be seen.

Events like this identified the man, his woman and his wallet. The money spent could be spotted everywhere. Couples were out in force showing off what the life could get you. This was the nightlife all of us hustled so hard during the day to prepare for. Everybody getting paid, anybody looking for a lucky connect, was there.

I felt good, especially since I looked more expensive than my pockets were really worth. I had rolled up in my black Cadillac truck. It was so unique. Everybody in town could identify it from a distance. I had the only one in town with soft gray and black two-tone leather interior. It had heated seats, but my trademark was the expensive Sprewell 22 inch-rims. This feature set mine apart from the rest.

I was wearing a $450 cashmere v-neck sweater by Sean John under my $1,500 rayon and cotton, one button suit by Giorgio Armani. My $3,000 full-length Sean John leather coat complimented my "big block" alligator shoes by Mezlan. With my glasses and a belt by Kenneth Cole, looking in the mirror had me feeling "fresh dressed like a million bucks." I could have been ripped right out of GQ Magazine.

What really set my look off was my "connects" matching platinum watch and bracelet set. I went by Rock's house last night because I knew he had these pieces.

"What's up Rock?" I asked, as I stepped inside his house.

"Nothing much homey. You the man with money! You blowing up my brotha he said as we laughed and gave each other daps.

"Yo, you remember the diamond-studded pieces you bought behind that robbery/homicide near the market?"

"Yeah," he said. "You really came through for me that night, helping me get the cash to make the deal."

"You actually did them a favor, Rock. Those boys had trouble big time on their hands. Bad enough they had hit the right mark, coming away with over $300,000 in diamond jewelry. But them crazy fools shot down the storeowner and an innocent bystander. They bought themselves a whole lot of trouble. They would never have been able to move that stuff quick enough through regular channels." *We laughed as we reminisce on the way we acquired that loot.*

"You're right about that, Fast Money. That heist was big news—fast! Cops were all over it, especially with the heat trickling downhill from the governor, to the mayor, to the chief of police. Everyone was leaning on the cops; those guys had to move that jewelry in a hurry or the whole thing would have been for nothing."

"No shit. They had to drop that stuff cheap, get as much

cash as possible and roll out of state."

"Those shots made this sale like buying stock on the day the market crashed. You came through with my $15,000 in a heartbeat and I got to take advantage of the $71,000 markdown with an ounce of cocaine thrown in for good measure."

"You mind if I hold them pieces to wear to the party tomorrow?" I asked.

"No problem, Fast Money." He answered, getting up quickly and heading toward his room safe.

But it was a problem the night we got them from the stick-up boys. While Rock went to get the pieces, I thought back to what happened...

I owed Rock 15 gran' for product, but when he called, I hadn't picked up my return from the streets yet. I called Outlaw to get the money quick, but he was out. Alize, his pregnant baby mother, was in and she took care of business. Now she had the smarts of a true businesswoman.

"I'll have it ready for you in 15 minutes, Fast Money," she said after I told her what I needed. When I arrived in 10, she had it counted and ready for me to cop and bop. That was why I really preferred dealing with her. I had given Outlaw a sweet hustle; lucky for him his woman was prepared to step in as he slowed down.

"Outlaw," I said as I laid out the strategy for him, "only sell the cocaine by the gram. No vials and no containers." I was getting the cocaine from Rock for $600 an ounce. "You sell each gram for $30."

Actually, only the first 28 sold were whole grams, which excited the crowd. The rest were ¾ of a gram, which meant he could get 35 bags from each ounce after the first, bringing a profit of $450 per ounce.

"If you work it like that," I told him, "selling 20 ounces in a few days brings us $9,000 in profit."

Outlaw and his crew had the hustle for the streets. I heard him selling: "Hitting in the hole. Hitting in the hole. No ones! No change! Straight line on the wall! Money out!" They did good business. It was just a shame Outlaw couldn't handle the back end as well. Guess that's why it was good he had Alize working with him out of her apartment.

Her quick turn around that night put Rock in position to cop those pieces real quick. Opportunity like that only comes around once. We risked a lot that night, cause those pieces were covered in blood . . .

"Here you go, Yo," he said handing me the pieces wrapped up.

Rock handing me the jewelry brought me back to the present, but did not diminish my amazement. He had gotten them for me just like that. No lectures, no questions about when he'd get it back. No balking, like he was going to wear them. Most guys with expensive jewelry like that guard it like the Secret Service does the President's wife. Rock was different. That jewelry put my look right over the top.

It was my birthday and I was flying high. The place was packed. You couldn't move without bumping up against someone. People were four deep all the way around the bar and it was loud, loud, loud. The scents of hundreds of different expensive colognes and perfumes where everywhere, but even that wasn't enough to keep you from following your nose to the buffet.

That table was as impressive as the clothing worn by hustlers who showed up to eat it. The brother I hired to cater had outdone himself. Even I was impressed and considering the picture I'd painted for him, I'd been unsure I would be satisfied. The spread stretched the length of two walls, with big punch fountains on each end. Along with the usual beef roast and ham, freshly sliced by line chefs as each diner walked up, there were these huge crab balls, steamed and grilled shrimp, seafood and surf-n'-turf kabobs, soft-shelled crab, a variety of cheeses, scallop and lobster dishes, baked and fried fish of four or five different kinds and, raw and cooked vegetables from broccoli to zucchini. Off to the right was the dessert table, a cake propped up in the middle, surrounded by an unreal number and variety of pies, cakes, cobblers, and puddings.

"Hey main man," said the guy matching his lady in Robert Cavalli lambskins coats, "is this your show?"

"Yeah, it is," I said.

"I thought so. That cake looks just like you," he said and pointed towards the dessert table. "Happy birthday man. This party is the place to be!"

His girl started chanting. "Ain't no party like a Fast Money party because his *Big Baller parties* don't stop."

"Thanks, y'all. I'm feeling that too." I thought to myself, whoever said it ain't no love in the city?

I was pleased and continued to appreciate the talent of the caterer. In the center of the food table was an ice sculpture of an exotic dancer spinning around a pole. I never knew such a thing could be created in ice. The chef surrounded it with every kind of fruit – apple, kiwi, nectarine, honeydew, cantaloupe, and watermelon slices, tangerine and orange sections, red and green grapes, banana sections, strawberries, passion fruit and pomegranate seeds. I had not been convinced the ice sculpture was a good idea, but the caterer insisted and now I was glad he had.

I was staring at how that artistry set the whole thing off and was feeling good. A party like this, with so many players flocking and looking for an opportunity, is a small reflection of the benefits of being high up in the drug game. Even though I was carrying it higher than I really was, the party made it clear I was on the way up. Image is everything at one of these parties, and this one was making mine. I didn't have these feelings often and decided to enjoy them.

As I stood there, taking it all in, the vision that had been haunting me since the last party crossed my line of sight.

Seeing her again boosted my already high spirits. I was filled with a "the worlds is yours" feeling and she saw it. She was gorgeous and being sexy was her gift. I already knew she had transformed her gift into a weapon. When she pointed her sexiness at me I became her prisoner. A quick glance confirmed what I already knew. Almost every man in the club was following her with his eyes, waiting for a chance to get at her.

The cake made it obvious that this was my party, but I had to do something besides act like I was playing the game to get her attention. At the end of the night, I wanted her to be mine. Then I had the perfect idea. I needed to get up close.

I made my way through the crowd to the bar. I thought I was going to have to elbow a few people, but I saw recognition in the eyes of folks who moved out of my way. I guess displaying my mug on that cake was a good thing. When I got the bartender's attention I pointed to Precious.

"What's she drinking?" I asked. "I know what Pretty is having."

He looked to see who I was referring to. "Sex with legs", he jokingly answered. *I nodded.* "Hold on, bro. I'll find out."

He walked over to another bartender and pointed at Precious. I saw the other guy nod his head and say something. Then my bartender walked back.

"Apple martini," he said.

"Send her a double from Fast Money," I said, handing him two C-notes, "and give Pretty another double shot of Hennessy and coke. You can spread the change around."

"Sure thing," he said.

A few moments later, Precious lifted her glass to me. I could see Pretty waving in the background. It was on . . . and I had to handle my business. I was nervous as shit, but I kept telling myself to "be like Nike and just do it."

I had everything planned out in my mind. I figured it would be OK for her to quickly luv me and leave like Black Face told me. Luv and life itself in the fast lane is always like that. It tricks you – causing you to chase an enjoyable pain until it or you burn out. So many have fallen off because of the chase. You-know-what-I'm sayin'?

That didn't bother me though. Pretty taught her like Marcella did me. I was taught to get it—whatever "it" was.

Never let the chase of it catch me! Once caught—it's over!

Since the last time I saw her, I'd been wondering what I would say to her when we finally spoke. I had studied my catch lines and thought I was ready. I made my way over to where she was. My walk wasn't right and I forgot my lines.

"Hey, Fast Money—meet my girlfriend, Precious," Pretty said.

"Precious, this is the man—Fast Money himself," she said to Precious while guiding her hand toward mine.

It didn't help that the party was very loud. The room had speakers on the floor and in the ceiling. It was blanketed in surround sound. She had seen me coming and just as I opened my mouth to speak, the DJ kicked a new track and everybody screamed. Damn, she looked good in those Chloe glasses. The first words I said, I couldn't even hear. I took her hand and led her to the front where we could talk in private.

I tried again. "Good to see you here, Fast Money," I said. "I'm Precious."

She smiled and I realized what I'd said. At that moment, I wished the floor could just open up and take me in. I couldn't believe I messed up so badly. It's funny because I've never been through this before.

"I know who you are, Fast Money," she said. "Happy birthday."

"Thank you." *At least this time I got the right words out.*

"You're welcome, and thanks for the drink. This is a really nice party you're having. You do do things large, hah?"

"I do what I can to make things happen," I said, trying to sound cool and redeem myself.

"Well, from the looks of this evening, you can do a lot," she said. *Precious looked me over. She didn't even try to hide her appraisal. She didn't stop smiling either. I must have passed because she reached out for my hand to look at the diamond studded watch and bracelet.*

It was my job to stay in control and I was failing miserably. My nose was full of the smell of her perfume. My heart doesn't't usually bleed, but lust was pouring out of every hole in my body. She was good and I knew it. I wanted Precious to take over and take me on the ride of my life and I think she knew it too. As I showed my weakness, in the midst of such a large evening, she must have sensed something, like a dollar opportunity.

"Oh," she said. "Look at this. Is the time on this beautiful watch right?"

"Yes."

"Well, I have to be rolling, but I hate to cut our conversation short. Perhaps we could do it again sometime?"

"Yeah, that would be good," I said. *And before I could ask for her phone number, she let go of my hand, took a card from her purse and put it into my palm, enclosing it in both of hers. I stopped hearing, smelling or seeing anything but her. That gentle touch was turning me out. Even though there was nothing sexual about it, I got rock hard just thinking about it.*

I couldn't look back directly at her. I was suddenly a bit shy. I glanced her way with a nervous smile, but I did nothing to remove my hand from her grasp. I took a deep breath and looked into her eyes, trying not to give in to my fears. I thought I would get lost in those dark brown orbs. She was so beautiful and I was convinced that if she was looking for a sucker, then I was her fool!

Almost without my noticing, she let me go, rubbed her hand in a brushing motion on my shoulder and walked away. As she disappeared into the crowd, I slowly became aware again of the other people, sounds and smells in the room. I looked at the card she gave me. It took all my energy not to call right then, just to leave a message and hear her voice on the machine. But I knew that doing anything fast would spoil all I imagined. I had to wait. The card had her numbers on it with a written message.

It read: "I've been waiting to meet you, too, Fast Money. Call soon. Precious."

Confidential

Internal Police Memo

At 10:15 PM neighborhood informant #519 reported that two armed gunmen with masks forced their way into Alize Wilson's Hollins Street apartment looking for her boyfriend, cocaine, and money. Outlaw, the suspect in question, was said to be the target of this failed kidnapping and ransom attempt.

However, he was not at home. Alize, a 24 year-old pregnant A/A female, was pistol-whipped several times before having a large caliber handgun placed inside her mouth. No leads, no arrest.

***End of Report*.**

Chapter 4

FAST MONEY

"I should've known better."
Jay-Z, "Streets is Talking"
The Dynasty

"Hello."

"Yo, Precious. I'm caught out here and I can't get with you this evening."

"That's okay Fast Money," she said. "I understand your business. Give me a call when you get in. I'll be waiting for you."

"I know I've cancelled on you a lot," I said, looking around at the traffic flying down North Avenue. "I want us to get together, but shit keeps happening. I thought we would have kicked it by now. I know Pretty told you already, but I'm giving you my word. Tonight is the night. We will be gettin' together, okay?"

"I'm patient, baby. I know it'll happen."

Her voice was soft and sultry and hearing her say she was patient, made me picture her naked on my bed. I could see her face buried in one of my soft pillows. Her shiny ass would be raised high in the air, waiting for me to bring her rough, doggy-style pleasure. I wanted her nasty ass right then, but there was no way I could get away. With all my energy, I wanted her. I knew I had to be more careful, but, for right now, I'm staying true to the game on these streets.

"Can you make it later tonight?" I asked before thinking about what I was saying.

"My whole night was set aside for you. Did you have something in mind for later?"

"Why don't you come to my house tonight?"

"That's fine with me. What time?"

"As soon as I'm heading in, I'll call you and send a car to bring you over."

"Please. With all of these cars, I can drive myself. Just tell me where."

I gave her the address and hung up. Well, this was it, no more stalling. It didn't matter anymore if I still had doubts. But it was more than that. My business was really taking off and it was making my schedule crazy. I had to be more careful since I spent all my time in the streets. It was worth it because those stamped bags of Dynasty were taking the streets by storm. Junkies were chasing us like an animal would its prey. Money was coming from everywhere and my pockets were getting fat. Pretty soon, that image I projected at the party would be the real one, and not just some props.

As crazy as I was about Precious without ever having spent time with her, it was probably a good thing we had been missing each other. It gave me a chance to project some self-control, to make it seem like I could resist her. I knew that wasn't true, and if I had any hope that it was, tonight was proof. That short exchange caused a bulge along my right thigh that was impossible to hide.

It was a busy night on the street, but the noise faded into the background as I thought about what I had done by telling Precious where I lived. It was a foolish move, bringing a stranger to the place where I lay my head. I should've known better! I know I was wrong since this was a rule I learned early and had never broken, until now. For whatever reason, I wasn't too concerned about the risk or the rules; I let Precious' voice and my other head lead me into temptation.

"Yo, Fast Money, we gotta roll," Outlaw said out the open window of my Cadillac truck. *We were not trying to fly under the radar this evening. Our business was somewhat legit. We swung by Outlaw's to pick up some money and then over to a garage on Harford Road. I had a connection that was going to hook Outlaw up with a new ride. His woman, Alize, was going to be using the other one; he felt too exposed in it. Too many people knew it was him--especially after what happened to Alize in their apartment building. Eventually he'd replace her car, too. He had to get low first.*

Business was starting to blow up for us and it was important that Outlaw be able to get around incognito. We had a quick quick stop. Things were going better than expected. In, out and bam, he was on his way to Norma Jean's down the Block for show-and-tell, but I was heading home.

As I pulled into my driveway, I dialed Precious.

"Hello," she said, her voice caressing my cheek as softly as the fur on top of a kitten's head.

"It's Fast Money. Give me an hour to get settled in and then come on out."

"Done. See ya!"

Standing inside the door I looked around. I didn't know whether an hour was enough time to prepare for the precious treat I was going to get, but I was sure going to try. I started by spreading scented candles. An old friend, Sheila, had turned me onto how those fresh smells excited human sexuality.

I had several different scents to spread around, all designed to excite passion and enhance seduction--just the mood I wanted for the evening. In each room, I placed one of my square candles. These were the pillar candles, the pink ones of ylang-ylang and mimosa, the yellow ones of neroi and rose, and the white ones of ginseng and ginger. I lit each room and turned off the lights before moving to the next. When I was finished, the whole house had this soft glow.

I took a quick shower. Dolce & Gabbana cologne was perfect for a night like tonight. I then put on my silk Winnie-the-Pooh loose brief-boxers to make sure my nature was unobstructed while experiencing Precious' magic. I dressed in my silk pajamas with matching robe--a marbled-navy blue. The color was so dark it could be mistaken for black, with a woven bright blue, yellow and red trim around the wrists, ankles, waistline of the shirt and pants, robe arms, lapels and the sash.

I ran a brush through my hair and took a look at myself. I caught a glimpse of the clock in the mirror and realized I only had a few minutes to finish my preparations. As I walked through the house, those fragrances from the candles began working on me, heightening my awareness of the events to come. I loaded the CD player with all the Luther I could find. His CDs always make the heat of passion in the night just right. I couldn't spend this time enjoying her without Luther being a part of our intimate night. I set the player to random and his mellow voice rolled out of every speaker in the house, singing "Here and Now."

"Everything is just right," I thought. *The doorbell rang. Precious was on time. History was in the making and I was ready.*

She was wearing a lightweight full-length coat, and was barelegged wearing red snakeskin shoes with 5-inch heels.

"Let me get that coat," I said as she looked around the foyer. *A barely perceptible nod of the head was all the answer I got. That same scent that made me follow her around the night I first saw her, wafted gently past my nose as she began to unbutton her coat.*

She worked from bottom to top, revealing with each button just how little she was wearing underneath. She looked directly at me as she opened each one, flashing me that beautiful smile. Her dark brown hair fell gently over her shoulders, bouncing lightly as her arms moved. I hadn't realized I'd stopped breathing. She threw her shoulders back, tossed her hair and slid the coat off her arms. All this revealed the sexiest red and black, leather and lace lingerie I'd ever seen. Luther started singing "So Amazing." I love me some Luther.

In that moment I had the craziest thought: "Lace covers everything and conceals nothing." I believed I was only reeling in my head, when I realized I'd taken a step backward to catch my balance. "Wow" does not come close to describing how sensational this woman looked in that outfit. My erection was flying at full mast and was hard as a roll of quarters.

On each leg she wore a black lace garter. These were attached to her teddy, which was framed in black leather and covered in red lace. The front laced up just underneath her breasts with a red leather strap. She had on a matching black and red, leather and lace bra. The teddy barely covered her breasts, and a matching front lace thong.

She glanced down at my crotch and said, "I take it you like my outfit."

I shook my head. I was feeling helpless like a poor kid in a Mondawmin Mall clothing store. Finally, I had the opportunity to play with my dream girl-toy, but I'm too overwhelmed to move. Lucky for me--Precious was ready and willing to take control. She gave me her coat and kissed me deeply. I felt her tongue moving around in my mouth. I got another surprise. Precious had a tongue ring. My excitement was so hard. Each heartbeat sent a racing pulse in my Pooh briefs. Throbbing against Pooh started to hurt a little.

As I hung her coat on the rack, Precious found her way to the music, blowing out candles and turning on lights as she went. I was dizzy with arousal-- all the sights, sounds and smells were doing a job on me; yet, Precious seemed perfectly in control. She switched off the Luther and turned on the radio to 92Q's club music. I had tried to fool myself into thinking it was a night of romance, but she was a straight shooter. It was on!

Precious slid her body up against mine as smoothly as oil and kissed me again. Her lace was as rough on my palms as my silk was smooth beneath hers. She rubbed her hands slowly down my chest to my Winnie the Pooh area. I felt her fingers on my flesh, first my stomach and then my chest, lingering on my nipples, rolling and flicking them with a gentle roughness.

I kissed her neck, nibbling softly at the tip of her jawbone, and my nose was filled with her signature scent. I was overwhelmed by all of this. She was really here and I would finally see if any of the rumors were true.

Precious worked me out of my pajamas with her mouth, opening each button from my shirt down to the three straining to hold my bottoms shut. As they fell to the floor, Precious, on her knees, stuck her tongue, then her lips into my boxers and kissed the saluting tip of my pulsating woman pleaser.

I guided Precious to the nearest chair and sat down, mostly to keep from falling down and looking weak. She took Pooh away, wrapped her hand around the base of my intense response and licked me like I was ice cream on a cone. As her head went up, down and around my bone and her hair brushed back and forth against my tummy and thighs, I watched as her thong separated one phat cheek from the other. I held onto the arms of my chair as she washed me down with that piece of jewelry in her mouth. She rotated it against the underside of my penis head, then swirled it all the way around.

"Ooooohhhh," I said and leaned my head back, ready to reward her expertise with what comes next. *But that was not her plan and as easily as she turned me out, she slowed me down. This was just the beginning of this roller-coaster ride.*

"Don't stop," I said, in a cracked voice that had no energy behind it.

"I'm not stopping," she said energetically. *She kissed the inside of my thigh with her tongue ring and intentionally teased what hangs between.* "It's just not time for you to have that pleasure yet. I want you to have all this, Fast Money."

She put me entirely in her mouth and forced a part of me to disappear. I'm sure my eyes were bulging 'cause I'm larger than average. I groaned, this long, low groan, before I could stop myself. My body frame trembled as she guided me deeper and deeper down her throat. The warm, wetness of her mouth kept my attention while she eased her hand along the sides on my thighs. This woman was giving me something I could really feel. Damn, her fingertips found my--Whoooa!! I jumped forward in shock. She tried to reward me by sucking it all in again, but this homey don't play that ass-and-finger game.

She had turned me out so far, I couldn't think. She flicked and bit and sucked on me until I wanted to scream and when I didn't think I could help myself, she backed off and denied me the ultimate once more. I wanted to release this steam she created inside of me. Not even making that finger mistake stopped my night.

The music controlled the fast pace. All of a sudden Precious stopped. She started to get up as if to leave.

"Hell no," I said. "Don't leave me like this."

She put her finger to my lips. "Shhhhh," she whispered. Her other hand was embracing Poo. "I'm not going to leave it like this forever. I feel real comfortable being with you--so I have more in store!"

She stood there feeling the music. Precious started dancing to the beat in front of me, gyrating body parts and rubbing her hands all over her body. She leaned over me, letting her breasts come to rest in front of my face and I kissed each one, sucking quickly on the nipples through the lace. She moved away and turned her butt to me. In time with the music, she made her cheeks clap. Then she made them jiggle, first the left and then the right, and then alternating. Finally, she vibrated both at will. El Dorado's adult entertainment show would be her only competition.

Moving to the beat, she unlaced her teddy and tossed it. It landed atop what extended from my body. She swayed over to the corner of the room, kicking off her shoes and tossing her bra in my direction along the way. She leaned her back against the wall and while massaging her breasts, she unlaced her thong, opening it just enough to get her hand inside.

She stuck her finger in her mouth, sucking it like she had me all along. When it was good and wet, she seductively slid her thong to the side. She stuck her fingers between her legs. Precious licked her tongue at me slowly and gyrated against the wall while passionately stroking her clit. She repeated the act with two fingers and rolled her pelvis to further stimulate herself. I wanted to join in, but she didn't need my help. Despite my lack of participation, her show was keeping me hot. I fought the urge to pleasure myself; I wanted Precious to do it. I couldn't wait for the next stage to begin.

She moaned in delight as she plunged her fingers deeper into her hot zone. Her once smooth movements become jerky as her excitement heightened. She would bring herself to the edge and stop each time to increase the pleasure. She spanked her naked ass while talking to herself.

"Hit that ass harder—harder Daddy," she begged.

I was on fire watching her!

"Take it from me, Daddy!" she screamed even louder.

I took off Poo! I was ready to go.

"This hot pussy is so gooood!" she said continuing to stroke herself in the corner. *Precious worked those fingers, squeezing her legs in between strokes. She reached that point when she started jerking wildly and slowly let her back slide down the wall.*

She took her thong completely off and walked over to sit on the top of the desk. With her legs spread wide, she motioned for me to come over. She spun around and leaned her back into my hairy chest, then wordlessly guided my hands, instructing me how to pleasure her as well as she had done herself. When she'd come again, we moved our game to the carpeted floor. She started by licking and nibbling on me from head to toe like I was a lollipop. My nipples hardened into buttons, and by the time she reached my feet and sucked on my big toes, I was completely hooked.

Precious lowered herself onto me; wet human pleasure dripped from her onto my stomach as she slid down. My body twitched and jerked inside her warm, wet hole, as it tried to adjust to being exactly where it wanted to all evening. I held onto her breasts as we bounced and gyrated on the floor. I tried sucking her nipples, but we were so sweaty they kept slipping out of my mouth. Our bodies made a sloshing sound as I pushed myself deeply inside of her, then out of her, over and over again. I took a deep breath; the smell of sex in the room caused me to want to rewind.

We rolled over so she was on her back and I plunged as deep as I could go. I pushed forward as Precious pushed back. She let out a low groan.

"Ahh Baby," she said, her words riding on heavy, jagged breaths. "You are in this--" *She stopped talking in mid-sentence and closed her eyes. Her head went back letting her hair fly free before trying to finish.* "So deep."

She wrapped her legs around my back, locking them at the ankles and put her arms around my neck, pulling my body flat onto hers and holding me there.

"Oooohhhh," she groaned again. "That's it . . . so deep . . . that's it."

It may have been it, but it wasn't anything I was doing. The force had me literally bouncing against the sides of her hole. It was so wet, warm, soft, tight . . . I wanted to move and plunge, but I knew that any more stimulation would interrupt it all and I never wanted it to end. With every tap of my hard thrust, it got wetter in there. Finally, my greedy nature got the best of me and I pushed my rear into the air and plunged deep into her. She cried out and I knew it wasn't pain because I felt her whole body give in. Her muscles tightened as it drained my strength. I was being flooded like the streets after a rainstorm. I didn't think it was possible to get more juice in there and all of it overwhelmed me.

Ivory colored excitement came shooting from me. I felt my body contracting while my chest jumped out of control. I looked at Precious. Her eyes were closed tightly as she got lost in her own pleasure. Everything about me became limp as I rode the wave of my orgasm.

"Damn," I thought, "I didn't use a condom. Shit! I broke two of my important rules tonight."

Those thoughts didn't last long because Precious was right back at it. It had to be the way she nibbled on me in little bites, touching my back, and licking my nipples that set me off. I was ready again. That's when I flipped her on her stomach and started with two fingers to see just how much she could handle in her secret cave.

I enjoyed getting that freaky sex from her. She used her talents to get me off two more times!! Man, I kid and joke, but I can't lie. She made love to me over and over that night like she knew what I needed. She had me hooked long before we stopped. Precious had me chasing her passion; she controlled all of me. We were like two animals, acting out of instinct, furiously pursuing pleasure. I'd never come three times in a night before; I didn't think it was possible until she coaxed the last one out of me with her tongue ring. I was so spent and satisfied, I didn't know whether I was coming or going.

I knew I was out of my mind later on that morning. Precious was using me to get what she wanted. I knew that, but I must've been crazy when I started thinking about doing something with her bath water other than letting it go down the drain. I was on dangerous ground and really didn't care. But I knew I had to be careful because her luv was said to be like fire.

Chapter 5

FAST MONEY

"Cocaine whiter now. /
Operation is sweet. /
Whole game tighter now. /
Moving a brick a week."
Jay-Z, "Coming of Age (Da Sequel)"
Hard Knock Life Vol. 2
(Feat. Memphis Bleek)

Ring! Ring!

"Speak to me," I said into my cell phone.

"Big Toney here. Can we meet, 10 minutes, at the spot?"

"Done," I answered.

I hung up and as I walked to the truck, I wondered what he wanted to see me about. He spoke to me in fast code setting up this sit-down. I really didn't completely understand. See, Big Toney and I had a run-in on the strip a while back. It was a good idea actually having a neutral space where we could be alone and work out problems so our West Baltimore competition would not end in blood and ruin business for both of us. Big Toney knew I would be on him and his crews whenever the opportunity presented itself, 'cause I was blowin' up. He knew if we kept hostilities down, there was enough to share and more reasons for me to keep my crews off his ass.

He and I pulled in the parking lot at the same time. Bennigan's on Security Boulevard was outside both our areas and public enough to be safe. According to our preset rules, he called the meeting so he fed the jukebox to add noise in case either of us was being policed. He also picked our seating--bar, table or booth--which indicated what kind of business we would be discussing, how long the meeting would be, and whether the possibility existed for someone to join us.

When he picked a booth, I was really intrigued. I didn't know someone else would be joining us, but he was acting with a strange caution. This move put my danger sign on blink. If he was crossing me, then I was tricked! I knew I should have picked the Breakfast Spot on Edmondson Avenue, but now it was too late. I had to go with the flow.

We sat down. The waitress came promptly and Big Toney ordered a Guinness Stout. I ordered my signature drink, a masturbating butterfly.

"How do you make that?" the waitress asked. "The bartender may know, but in case he's never heard of it before, telling me will keep your drinks from being delayed."

I smiled to myself. Every time I order one this happens. I probably should have been more on the down low, but it had been a while and I was trying to settle in for what Big Toney was bringing.

"A jigger each of Midori, Absolute Vodka and sour mix, and a splash of Sprite. Mix well and then float a shot of Jaeger on top."

"You mind if I have him make one for me, too?" she asked.

"Naw, but if you're not a drinker, make sure you have a designated driver," I said to her. "I'm not trying to be responsible for a car accident. Plus, you just earned yourself a big tip!"

We were sitting in the smoking section and the back of our booth was against the hallway to the kitchen and restrooms. Big Toney was seated facing the door; I had my back against the side of the booth so my back wasn't to the door; I could see it to the right. For a Thursday evening, there were quite a few people, but it wasn't what I'd call packed. Near the bar, a group was forming. A crowd of people seemed to be celebrating something after work. The stragglers to this party needed to get a move on because the folks in the house were getting an impressive lead in the alcohol department. Alcohol blood levels were starting to show. They were loud, laughing and falling all over each other. Three women were dancing together without a man.

I purposely did not initiate conversation. He called the meeting and when the time was right, he would talk. He lit a cigarette and offered me one, but I wasn't interested. I didn't want smoke interrupting the smell of food from the kitchen. It's a shame to sit that close to the preparations and not get the perks.

The waitress brought our drinks, a bowl of pretzels and a menu.

"I'll put these menus here in case you decide to order later," she said. "And he knew how to make a Masturbating Butterfly."

Big Toney took a drag on his beer and belched real loud. You could tell he was from the hood. I enjoyed my drink trying to keep up with him. After we finished our first round, the waitress cleared the table.

"Give us another round," I said to our waitress.

"Yo, you remember that guy from New York I was with at your party, Dominican, real flashy?' he asked.

"Man, that night was a blur," I said. "I know you were there, but there were so many people in that place I can't remember who I saw."

"You had to see him that night. You don't remember?"

"Naw, I don't remember."

"Well, he is looking for another out-of-town pipeline. That's why I got you here so you can listen to his deal . . . I think it might interest you."

"Oh, yea. I hear that," I said before I took a sip of my new drink. *That bartender knew his stuff. The liquor mixture socked it to my mouth and then to my throat. It was just like I remembered it.*

I wasn't much for small talk, and I gathered, neither was Big Toney, because he just sipped his drink and smoked cigarettes while we waited. I didn't think we would be waiting long. As I savored that masturbating butterfly, I wondered if a butterfly did it anything like Precious did, and if those two might share a technique or two.

We had become a somewhat regular thing. Every time we got together the sex was hot and sloppy, the kind I could still smell in the house a full day later, but I was beginning to see that sex had a cost.

It wasn't out of the ordinary for me to pay for sex. I'd done it before, but not all the time. It wasn't the normal way it happened for me, but I understood the process, and set the price high on this one.

I remember after our first night together. I asked her if she was okay as we were saying our goodbyes. If she had needed or wanted some money, all she had to do was say so. I had several hundred dollars, ready for her to play herself. I didn't know what she might need, but I knew she was going to the hairdresser because she and I sweated her hair out. She was also going to the nail shop, because she broke one of her fingernails on my desk during one of her wild performances.

I thought she'd want the money and I was more than surprised when she turned me down. She had that "get the money" look in her eyes. When she turned me down the next couple of times, I began to think that maybe something else, something more, was going on between us, not just a business transaction. What she did was smart. Saying 'no,' she became more valuable to me. Turning down the money, she made me think that my reports of her being a hustler chaser were all wrong. I liked that thought and it blinded me to her real motives for a while. When I started paying, though, it cost me big.

Once she wanted to go on a shopping spree with Pretty. I was paying Pretty a whole lot for what she was doing for me, so Pretty had shopping money. Precious told me she only had twenty-five hundred dollars. She played like she was okay with that amount, but I knew how she shopped. Her comments were a hint that it was time to play my part in our situation. Once again, I messed up and overplayed my hand, counting out thirty big Franklin faces. Three more thousand is not a little bit of cash, but it was a small price to pay for her. How she made me feel was worth double that. Little did I know that the ease with which I handed over the cash that time would set the stage for each session to come.

I was carrying it large, no doubt I was doing well, but damn, Precious was cutting into my wallet. And it didn't help that despite how well my crews and I were doing, I couldn't get over the hump to the big time. I needed a better source because Rock's prices were high. I was trying to make a dollar out of fifteen cents, but his prices kept it just out of reach. I knew that six flips were ninety cents and I needed just one more to crack that dollar, but it never worked out that way.

Rock was always the man with the money, not me. I was doing too much grinding, but I kept doing business with him because I didn't find a better way. Debts and Precious kept me pushing with Rock, but the big time kept me hungry and had me looking for another way. That thought brought me back to Big Toney's proposition.

As I was finishing off my drink, I saw a guy fitting Big Toney's description heading for our booth. I glanced at Big Toney. His look told me that this was the guy. I looked at the brother again, but he didn't look familiar to me. He was on the short side, not overly handsome, but he was clean. His clothes were expensive, but the look he put together was purposely understated. He had dressed carefully. The only thing on him that might attract special attention was the blinding platinum bracelet he wore on his right arm. It caught my eye as he walked toward us. He put his arm out to keep a lady at the bar from knocking him over and I saw it again. It was definitely a custom made piece, with a shine that was definitely a platinum chain-link, about 3 inches wide, made of 4 thick chains connected to each other in a yellow diamond setting.

"Fast Money, meet Raul," Big Toney said as Raul slid into the booth beside him. "Raul, this is Fast Money."

He stuck his hand across the table and I shook it.

"Thanks for your time Amigo," Raul said. "We can get a lot of fuckin' money, but I need your help-- just like you need mine! But before we get into that, let's get the waitress over here to refresh your drink and get me started."

Big Toney signaled for the waitress and she zipped right over.

"Another masturbating butterfly," I said. "And give my compliments to the bartender."

"What is a masturbating butterfly?" Raul asked.

"I'm not messing with that! The name don't sound right. It sounds like something you take when you can't shit right!" said Big Toney. "Just give me another Guinness Stout."

"Now, that's something I'm going to pass on," I said.

"He don't know something good when he sees it," the waitress said. "The drink has Absolute Vodka, Midori, Sour Mix, Sprite and Jaeger in it. I have never tasted one, but the bartender told me it would put hair on my chest. And I believe him!"

"I got turned onto them a few years ago," I said, "but I don't drink them regularly. You definitely take a hit, but if you like adventure . . ."

"Give me one of those . . ." Raul said and looked at me.

"Masturbating butterfly," I said.

"Masturbating butterfly. Thanks," Raul said.

While we waited for the drinks, Raul talked.

"I really like Baltimore, but I don't travel this way often. There are some great hotels and restaurants here. New York is still better, though. I was here for your party; I am surprised I've had a chance to get back here so soon. I was impressed, my man, by the way. That's why I asked for you."

"Thanks. I always try to represent West Baltimore and put us on the map for big baller parties."

"I bought my last two cars here. And I'm picking-up a Miata tomorrow to drive it back to New York. Big Toney will keep my Mercedes for now. I'll send for that later. I was supposed to be going window-shopping, but I couldn't resist. I have a soft spot for small sports cars."

The restaurant was getting busy. That group at the bar was over the edge. Some were being loud, but many were straight up drunk. Staff was flying back and forth into the kitchen and I was starting to smell real food coming out. The smell made me hungrier, but I decided against ordering because I wanted to get to the reason for this meeting.

The drinks arrived; the waitress quickly left them. It was too crowded to dwell and flirt at a table now. Raul took a cautious sip of his drink.

"Splataklacklow!" Raul said. "That drink packs a mean punch. But it's good. Masturbating butterfly . . . I'll have to remember that. Wheeeew!"

I took a long drag on my drink and waited to hear where this was going. Raul set his drink down and, suddenly, he was all business.

"I asked Big Toney if he knew of another good connection in Baltimore for the stuff I want to move," Raul said. "I've got a sweet set-up, but without some contacts outside of New York, it won't work. I don't know if he told you or not, but I get so much shit that I have to use the scales they weigh the fuckin' whales with!"

"That's why I came to you Fast Money," said Big Toney, "because your crews are blowing up and we're both in West Baltimore territory. I was thinking we both could move large amounts of dope and cocaine."

He was right. Baltimore was No. 1 in so many categories – teen pregnancy, prostitution, sexually transmitted diseases, HIV infection, drug addiction, homicide—and all of it, in one way or another, was related to drugs. Here, death from drug overdoses exceeded homicides. The city was big on providing help, but with sixty thousand or so addicts in the methadone maintenance program alone, it was clear no one was making a real dent in the problem.

"I want to take full advantage of the demand for heroin and cocaine in Baltimore," said Raul. "My operation is sweet! I can get you as much high-grade dope as you can handle at the best possible prices. With a high volume area like Baltimore to sell it in, we can all get paid, large. Comprende?"

I didn't take any time to think about it. My whole game would be tighter now. "I'm in!"

Raul waved his hand. This dude was a big boy because Big Toney dropped two fifties on the table to cover the tab and rolled out. He didn't need to stay for this part of the meeting. The details of my connection with Raul were not his concern.

"Here's the deal. I can front you the merchandise. I'll do that for twenty thousand a brick. This is your start price until you start moving a lot more. Twenty g's leaves you open to front for your crews and still get crazy money for yourself. I'll pull as much as you can handle from my source. You push that shit, but you-gotta-come-get-it!" Raul said.

Our meeting was about the details from then on. All I knew was twenty thousand a brick was a steal. Raul wanted to make all the arrangements on where I would stay when picking up merchandise and how we would connect. He provided me with codes so I would know where to go when he called me. I could barely concentrate on what he was saying, 'cause I was thinking about all the fast money that was about to come my way.

Even charging my crews a premium price—between twenty-five to thirty g's--would still be below what it would cost on the streets. None of them had twenty-nine g's to spend in town. The best part is not having them use their own money up front. We would all be blowing up with this deal. I couldn't believe my luck. No more getting close for me! This deal could put me over and move me into the big time for real. We talked a little while longer, and then left.

It was only a few days after the meeting when I got my first call from Raul. He hit me up on my cell.

"Paso, Fast Money?"

"What's happening?"

"Leona and I want to see you soon--like tomorrow! This time I have a big surprise for you. You'll understand."

Just that quickly our conversation was over. Raul was careful on the phone and kept all conversations brief. But what he said was enough to know that he'd made arrangements for me at the Hemsley Towers hotel and that information on the drop would reach me there.

The first two transactions went off perfectly. I was thrown the third time when I saw 'NYPD' evidence logos on the bricks. Raul picked up on it and smiled. I looked at him, my entire face a question and said, "New York Police Department? What the fuck is going on up here! What, Raul—if that's your real name! You trying to set me up--NYPD!"

"My friend, Big Toney didn't tell you my scheme?"

"He said something about a sweet hustle, but he ain't say shit about no police department, NYPD shit!"

"My prices are so good," Raul said, "because of the scheme I have set up."

"Apparently," *I said while still having my hands wrapped real tight around those kilos. I wasn't strapped. If I were going down in a setup, it would be after trying to get away with those bricks. I was looking for the nearest exit and the bricks were coming with me.*

"Whoa! Slow down, Fast Money. I'm a master electrician on call for several precincts of the New York Police Department," said Raul, "with special alarm and locksmith skills. My job gets me through locked doors and high security areas without a second glance. That's how I get so much of this shit, man.

"I can get into evidence rooms without signing in and out. I can sneak in these areas without supervision. They gave me, of all people, keys and codes! Because I don't have official clearance to be in these areas, no one ever looks at me when the drugs they snatch off the streets are missing. No one ever remembers I was even near there if there are problems."

Raul continued to explain his hook-up but his voice faded into the background. My mind was racing a mile a minute. I had been beating the streets for another connection, to take my business to the next level and now this just drops into my lap. This was the break I was looking for. Raul was getting it like the Colombians who made it, just picking it from the NYPD field. Getting his drugs straight from the police gave meaning to the cliché "something for nothing."

What he did, put the H in hustling. He was taking the risk of stealing the product, and I took the risk of smuggling it across five state lines. He passed the cost of his risk on to me and I passed mine on to the crews. But it wasn't until then, that I was really aware of how sweet this deal would be for me.

Raul and I had a good system and our transactions were easy, right from the start. I'd come to New York for a few days, get caught up on some shopping, and experience a new way of living. My business blew up with our first transaction. He and I proved that our business together had much greater potential. Everything was different compared to my business with Rock. I was on my way to the top now. I had my secret contact helping me deliver discount prices every time I moved. Nothing could stop me! The big risks resulted in big money, and I was getting it.

Raul and I had done business a few times and everything had gone the way he had planned. I needed to know where his loyalties were, so I over counted on purpose. I owed him $200,000 for 10 kilos and I gave him an extra $5,000 before leaving New York. I was just pulling in to Baltimore when my cell phone rang.

"Fast Money, it was good to see you," he said.

"Yea, I enjoyed myself. And I ate just enough to keep me phat."

"You left too much for me to listen to. I keep going over and over and it's just too much."

"Oh, yea. Damn. My bad," I said trying to sound as if I was surprised. "Moving too fast probably. I trust your ass—for whatever reason. I'll holler back later."

His call let me know I could trust him, at least with money. Loyalty was his way of protecting himself and those who trusted him. His method of doing things made wise financial sense. He dealt with out-of-towners only. The only thing he did locally, was pass kilo opportunities to other East Coast hustlers. Nothing was done in New York. He made absolutely sure of that.

After my partnership with Raul took off, I started making crazy money. His cocaine produced cash. His dope generated bank. It was so plentiful, I felt like a cash money millionaire. I wasn't rich, but I was on my way. My horse was high, just like my status. Riding it made me powerful.

When I got to New York, the only thing more important than spending the money needed to look like a millionaire, was getting that powder. I spent money at places like Lord & Taylor for Claiborne and Bill Blass suits, going to Madison and 60th Street to shop at Donna Karen New York for colored leather outfits, hitting Lorenzo Bonfi's for shoes and DKNY Apparel for other items to satisfy my lust for a high-priced wardrobe. No more fronting at clubs for me.

I also made a special run in Manhattan's diamond district to purchase my first Audemar's Piquet timepiece for $52,000.

Shortly after that, on one of my weekly runs to New York, I picked up an Art Deco platinum bracelet and matching necklace. A sweet deal, only $45,000 cash under the table. Rock's jewelry was nice, but now he was buying weight from me and I was worth more. It was time for me to look the part, to give some credibility to the rumors on the street. Showing up, looking like a millionaire on the streets of Baltimore was more important than being one. And I wanted the look cause I had thousands to match *it now. A few weeks later, I picked up my platinum Superman-shaped medallion with FAST MONEY in diamonds. Scarface's movie theme had finally come true in my life— "The World Is Mine" —and I had color, carat, cut and clarity to prove it.*

POLICE BLOTTER

Western District Drug Arrests:

Western District drug enforcement agents posed as drug dealers yesterday at North Avenue and Dukeland Street and arrested 38 people. Eleven dealers were arrested and charged with various offenses including possession of CDS and distribution charges.

Two juvenile offenders were taken into custody for possession of CDS and released to the custody of their parents. Twenty-four others were arrested for buying narcotics.

Kev "Black Face" Abbey was also arrested in the sting on a warrant for attempted murder, drugs and possession of a chrome Davis .380 semi-automatic handgun.

Officers also seized 11 vehicles, including a state government vehicle used to illegally purchase drugs, $4,314 and different amounts of heroin, cocaine, and marijuana. A small amount of Ecstasy was recovered from a Virginia resident caught in the drug sting, but authorities were unsure whether it was purchased here.

Chapter 6

PRECIOUS

"It's my biz how around ballers all day I spend my time /
And don't have to spend a dime."
Jay-Z, "Would You Love Me "
Life & Times Of S. Carter Vol. 3
(f/Amil, Beanie Sigel & Memphis Bleek)

After another night of hot sex, Fast Money and I got up and just kind of lay around the house until he started counting some money he'd collected the night before.

"Fast Money," I said as I sipped my steaming cup of coffee. "My girls at the beauty shop were talking their heads off yesterday. The word is that you are becoming the go-to-man in the city."

"I know my rep is growing, and so is my money. Here, this is a few dollars for you," he said bragging with that self-centered smile.

"Thanks baby. That's what they were saying about you."

I had to find something to do, too. I grabbed the nail polish remover and file from my pocketbook after stuffing the money inside. I sat at the table on the opposite end.

"I'll be out of this shit in no time if it keeps stacking like this," he said pointing to the rest of the money he was arranging.

"Get in and get out. Everybody says that, but nobody can pull it off."

"I never said it Precious. That's what I'm gonna do, though," he said stacking his first pile.

I could see he was trying to convince himself of the lie he wanted to believe. I started taking off those loose nails that I get done every week.

"How are you blowing up so fast anyway?" I asked—acting like I didn't know.

Lately though, he has been avoiding the question. Fast Money went from being a hustler on the way up to a man controlling the game--with a serious connect--in a matter of months. His climb was faster than anyone I had ever seen, including Dollar Bill. Although Pretty was giving me all kinds of inside information about him, I wanted to know his secret because I wanted to continue to ride this train as long as the money was right. He was making mad money and so far, didn't hesitate to spend it on or share it with me. I didn't want that to stop and we all know that information is power.

"It's just my turn, I guess," he said, without even looking up from what he was doing, continuing to avoid answering my questions.

"Say, Precious. I'm going out-of-town this evening. *Wanna* just get away and get some shopping in?" he asked.

"You know I'm down with that," I answered springing up from the chair. *I knocked the remover over on the table. I took one of his kitchen rags and wiped it up real quick. I realized one thing. I love this life and all that it brings.*

I know he offered me the shopping to divert my attention and while I know that what he intends, I never refuse to allow it to work. I always knew he was gonna make it big. That's why I made sure I latched on to him in the first place. I know how to pick a winner, starting with Dollar Bill. I can see a man with the potential to make big bucks and a weakness for good pussy, and Fast Money sure did fit the bill.

He offered me money after our first night together and I turned him down. I was able to live okay with the money Dollar Bill and Caine left behind even still, that has always been my bait. I never take money after the first night. That way they'll think I want them more than their money. All it took was a couple of sex sessions that seemed to have no strings attached and BLAM! I had him.

From then on, all I had to do was suggest I was going somewhere or doing something and didn't have enough money and Fast Money would open his wallet. Even before he really started blowing up, he was bank rolling half or more of my shopping sprees. All I had to do is tell him sadly how little money I had to go shopping with my girls. He'd just hand me ten Benjamins to add to my pocket. He always broke me off hundreds of dollars--what he called pocket change whenever I spent the night. After all, someone had to pay for repairing the damage to my hair and nails from our wild sexcapades.

When his business really started to take off, he began to take me with him on trips to New York and Georgetown in Washington, D.C. We shopped together all the time. I never had to spend a dime and I never turned him down. He kept me looking just right and, more important, he keeps me from dipping into my money stash.

I left Fast Money's crib in a hurry. I couldn't get ready for this trip fast enough. I came rushing into the house. As I rushed up the steps, my shoes made a familiar clicking sound against those hand-painted ceramic tiles on the foyer floor. I quickly glanced into the living room, like I normally do. I really liked that room with everything colored either hunter green or peach in the textures of leather, velvet, wicker and marble.

I blew into the master bedroom, yanked a suitcase from my walk-in closet and threw it on the bed. One of the seven pillows that live on the bed bounced to the floor. I kicked it out of the way as I went to the dresser, tossing lingerie, pajamas and other small items into my bag. I had no idea where we were going, but I was starting to get used to that. Fast Money's business was apparently expanding and with it, his need to travel out of town. Word on the street was that no one had better prices or higher-quality blow for sale. And now everybody was flocking to his enterprise for personal supplies.

I went back to the closet and turned on the light. I grabbed several outfits, a few for warm weather and a couple for cool, and folded them into the suitcase, hangers and all. I decided to take just a few outfits out because Fast Money always buys the clothes I need on these trips anyway. I closed my suitcase and turned to my full-length mirrors and tried to dress my nude body in my mind.

"What will I wear," I said to myself out loud.

I walked through the closet a few times until I settled on a bright red dress. I tossed it on the bed and then took a steaming hot shower. In about a half hour, I had repaired my hair and fixed my make-up. I slipped into my newest spandex dress that fits perfectly and of course no underwear was needed for this one.

AsI spun in front of the mirror, I knew this was the correct choice. The dress was a sparkly red and covered with sequins. The hem fell just above my knee, but the splits on each side would have shown the leg-hole seam of my French cut briefs if I was wearing one. The dress had long sleeves, and a turtle neck collar, but the shoulders were out with a diamond cut out to display my ample cleavage. To top it all off, my back was out, all the way down to the top of my butt.

I slipped on matching red pumps, dumped the contents of the bag I was carrying into another purse and put on my floor-length black sweater jacket with the hood. Just as I picked up my suitcase, I heard Fast Money on the doorbell.

"You ready Miss Beauty Queen?"

"I sure am," I answered, already starting with my flirting that always gets me so much more.

He carried my suitcase to the car. Outlaw was driving us to the airport, we both hopped in the back of the car and as soon as we pulled off, he began talking to Outlaw. For most of our way out of the city, he was giving Outlaw instructions on what to do while he was gone. We were on MD 295 South before he turned his attention to me.

"Where are we going this time?" I asked. "I didn't know what to pack."

"I always wonder why you pack anyway. As much as we shop, we might as well pick up everything you need when we get there."

"That doesn't answer my question, Money. I don't know where we are going or what we are going to do."

"So, would you like to stay home or are you going on this spree with me?"

I pouted for a second and turned my head, but I didn't ask again. He knew he had me and it ticked me off. I liked being in control and these little games undercut my power a bit. He would pay later though. I knew I'd be spending much more cash since he said the magic word spree.

His secret wasn't secret for long. Heightened security related to 9-11 required me to show ID in the airport before he could purchase my ticket. That's when I found out we were going to Los Angeles again.

I was wearing my sweater coat until I settled into my seat on the plane. It wasn't until I stood on my tiptoes to store my carry on things in the overhead compartment that Fast Money really seemed to notice me.

"Excuse me, miss sexy-as-I don't-know-what," he said, "Are you wearing any underwear with that dress? There doesn't seem to be any room for it under there."

"Well sir," I said, "there isn't any room for it, so no."

"Hotel room, here I come," he said laughing and grabbing my butt.

Our flight from BWI to LAX was not full. We had empty seats in our section. The seatbelt lights were barely off before Fast Money had his hands up and down my dress.

"Baby, I think we should get busy in the bathroom or try something right here?" he whispered in my ear.

"Do we have to choose?" I said, positioning myself so my body was even more accessible to his hands. "It's a five hour flight, won't we have time for both?"

I knew I had him then. Didn't I say flirting gets me everything?

"That's what I'm talking 'bout girl!" he moaned.

I must have drifted deep into my thoughts, because the next thing I heard was the sound of my own moaning. Fast Money was causing a spill underneath the blanket that was supposed to be keeping me warm. Finger exercise between my legs had me shaking. I continued to play like I was sleeping believing I could continue moaning a little without drawing too much attention.

I pointed to the rest room and he promptly got up and went. I watched him enter and then I walked down the aisle to the same one. Once inside, I knew what I was going to do in such a tight spot. Fast Money dropped his pants and boxers to the floor and sat on the toilet.

"Do you have to go, now?" I asked.

"Hell, naw!" he said. "This just seems easiest."

I nodded, kicked off my shoes, and put my left leg on his right shoulder. I hiked my dress up over my butt, exposing my crotch and leaned forward until my hairy forest was right in front of him. He stuck his fingers in and rubbed me gently, so lightly that at first I wasn't sure whether it was his tongue or finger. He stroked my crotch until it was covered in moisture and then suddenly tried to take my nipple into his mouth, but couldn't because of the dress. I was feeling so excited, I had to put my hand over my mouth to stifle a scream.

I took my leg down and kissed him. He was sticking straight up so I played with it a bit with my fingers. Then I turned my back and sat down on it quickly, plunging it deeply into me. Fast Money let out a yelp and then moaned. So did I. He was so far inside me. It felt like I'd eaten him for a snack.

I tried to hold on, but there was little to grab in there. I had to try and remain balanced and braced. I was managing it, despite the shivers he was sending through my body with each push of his hips, until we hit a pocket of turbulence. The sudden movements of his mouth and fingers pushed me over the edge and made me weak in the knees and caused me to cum at the same time. It wasn't long before he clamped both hands over my breasts, holding me down against him and came himself.

I left the bathroom first and when I got back to our row, I took down another blanket and covered up in the window seat. It was really evening now and dark outside the plane. The cabin lights were turned down for those who wanted to sleep. I got comfortable under the blanket and closed my eyes. I remember thinking that usually I am more in control than this and wondering what it meant. Something was different, not a bad different, but definitely something had changed.

We were met by our limo driver at the baggage claim area. His sign had our name on it. He knew the layout because he took us to the Hyatt West Hollywood Hotel. Fast Money was really out to impress me this time. His attempt was fine with me. I was open to the experience. It was just midnight in LA when we headed up to our room. In the elevator, we ran into Wu Tang Clan. They were eyeing me, but they were cool, like homies around the way. They offered to autograph my bag because none of us had any paper. The only paper Fast Money had was cash.

The next morning, we had room service bring us our continental breakfast. We had just finished dressing when the call came up from the concierge; our chariot had arrived. We hopped into the limo and I was stunned. It had been transformed since last night into much more than I was expecting. In the back, along with a well-stocked bar and refrigerator, was a brunch buffet table, and the most beautiful roses I've ever seen. The scent of the rose petals literally took my breath away. Along the top of the rear window was a banner that read, "Welcome to your exclusive shopping tour!"

Fast Money poured me a glass of champagne and himself one of those masturbating butterfly things. He apparently ordered a pitcher be stocked.

"Here's to your biggest shopping day ever," he said.

I touched his glass and took a long sip. Then I looked at the buffet. There was everything from miniature croissants to a sushi and sashimi platter. Everything looked delicious. I picked up a croissant and started eating.

"Where are we headed?" I asked.

"The sky is the limit," he said. "Sit back and enjoy the ride."

It didn't take long for the limo to stop and when I got out we were in front of the Polo Store. Fast Money helped me from the car and when we entered, a sales lady shot across the room.

"Good morning, Precious," she said. "I'm Julie, your personal Ralph Lauren shopper. Based on the information we have for you, I have prepared a special line for you to look at today. This way, please?"

I turned to look at Fast Money who was smiling ear to ear. He had outdone himself this time and all I could do was follow Julie. She seated us in the back near a short runway and the show began.

"Using the measurements, photos and preference information supplied, I selected these items from the current line for your review," Julie said. "As the models pass, just let me know about any items you want to try on."

And with that, about six models, all African American and about my size, modeled approximately 20 outfits. For the first 15, I was in too much shock over this whole surprise to really remember the clothes. I had to ask to have them shown again at the end. I chose at least 6 outfits to try on. Julie showed us to a private fitting area, where I had my own dressing room and stage to show off my outfits.

"What do you think of this one, Baby?" I asked as I looked in the mirror to see the dress from different angles.

"It looks good and it fits as well as the one you were wearing last night," he said. "But I think the color is stank. Julie, do you have this in another color, any other color?"

"Coming right up sir," she said.

We repeated this ritual I-don't-know-how-many-times before I came away with 12 complete outfits and I do mean complete, with accessories, shoes and even underwear. I had my boxes taken to the limo. By now, I had an appetite for the buffet. We boarded the limo to our next destination, Gucci. Much to my surprise the same ritual--personal shopper and fashion show--was repeated until I found exactly what I wanted. And I didn't have to spend a dime. I know people are always wondering why I spend so much time chasing these ballers--if they only knew.

By the end of the day, we had only visited about half the stores on Rodeo Drive. Fast Money assured me that the other stores were scheduled for the next day. All in all, we shopped in Polo, Gucci, Saks 5th Avenue, BeBe, Tiffany's, 9 West, Kenneth Cole, and Bally's shoe store before we were done. When we were done each day, the trunk and inside of the limo were filled with packages from the best stores in Hollywood. We spent another half day getting all the stuff shipped home by the hotel manager at the front desk.

At first I didn't know Fast Money had booked us into the hotel of the stars. But during our visit we saw Little Richard, Spike Lee, Master P., Mary J. and Shaq.

After shopping with me for a few days, Fast Money announced he was going to Huntington Beach to shop for himself overnight and he wasn't planning on taking me with him. That was too personal for me, so I tried to start an argument. Most times it gets on his last nerve and I get my way, but this time it didn't work. Things felt different to me. I was sure he didn't think I would notice because I was so busy shopping and spending his money, but I did. He seemed to be avoiding me, sexually. No matter how many times I had come onto him since arriving in L.A., he seemed to be avoiding me. I felt my control slipping, but I dismissed it. Because he was spending so much money on me, I didn't think what was wrong had anything to do with me. I began to wonder again why he wanted to shop without me, but I suspected it was business and he was shutting me out of it again. Anyway, I let him go without a fuss, mostly because there were stars to be seen in Hollywood. Once when he was out, I took in the sights and sounds of the hotel bar. One of the famous L.A. Lakers made a play for me. After leaving his room he gave me two tickets to a home game at the Staples Center and a private after-party.

I had just stepped out of the shower when he came back from his trip loaded down with clothes and that feeling came back again. He really was shopping, no business. Why not take me?

"Did you have a good time," I asked, as he put all his bags in the new luggage he bought.

"Yeah," he said. "I'm glad I went out there shopping and hanging out a little bit—just seeing the world."

He started looking around the room as if someone else was inside before he started talking. "We come from a real ghetto in West Baltimore. Once I tell people where I'm from, they start asking questions."

"You're a real celebrity now! Is that why you left me by myself?"

"Naw, I was just able to see a lot of the stuff I wasn't able to yesterday. I needed that time to myself to arrange some things."

"I ain't see any of the stuff you bought. I could have helped," I said.

"Precious, I think I can dress myself," he said. "I don't mean it like that, but I wanted to do this myself."

"OK! OK!" I said changing the subject.

"Look what I picked up today. Two tickets to a Lakers game, straight from a player."

"How did that happen?"

"A Laker's player who was in the hotel bar waiting for a friend from college tried to hit on me, but I told him I was here with you, so he apologized with these two tickets."

"Oh, yea," he said without real interest.

"Oh! I forgot to tell you. Outlaw called. Him and Alize had a little boy!"

"Now that should have been the first thing you told me instead of that Lakers bullshit," he said before walking into the bathroom and slamming the door.

I didn't tell Fast Money I drank too much and can only remember part of the night. I do know that the apology came after my player and I spent a few hours in his suite. From the bar we went upstairs. He tried his best to get me in that big bed of his as soon as we got upstairs, but I played the game of hard to get for a good while. I do remember teasing him with touches and kissing on his ears, but I don't think anything happened. I can't remember the rest. He gave me those tickets to entice me to see him again. The last thing he told me was he'd find me if I didn't show my face.

* * *

It wasn't long after we got back to Baltimore that I spent my last night with Fast Money. I should have seen it coming, but things seemed back to normal between us once we hit home turf. I thought I was back in control. But I think I went too far.

I had driven over to Fast Money's house in the early evening. I spent the night with him as usual. He seemed to have something on his mind because his performance was different. We spent more time on sex than sleeping. When we'd exhausted ourselves, I fell asleep in his arms.

The next morning I tried to get Fast Money up and out of bed--perhaps for a little more play before leaving. He had to be still feeling the night before, and was content to stay in bed.

"Do you need a few dollars?" he asked me as I put the finishing touches on my outfit.

"Yeah," I said, "I'm behind on a few bills."

"I've got money on the dresser. Take what you need," he said without opening his eyes.

I walked to the dresser and saw a bunch of money counted out already. I thought a minute about what I needed, which was really nothing at all, and decided to take a couple of stacks. It's only money, anyway. He was getting it, so this little bit wouldn't hurt him.

Chapter 7

FAST MONEY

"I'm just trying to show her how I ball and a roller."
Jay-Z, "All Around the World "
The Blueprint 2
(Feat. Latoiya Williams)

Chicks like my girl Precious come with high maintenance costs. Her time could eventually cost me more than the price of a high paid criminal attorney. She spent time with me. I spent cash on her since I balled and was a roller around town. That too is the game. One need satisfies another. I needed top quality; she needed top dollar.

A hustler like me has to refrain from losing control. At all times we must master our strengths while masking our weaknesses. Although each one of us has certain soft spots, we should never show them openly. I was taught this principle very early on in order to help me avoid getting "strung out" when chasing my fetishes. But Precious was my fetish, and I was in danger of getting strung out. She was taking me out of my game.

This all caused me to think how a woman's forbidden passion, a partner's clear signs of betrayal, greed for someone else's money, wanting something or someone you can't have, all end in tragedy. Facts like these are, in some way, responsible for every fallen empire and every life that's lost in this game.

That could never happen to me because things in the streets were blowing up for me. So, I decided to treat her to something special since she was putting work in herself. This would be something big for her and me both. My need to impress, have fun, and spend money had us shopping in Los Angeles, California. Exclusive arrangements were made with a customer who was also a travel agent for us to shop in Beverly Hills. All this would be a surprise.

The Hyatt West Hollywood Hotel was our first destination when we got in town. The hotel concierge and I hit it off. Davidson was his last name, but he wanted me to call him Clark. My travel agent had already told him about the purpose of the trip.

He had a limo arranged for us to travel Hollywood style early the next day. We went all-out shopping at several classy stores for Precious. We saw different stars during our first few nights of stay. They all were like friends from around the way. I was used to it because of all the trips to New York. The one star I enjoyed seeing was Mary J. She was just as beautiful in person as she was in the magazines. I had that look of lust in my eyes as I watched her move through the crowd. Precious probably noticed, but said nothing.

On a couple occasions, I went downstairs to drink at the bar with Clark.

"What's your drink, Craig? The treat is on me. Jennelle, I'll have a Hennessy & Coke on the rocks. And give him whatever he wants," he said without a care in the world.

"Give me a masturbating butterfly. I know he knows how to make that." *We sat there comparing some of our life experiences while she made our drinks.*

"I know you told me that your name is Craig. But what is your street name, if I can ask without sounding nosey? Mine was C-Rock before I quit."

"In Baltimore they call me Fast Money. I took on that name because of my fast hustle. They should name me Mr. Opportunity, know what I'm saying?" I said as we both laughed.

"Craig, there is a lot more opportunity here—if that's what you're looking for. This town is large when it comes to action, but there are not many who can be trusted. I'm going to give you my information before you leave. If you ever consider expanding beyond Baltimore, just give me a holler. You are all right. Plus I like the way you think."

"I feel that, Clark. I'm telling you, I could hang out with you all night, but I got to get back up there to Precious. She hasn't seen me yet for the day." *He was the one who suggested I go shopping for myself at Huntington Beach. He'd seen all the boutique gifts Precious had received and mailed home. It must've shown through that I was a baller and rolling in dough. He thought it would be a highlight for me. I took heart at his ideas and followed them.*

Precious wasn't feeling it, but I did it alone, anyway. That hold she tried to exercise wouldn't work—no matter how hard she challenged me this time. The consensus was that if I did my thing, she had a right to do hers and socialize without me.

I visited most of the stores Clark suggested. Clark told me about Mezlan and Bacco Bucci shoe stores and their exclusive showroom. I could have traveled to New York where I usually shop for shoes, clothes, and jewelry, but I wanted to do something different this time. Going up to New York would have saved some money. I probably wouldn't have spent more than thirty-five g's as I did in Hollywood splurging.

On the way back the next morning, I had Precious on my mind. I had taken the whole day to myself. When I returned, Clark called me to the desk.

"Craig, I have a package with your room number on it. I saw your lady guest go upstairs, but I held it for you. It came courier about three hours ago."

"For my room? I'm not expecting any packages."

"I think it is."

"Before you make a mistake you should check again to make sure the package is for room 208. By the way, I went to both of those stores." I said. *He had his back to me while he checked the package.*

"Sure is—room 208. And here is a card to go with it. It has Precious' name on it. Here, see for yourself?"

I took the card and flower arrangement to the side so I could see what was happening. I couldn't believe my eyes. I poured my heart and my pockets to make sure she experienced her dream come true. More than thirty-five thousand—all for nothing!

The card read: *"I told you I could find you. Those tickets to the game were the first. To share that special time with you in my room was something like a dream to me. You felt so perfect in my arms. I know you said you were with a friend, but I want to show you what is real. Call me at the Staple Center or at my home. You have the numbers.*

P.s. I want to see you again before you go back to Baltimore."

That was it! I checked the phone records on my room. She had a lot of nerve -- dialing his numbers and staying on the phone for more than two hours off and on. All I could think about was what Black Face told me about her in the first place. I hate to make him right. I love him and all that, but the first thing he'd say was I-told-you-so! I hate that!

I said nothing about what had me heated! This was just like everything else in the game. All good things will come to an end. I didn't really want to, but passion had no place in the life I was trying to lead. Being in the streets, I had to be able to walk away from arrangements like this in thirty seconds. Whenever threats surfaced, then it was time to go. I didn't want to end up like all the others Black Face warned me about.

A few nights had passed since we got back from our trip. I was still trying to hold her secret inside, but it was bothering me. We had finished our night the usual way. Our ritual was going to sleep in each other's arms, waking up beside her and her good morning kiss. I usually got her picked up, but this night she had driven over to my house. She took me on one of those wild rides that drained all my energy. I quickly went into a deep sleep.

I was still in bed when she was ready to leave. Worn out and relaxed, I asked her whether she needed a few dollars. A few dollars ended up being a mortgage payment and some.

She said she could use the help because she had fallen behind in some bills. I had, I know, around 8 g's on my dresser laid out. I had another twenty-five hundred placed on my night table, not far from my mahogany dresser, for a debt I owed. I picked that money up from Weeda the night before.

I made the mistake of telling Precious to take whatever she needed. That wasn't me actually talking about taking whatever. That was the sex making a fool—No! —a damn fool out of me! She had to have had some big ass outstanding bills because she took more than two thousand. What was her problem? Better yet, what was mine?

Later, she called me to see the next time I wanted to see her.

"Hey, baby," she said softly.

"I don't wanna hear that *hey-baby- shit!*"

""What's wrong with your ass, Fast Money?"

"How much of my fuck'n money did you take? Dat's what wrong with me!"

"I only took a few dollars."

"Well, I hope you enjoy that money just like you enjoyed that dude's hotel room in L.A."

"Money, I ain't do nothin'!"

"You didn't do nothing, but trick the shit out of me! Bitch, go find another sucker 'cause you got the wrong one!"

I hung the phone up on her and avoided her like the plague because I had too much to live for.

Carl Thomas had me singing, "And I wish I never met her, at all!" The only thing that could keep me away from her was space and time. She tried different ways to get in touch with me, but I ignored her. My team knew what the deal was. They would say whatever was necessary to protect me. Enough was enough.

Confidential

Internal Police Memo

At 2:30am I met with neighborhood informant #519. He reported that Craig "Fast Money" Carter is traveling to New York or New Jersey to purchase large amount of heroin and cocaine. Prior to this report, this suspect was not a major figure. However, informant #519 has dealt with the suspect in question several times prior and is still heavily involved in West Baltimore's drug trade. Prior information provided by #519 was positive intelligence leading to other arrests. Information on the suspect in question, his residence, contact numbers and family/friends are attached to this report and will be forwarded to the Drug Intelligence Unit.

End of Report

Chapter 8

TAVON

"They call me dope man, dope man. /
I try to tell them I'm what hope floats, man-- /
A ghetto spokesman."

Jay-Z, "*Dope Man* "
The Dynasty

I was ready when my mother, P-Nut, knocked on the door. I really don't call her mom. She was more like a little sister I had to look after, so calling her P-Nut felt more comfortable for me.

She was dressed up as best she could. That was unusual for her these days, but I could still see how the streets were wearing her down. She was too thin, so when her ankles swelled, like today, they looked deformed. She stood barely over five feet, and I could look down into the top of her head. She always bragged about her back-in-the-day figure and smile when she told me stories about her youth. Man, I heard those stories over and over from her. She always promised me she'd get back on top. Now there are dark circles under her eyes and her neglected mouth makes her smiles unattractive.

I wanted her away from the life she was leading. She was said to be selling herself and chasing dealers for drugs to support her habit. Bag food wasn't proper nutrition, and good hygiene was a thing of the past. Truth be told, P-Nut's a damn mess most times. Today though, I was almost proud of her. Today she smelled like soap and roses, instead of stale sex. She usually smelled sweaty from chasing a high and drinking cheap wine when I hugged her.

"I'm glad you're ready," she said while tugging gently on my right shoulder to get me to turn around. *Even though I was wearing my regular, everyday gear, she was fussing over me like I was wearing a tuxedo. She even pinched my cheek.*

"You are my handsome young man. You remind me of your father with your strong jaws and bright eyes. And I think cutting off all your hair for the bald look makes you handsome," she said. "If you weren't my son, I'd be sweating your chocolate ass myself!"

"Don't talk to me like that," I said right away. "You gave birth to me, P-Nut, my goodness!"

"Boy, I'm just playin'—Damn!" she screamed before swinging at my baldhead.

Momma was excited because opportunity would be coming through my hands now since my father was long into his prison sentence. At least my selling drugs and getting money would now remind her how things used to be when my father was home. That's all she ever spoke about. All her conversation was about how things used to be when my father was home. For years since then, she has been the first in the dope line spending money she didn't have. That would change almost right away.

"You know, Fast Money doesn't like it when I flirt with him either," she said fixing herself up in the mirror. "Aside from really taking off in the business, he's FINE. I'm looking forward to seeing him this afternoon."

"I heard that, P-Nut."

"Going with you is my excuse to get a glance at his butt. Back in the day—that young boy would be mine! I can still get him, as soon as I get myself together."

"Let's not keep the man waiting then," I said. *I stood there shaking my head and trying not to focus on how uncomfortable this kind of conversation with her makes me feel. Imagine that--my mother was turning me on to the game.*

P-Nut kept talking all the way to the meeting she had arranged. At first she was talking about this and that, but then told me about stuff I should know about Fast Money and the business. I heard her but I couldn't focus on what she was saying. All I could think about was how I was finally in the right spot to make my mark. I was being introduced to the man himself.

The truth is, I had hustling in my blood and had been preparing for this opportunity since middle school. My stepfather and father were both heavy weight hustlers back in the days. The streets remembered how P-Nut and King moved heroin in the hundred thousand dollar range. They had their thing together like Bonnie and Clyde. My mom was the shit!

I started early just like my father. I was pushing weed in middle school and turned my partners, Juvenile, Carl and Andre, onto the racket. And I was smoking with them too. We would get a stash, sell half and smoke half, which was not the way to do business.

"If you want to be big time, you can't be high and you have to turn all the product into cold hard cash. Neither can you get high, and get money at the same time. The two don't mix. You can't be your best customer selling that reefer," my stepfather King said to me one time.

I stopped smoking and so did Juvenile and Carl, but we didn't stop hustling. For a long time now, I have been doing my hustle--selling whatever I could get a supply of. It's been rough. Lately, I had barely enough to keep P-Nut's habit satisfied so she'd stay off the streets. But now, I guess she thinks I'm ready to move up. I tuned back into what she was saying.

"When I spoke to Fast Money last night, he said he didn't know you were my son, but he'd noticed you hustling. He said you had more drive than most people out there."

"He's seen me? I knew he was watching me, P-Nut!"

"He damn sure did! He said he could put you on with work just like he does for all his main workers. You know he looks out for me, and a lot of other people. He can really do something big for *us*. It's up to you to make things happen after I introduce you to him."

"P Nut, I'ma' make this work and take care of you. I want you off the streets. Let me do this now."

"I know you're gonna take care of your mother, Anthony?"

"I wasn't even called that in school P-Nut. I prefer to go by Tavon," I said to her in a serious tone. "And, yes, I'm gonna take care of you and both of my fathers."

There wasn't any more time to discuss my name, Anthony Tavon Truston, because we had arrived. I don't know what I thought, but it seemed strange to have this sort of introduction on a corner. My mouth was dry and my heart was pounding. This was it!

P-Nut hurried out of the hack after having me pay for the ride. She rushed over to where a crowd of people surrounded somebody that I couldn't see from where I was. Being around the game for about a decade, I knew what Fast Money looked like, even though we'd never really met personally. He was a real dope man—and I was determined to be like him. He was the reason why a lot of guys remained hopeful of making it big. He was our ghetto spokesman who everybody listened to because he controlled the flow of things. Having what people enjoyed, controlling what junkies fiend for, makes dealers like Fast Money a superstar.

That was how it was. And was the real reason why everybody surrounded him all the time. If you wanted to be in the game, you had to be aware of the players and not just those on the top. And to survive, you had to hustle hustlers from the bottom up. That's how you gained recognition.

I really wanted to bring Juvenile with me, 'cause it was my plan that we work this together, but P-Nut was only trying to get me in, not my partner. But for real, Juvenile and I share everything, so there was no way he wasn't going to be a part of my start in the major league. What my mother had told me about Fast Money was too big for me to handle by myself. I needed Juvenile.

The corner was real quiet, or at least I thought so at first. Then I realized that I was so focused on Fast Money and the action at his corner that I had blocked everything out. P-Nut was waving for me to come over and as I walked across the street, I studied Fast Money. P-Nut and King taught me that the way you look is important, and Fast Money had the look I wanted. He looked like he was more than making it. Even though he looked relaxed, having a casual conversation, I could see he was still watching everything around him, picking and choosing his opportunities, constantly making choices. It was all working for him and I knew for certain I would be going places because I was sure he was.

"This is my boy Anthony--I mean Tavon, Fast Money," she said as she gently guided me forward. *Fast Money put out his fist for daps and I obliged him.*

"What's up Black?" he said.

"You the man, up and coming," I replied.

He turned first to me and then toward my mother.

"Yo', moms said you're interested in joining my crews. She thinks you can handle it and so do I. I've been watching you doing a thing or two, but nothing heavy. I could have pulled you in, but I didn't know you were her son. P-Nut, are you sure you want this for your son?"

"Oh, yea. My boy can handle himself; he can make us all a lot of money."

"What do you wanna do, Tavon?" he asked as he turned to me again.

"To start. I wanna be your right hand man and start running some of your crews."

Fast Money raised his eyebrows and smiled. "I like your ambition. It ain't that easy kid. I'll put you where you need to be and we'll both go far. I'm too busy right now to do anything today. I'll tell you what, kid, here," he said extending his hand. "Take a couple dollars and meet me here tomorrow about noon and we'll get you set up."

"Here Fast Money. I can't take that because I *ain't* earn it. I'm down for the cause—that's why I can't take it."

My father always told me you gotta work for what you are worth on the streets. Nobody is gonna give me somethin' for nothin'.

"Good thinking son--and, for that, Tavon--here is some more money—and I'll see you tomorrow for sure," he said as he walked away toward a guy waiting for him. I noticed the other guy was wearing a spray-painted t-shirt with the name "Outlaw" written on it. My mother smacked me upside my head at the same time to make a statement.

"If you don't want the money--then I'll take da shit!"

"Here, you take it—and make sure you send my father a money order in the mail," I said knowing there was a strong possibility she wouldn't.

And that was it. Down the street, one of Fast Money's guys caught his attention and off he went. Put-Nut and I caught another hack and I dropped her at home with the money. Then I went to find Juvenile to tell him what I had done and how we were on our way.

The next day at 11:45 in the morning, Juvenile and I were at the corner waiting for Fast Money. We didn't have to wait long because he pulled up in his Black Cadillac truck about ten minutes after we did.

"Who dis?" Fast Money questioned. *He was clearly talking to me, but looking Juvenile up and down.*

"This is my partner, Juvenile." *I took a deep breath while uttering a silent prayer asking God to keep Juvenile quiet. It worked because Juvenile stayed quiet as Fast Money continued his intimidating scrutiny. It seemed to me like fifteen minutes even though it was really less than 30 seconds.*

"Well," Fast Money said.

He never took his eyes off of Juvenile who is a head taller than both of us.

"There's enough to go around, but I'm dealing with you and he's your first crew."

That's how it all got started. To Fast Money, Juvenile was just another person in my crew. He really wasn't feeling him--but between Juvenile and me, we were partners. I promised to share everything with him since Fast Money promised to take me under his wing from that very first day.

"J," I said after one of my lessons from Fast Money, "we can't be selling to just anybody anymore."

"Why not, Tavon?" he asked. "Money is money. We need to get all the money we can."

"Naw, man, it's not. If we get some of the wrong kind or serve the wrong people, it could shut us all down and get us locked up. Fast Money laid it out for me asking me a question I'll ask you. If you robbed a bank and on the way out the door with a bag of cash the manager called you back to give you another bag, would you go back and take it or would you leave?"

"I'd go back and get all the money. Why leave any money in that bank?"

"That's what I said too, man. But that's not right. That manager would have put a dye pack in the money he was giving you and if the money got mixed, none of it would be any good. The whole robbery would be for nothing. Think about it."

Juvenile listened, nodding his head in thought.

"It's like that on the streets too," I said. "If an undercover cop starts passing marked money around the neighborhood and we are not on top of our game, we could get some of it. If we pass it, they can trace it to us and lock us up. That's why all money ain't good."

Fast Money also taught me a few things I couldn't share with Juvenile. He told me to trust no one, not even Juvenile. The truth was, I didn't know how not to trust him. We had been partners for so long, that sharing with him and trusting him were like breathing. I did it without thinking about it. Being a team went without saying. I did it because we're like brothers. That's never going to change!

Coming in with Fast Money meant I had to build a new clientele. Before meeting him I dealt in small quantities, and an unreliable supply kept me dealing with nickel and dime action. But now, I was moving into the big time and I needed to step up. Fast Money showed me how to do it. His product was premium quality and an expensive but reasonable price. To get people to pay for it, he was not afraid to give them free samples of his products. He showed me how to use testers to spread word in the streets of what I was selling. Giving dope to addicts translates into regular clients—and cash money!

I took to using testers naturally, for some reason, addicts like me and they're cool with the way I do things, too. I feel for them because I feel for my mom, and I want to make them comfortable. I don't like to see them sweating and suffering. I know what my mom goes through. That's why I try to take care of them. Not, of course, at the risk of not making the money, but in a way that takes care of us both.

I think this gift and Fast Money's training is going to help us blow up. I am golden on the streets. Juvenile and I are making real money, fast, for the first time. When people heard that we were working for Fast Money, they came from everywhere.

There was really only one problem for me from the very beginning, and the bigger I got the more concerned I became. Stashfinder was still trying to set me up—almost any way he could. This Baltimore's finest law enforcement officer got his nickname by taking stashes he found and planting them and the accompanying charges, on someone else. He would take Paul's dope and give it to Peter on the next corner. But that's not all he did.

The city officials wanted guns off the streets under some new program called Project Disarm. The police would lock people up under the suspicion of guilt. Those arrested like that had to give them a gun in order to walk away from some trumped up charges. It was either give up a gun—any gun—or face drug charges and need money for bail, a lawyer, a trial, or parole and probation. Stashfinder would use this powerful position to extort information and anything else he thought he could get from us.

Lately, he and his undercover team were said to be kidnapping drug dealers. Holding hostages for ransom was common in the game, but it was now crazy because police were doing it. They would snatch a drug dealer and make him call his people to get drugs, guns and money. No dealer really cared about where the money was going. There was no report or receipt for the confiscated property.

Officer Crupt had been trying to lock me up for a while, but I was too fast for him. I wasn't really hustling consistently back then. Neither did I have a gun to give up. And I think I was just lucky too. Anybody with a hard-on for you, as bad as Officer Crupt's was for me, is bound to get you. But I just stayed out of his way. Moving up Fast Money's operation made me more visible and exposed us to more trouble from Stashfinder.

It was the first of the month. J and I were working out on the block in West Baltimore. We were set up on the corner of Lexington Street and were running a lot of product that day and were thinking of closing down a little early so we could have another big day on Thursday. I was leaning against the stoop, watching the street from both directions, when my favorite dope fiend, Big Roy, rolled up.

"Where you been, Big Roy," I asked. "I haven't seen you in about three weeks. You didn't go into a program on me, did you?"

"Naw, Tavon," he said. "But I was put in a program when Stashfinder picked me up for loitering and claimed to find 'caine on me. You and I know I don't even get high off of 'caine. Dat crazy ass cop set me up and took my money. I sat in lock-up almost a five days until I gave him my gun. He got the State's Attorney's office to throw the charges out at Central Booking. It was like being in a program."

"I bet, ole soldier. So, what can I do you for?"

"Man, I want to forget that place, sleeping on the cold floor and the smell. Give me all a hundred will get me."

"Done," I said, *as I signaled Juvenile to bring it up from the storage spot.*

"I have to tell you what Stashfinder wanted with me," said Big Roy.

"He wanted more than just to snatch you off the street?"

"Yeah, he wants you! He was flashing your picture with a few other mug shots of people I didn't know. "

"Still. That clown has tried to get me for years. I hadn't seen him around in a while, so I thought he'd moved on. "

"He kept police coming to me on lock up, trying to get me to give you up, saying that if I helped, he would let me go. He even talked some shit about having me work for him in the streets. All I know is he's got it in for you bad. I'd still be sitting there if I hadn't given him a gun."

"Should I be running?" I asked. "Is this the set-up?"

"Man, please!! Fuck Stashfinder! I have a habit that could knock an elephant to its knees and you always make sure I am alright, even when I am a little short. I may be a junkie shooting that shit, but I ain't dumb."

"Well, for dat' shit your loyalty will be rewarded," I said. "Today your money buys you double, so you can get a few dollars too."

Juvenile gave him what he came looking for after a quick handoff. He gave me one last warning before leaving.

"Boy, I'm telling you—you gotta be more careful with dat' crazy ass police on the loose."

"You got dat', ole' timer."

Juvenile spoke at the same time, "Good looking, Big Roy."

A few days later, Juvenile spotted Stashfinder circling our corner. We moved on for the day. As a matter of fact, we shut down! When our sales fell off, I had to tell Fast Money about Officer Crupt and how he had it bad for me. I learned my next valuable lesson. If I was going to succeed in the game, I needed to keep good defense attorneys on retainer.

Fast Money had a team of good lawyers and he turned them loose on my problem. Those guys called my problem with Stashfinder harassment. The next thing I knew, I had to sign some judgment papers complaining to their internal affairs about his tactics. Stashfinder got the message real quick. He seemed to have moved onto another target. I knew it wasn't over, but for once I had some protection from his crazy police tactics. With him gone, I was ready to take off in the business. And Fast Money was showing me he was ready to make it happen.

Chapter 9

TAVON

"Any [hustler] trying to harm [Tay] /
I'm feeling for you /
I'm not only touching you /
I'm touching your crew."

Jay-Z, "Coming of Age 2"
Hard Knock Life Vol. 2
(Featuring Memphis Bleek)

"Yo, Tavon, you can't be worrying 'bout Stashfinder trying to set you up anymore, man, because you know that shit slows up our business."

"I know," I said, "but I ain't letting him stop me. I'm going all the way with this!" I said pulling money out of my pocket.

"That's good," he said, "because I think you are ready to move up. I wanted to hear from you what you want to do. This shit is serious."

"I'm in this all the way to the top, so I'm ready."

"Well, there's a lot of stuff you need to know. First, I'm giving you a different strip. You have to have a base where all of your real money comes from."

Fast Money set me up with some crews in strategic hot spots in West Baltimore. I started with five crews. He never told me who his supplier was, but he did show me the ways he flipped the product into BIG money for us all.

"Do I still get everything from you or"—I tried to ask before he cut me off.

"You get it straight from me! I'll still front everything to you and you pay me when you come back for more. We're doing shit the same way, but you'll be getting more. For you to make a profit, the crews need to make at least 35 G's a brick on the street. They work a week before they get paid and turn everything in every night. We're doing this on salary. I pay you. You pay them."

He laid it all out for me, telling me about the two types of sales I would be doing--direct sales to the addicts and selling weight to other dealers. He explained that even though an ounce weighs 28 grams, we cut ours, dope and cocaine, and sold 30 grams to the ounce. If somebody was trying to buy some brown dope, we could manufacture that too. Coffee grinds and cutts do wonders in the dope game.

Everybody had regular street prices for an ounce of coke. The going rate was $1,000, but ours went for $1,100. Our higher price didn't seem to matter because hustlers buying from us felt they were getting value in quality and quantity. He taught me never to sell the competition the same grade of product we had to sell to our customers. The extra weight we sold definitely put extra money in our pockets.

"How are you making out," Fast Money said to me a few days after he turned over those spots. *He had run up on Juvenile and me at my 24-hour shop on Franklintown Road.*

"Things are cool," I said. "J and I are moving through those bricks you fronted us and we'll be in to settle up and get more before the end of the week."

"Dat's cool. I could see that you would make it happen. You got that shit tight. The set up is perfect using the dead end streets. That gives you a full view of all the police traffic. Looks like you are handling business my man," he said patting me on the shoulder.

Sometimes he tried to act like my father. At first it was weird, 'cause he's not much older than I am, even though he is Big Time in the business. But now, I see, it's not like he is being my daddy in all ways, but being my father or much older brother in the business. I can see now that he is paving the way for me and moving me forward fast.

Fast Money was also softening on Juvenile. At first, he didn't believe I should trust my partner. Then, after he saw that I was serious about sharing every opportunity with Juvenile, Fast Money lightened up a bit. Even though he still dealt mostly with me, he began to see us both and to even do some of our business with Juvenile.

I remember the conversation Fast Money and I had that let me know he was finally accepting Juvenile. I was settling up after moving damn near a week's worth of product in two days at our 24-hour shop. I sat at the table counting the money while he finished a cell phone conversation. As he finished his conversation, he walked over to me and started talking about J.

"Tavon, Juvenile is off the hook, but he's your man—and he's got your back," Fast Money said.

"I told you he's been my partner forever Money. I'm glad you see I'm not crazy for sharing everything with him," I replied, still counting out money.

"Well, I saw it first hand and I have to believe my own eyes."

We laughed and then he continued to talk.

"Check this out. The other day when he came to pick up the product, Juvenile and I stopped in at the sub shop on North Avenue. We ordered and were waiting. Man, they are slow as shit up in that joint. It took them 20 minutes on cold cuts."

"Yeah they are always slow. But I keep going there because the food is slammin'."

"Well, I wouldn't know. Going with Juvenile was my first time and I never got to eat the sub.

"Hol' up. What happened—because he told me some gangsta shit about how he carried it up there," I said.

"Sme guy, Rabbit, I think it was, was in the joint talking just to hear himself talk, running his mouth to some other dude in the place. I really don't think he saw us in there when they came in. But whose name did he have on his lips but yours. And he was talking shit about you."

"Yeah, I know Rabbit. He's just mad because I won't sell him weight."

"Why not?" Fast Money asked.

"Mostly because of what you told me about all money not being good. He can't hold water and would give me up in a heartbeat. Also, he's small time, trying to find a break, but I'm not the one. That kid's not ready. Selling shit to him is too big a risk. And I was straight with him when I turned him down."

"Oh, now I'm feeling that. Anyway, he was going on and on about how you thought you were big time but you were just like one of them--trying to make it. He said shit like you only had two crews and that didn't give you the right to think you were so much better than anyone else hustling a corner. He was pretty much saying stupid stuff that was coming from someone who didn't know what they were talking about. He was slipping and didn't know what he was getting himself into.

"I expected Juvenile to do something, because we have to protect our name, product, and image. We've worked hard to get our respect on the street, so this guy had to be dealt with. But I didn't expect that."

I stopped counting and looked up because of Fast Money's serious expression.

"Before I knew it, Juvenile had moved," Fast Money said as he moved across the floor imitating Juvenile's actions. "He pulled out and shot him down at point blank range. I was locked with shock. It was so sudden, I was sure I heard the tearing of his skin and the cracking of the bones in his chest. Rabbit screamed like a woman testifying at a Friday prayer service!

"Juvenile hauled ass out of the sub shop and I was right behind him. It all happened so quickly! The most shocking thing was how Juvenile didn't care whether Rabbit lived or died. We ran straight to the car. We got da' hell out of the west part of Harm City before the police came or something else happened."

"He burned him up?" I asked like I was hearing the story for the first time.

"Did he—Yeah, he burned his ass up!! He did us a favor because the fool didn't have sense enough to die. He's still in the hospital."

"Now, all I have to do is protect my main man—and make sure he is all right," I said. "It took us too long to build this up. Now this is ours and we have to watch each other's backs so we can enjoy it all for what it's worth. He's just like I told you from the beginning—a brother to the end."

It was then that Fast Money started treating Juvenile like my right hand instead of just a member of my crew. While he still saved his fatherly talks for me, he seemed to accept that when doing business, Juvenile and I were one and the same. He and I had more than money. We had each other, and now loyalty. It's all a part of being true to the game.

Things were going right for us and business couldn't be better. Fast Money looked out for us. He provided a good product, great prices and a rep that had customers begging for more. He sold to me and I pushed everything to J. It was just like he said. As long as we pulled in at least 35 g's a brick, we'd be gettin' crazy money.

But working for Fast Money was full of surprises, especially where money was concerned. My first real glimpse of his financial power was when one of our crewmembers was killed in a car accident. He took me with him when he went to visit the brother's momma. He was just like State Farm, there when you need him. He walked in with the cash she needed for everything and never batted an eye. He always managed to have money ready for whatever might happen—like bail, lawyers, fugitive "fly" money, vacation or whatever.

He was my kind of man, too. The first Christmas after I started with him, he showed up unexpectedly at my crib. I was taking a rare afternoon off, just chilling, eating a chicken box and drinking a half-n-half while watching a black market video when I heard his knock. I checked the peephole to be sure it was him before I snatched open the door.

"What's up?" I asked as I moved aside to let him in.

"Well, you've been pulling down weight with me for a while and making us both blow up. So, I have something for you and didn't want to wait. I wanted to put it in your hands now," he said.

"Ah, good looking out!" *He handed me a thick manila envelope. I didn't know what it was, but it had to be something good. He kept watching me so I opened it. It was lucky for me that I was standing by a chair because I just sort of sank down into the seat. The envelope was full of bundles of hundred dollar bills. I just kept staring into the envelope and somewhere in the distance. I heard Fast Money laughing.*

"Aren't you going to count it?"

I looked up at him 'cause the thought of counting behind him never occurred to me. I had never seen so much of my own cash in one place before. I reached in and counted the bundles.

"About fifty thousand?"

He laughed at me again. "Yea, Tavon. Fifty thousand. You looked out for me. Plus, you worked hard, charmed the customers and learned everything I have taught you. That's all you."

I sat quietly for a minute, taking it all in. I wanted to be in the big time and was working hard to get there. But this meant I was getting there, really on my way and that being on top wasn't just a dream, but a real possibility. I looked up at him.

"Can you take me someplace? Now?"

"Well, I have some other business," Fast Money said.

"It won't take long. And you probably don't have to stay with me. I just need to get there without having a car with me."

"Okay. I can take care of that."

I grabbed my coat and asked Fast Money to head out Route 40 West. We didn't talk much on the way to Russell BMW. Every now and again he would glance at me clutching the envelope in both hands and smiling like a kid on Christmas. By the time we pulled into the lot, I had gotten used to the idea and was laughing with him.

A trailer full of cars was just coming in from the Dundalk Marine Terminal. I saw what I wanted before I got out of his truck. It was a BMW M Roadster, metallic steel gray, with a deep black leather interior.

"I want that one," I said to Fast Money. *I was pointing at the car still sitting on the trailer. I started walking toward a guy who looked like a salesperson, with Fast Money in tow.*

"You want another car?" Fast Money asked me.

"No," I said, "this is for Juvenile for Christmas."

My next Christmas gift should be for Tiffany, but her mom wouldn't allow me or Juvenile to buy her anything. She was not only Juvenile's daughter, but also my goddaughter. She's my heart. Baby girl gets most of her qualities from her mother, Jameel, who has raised her well, despite how crazy Juvenile acts sometimes. He loves his ladies, but can't find a way to be with only them. I don't understand it really. If I had what he had to go home to, I would find a way to make it; I would be with them, no matter what it took. But, he was still my boy and he and his family deserved the best from me. And this car was it.

I snagged the salesman and he was more than happy to make this sale. I was sure it was making his Christmas, his month and his year.

I don't know what business he had, but Fast Money stayed with me until the deal was done. The car never made it to the showroom floor. It was wheeled straight into prep and brought to me, with a full tank of gas fairly quickly.

"Tavon," Fast Money said, "It's good to see you taking our family concept to heart. This is a big plus for us taking over the streets."

"No bigger than the one you gave me. I had to share my good fortune with my partner." *It wouldn't have been possible without him. He and I will find a way to share it with our boy, Trigger, on lock down, because he made this possible for us.*

"Man, you gotta meet our man Trigger. I'm telling you-- You and Trigger would hit it off. Plus, I talk to him about you on the phone all the time when he calls collect."

I got into the car and put the top down.

"Thanks for everything, man," I said.

Fast Money threw up his fist as a symbol of one love between two and pulled out.

Chapter 10

FAST MONEY

"I'm everything.../
the when's, why's, who's and what's!"
Jay-Z, "It's Hot (Some like it Hot)"
Life & Times of S. Carter Vol. 3

"Hey, Fast Money, my friend. I knew you'd be calling me," Raul said calmly after his wife put him on the phone.

"What's going on up there, my friend?" I asked. He always called me that I guess as a way of letting me know we were in this thing together. "I'm waiting to do it here, but I can't get it done without you. You know what I mean?"

It had been more than a month since he had sent me something heavy down. My job was to keep the work coming in and managing the money going back up to him. For each kilo I was pushing, I always put a few extra G's in the safe to pay my bill. This didn't include the heroin we sometimes sold. That remained separate when it was sent to me. Lately, nothing was coming, though.

Big Toney turned me on to an in-town connection. Raul forced me to start making local moves with this big crew called the Jamaican Posse from off of Park Heights. I had to buy my weight from them just to keep things going. Most times it was just a waste of money compared to what I was getting directly from New York, but at least the Posse was reliable.

They have the slickest operation I've seen in Baltimore. The Jamaican Posse has been doing it big for the longest while, 24-7, 365. I get a kilo or two from them each time a drought comes. Their product was OK but not as good as Raul's. Rumors had it that the Posse gets big shipments straight from Jamaica. They used to smuggle through cargo ships from Florida, but after a while that kind of got too costly because they started getting knocked off a lot. Big Toney told me how one member was bragging to him. He said the Coast Guard started shooting up the engines in their speedboats off the Florida Keys. That's when they started getting 300 pounds of weed and crazy kilos through our Dundalk Marine Terminal and the Chesapeake Bay shoreline. The Jamaican Posse had the perfect hustle getting shipments picked up by Baltimore City trash truck workers, but that was theirs. Raul was mine.

"I sent you a copy of the memo by Poncho of what I found. There are some people investigating my house. You didn't get it?" he asked.

"Yea, I got it." *I wouldn't say anything else about it over the phone, but Poncho dropped it off to me while he was here picking up money from Big Toney. Poncho and I both agreed that Raul had nothing to worry about. He was being too cautious. Besides, it's just too much money out here to be made for him to be slowing down now.*

"My friend, this situation is something big and it scares the shit out of me! That's why I am staying low, for right now. I'm telling you all my coworkers are running around here like chickens with their heads cut off. Although no one has said anything to me and they are really scrutinizing each other, I'm still gonna lay low a bit longer."

"I'm telling you Raul that shit has nothing to do with you," I said speaking forcefully into the phone trying to convince him to forget about what was happening amongst polices. "Man, I told you how paranoid you are." *I had to tell him something since I read that Joint Task Force Commission Investigation memo he sent. It said something about how veteran police created a culture of corruption in the force and crime had gotten out of hand. His fear was having his precinct on the investigation list. This investigation started when high profile district attorneys started losing cases because large quantities of evidence logged in as exhibits in drug cases mysteriously disappeared from police storage departments.*

Raul wasn't even a suspect. I told him what we were doing was nothing compared to the shit Serpico exposed— against the NYPD in the 70's.Corruption didn't start with him. Neither would the New York Times want the story of a master electrician stealing police evidence.

"I told you, dammit! Nothing is done until I find out what is going on up here!" he shouted. "This is my ass, not yours! Let me think--let me think," he said sounding frustrated and scared.

"We're losing by the minute down here my brotha! All that money is walking right by us!" I snapped back pushing him even more to the edge. *But at that moment I was thinking about the Jamaican Posse and all the money they were getting.* "They *ain't* waiting for our scared asses! If we don't move in a minute, all the spots I have now—I'm gonna lose! Everything we do involves chances—and those are the chances we have to take, my friend. You know that!"

I was talking my ass off trying to convince him things were clear since Poncho already told me he had 15 bricks for me, but was scared to move. I wanted to get that paper money and those G stacks that put me on top. His fear was holding things up.

"I'm not without," he said. "I just don't think it's good to move. I may be looked at—know what I mean? I still have fifteen—but, umm--" he said. *He was counting money and possibilities.*

"Get that shit to me, Raul. I got this bag waiting for you, so call me back with the details," I said quickly before he changed his mind.

That's how things go in the game. Raul was making it happen not only for me, but a lot of other hustlers, too. We were all getting' paid—quick, fast and in a hurry. The only problem was Raul having to make strategic stings. He couldn't always be sure when a major police bust would go down on international cargo ships and speedboats traveling into New York ports. There was no telling when a multi-kilo confiscation would occur. Then, too, he couldn't just walk in and remove evidence from lockers at will. So, we were sometimes off for weeks at a time. This time it was taking him too long to get his nerve up.

"I hear what you're saying Fast Money. And I'll get back to you soon. Let me see what's happening and if I can--I will! You have to come up and we'll talk more. Just let me get back to you," he said in frustration.

I could hear the fear in his voice. After I hung up the phone, I thought for a minute that I might have leaned on him a bit too harsh. But those consequences were on his end. Money was on mine. And besides, if I had bricks belonging to him at the time of his arrest—well, you know how the game goes! I'm rich!

The streets were locked down! That's how I "sewed" the blocks up and cornered the market within our West Baltimore borders. I kept it coming while they kept pumping. We all shared big dreams of being better than our fathers and those we competed against on the streets. It was competition like this that kept us tight!

I stood right beside my crews on the strips. They didn't mind paying the extra prices. Weight sales my crews did on the side added up to extra money. I was in control of distribution around most of our high traffic areas. I always had somebody doing something.

I was a chemist by street trade because our 30-gram ounces made us blow up! Two extra grams of cutt for an extra one hundred dollars wasn't bad at all. That's how I kept home team advantage.

I got this idea from Philly hustlers who I met through Raul while in the Big Apple. I started using the "Get down or lay down" tactic. Any hustlers in any of my areas had to get down with me and my crews or lay down the hustle, period. Imitating them and doing it effectively was working for me. I wanted it all. My strategy was fair game—and anybody who was a major player in weight sales, in one way or another, played the game by my rules!

See, the whole damn thing out there is a game. Running game is the mental aspect of our street activities. Everything we do is a hustle. True paper-chasers show talent each time we transact business. We have customers thinking one-way when, in fact, we are doing something completely different. Each player watches the street economy and measures his or her ability to create get-over opportunities. Having this talent and the competitive mind to make a get-paid dream a reality is not as common out here as many may think.

Each crew needs a special leader. This one person is the brain in every illegal organization. He is the "who" in a conspiracy. In my organization – that person is me—and it is within my power to determine the when's, why's, and who else does what. The government labels me as evil, since I'm creative in distributing large amounts of death and destruction on the streets. They say a man like me is responsible for our community demise. Picture that?

Hustling is the action we create on each street corner. This is what you read about in the papers. Each plan of action is carried out like it's a big business franchise. Products and creative selling ideas become necessary to make every distribution dream come true. That's why I put names on my bags and cap my vials with purple tops. This is how we make bargains, give wholesale discounts and have crowds of people chasing our drugs all over the city. This is our make-it-happen, get-that-paper mentality.

With all of the problems Baltimore had, we took advantage of them all. The rewards outweighed the risks. Short-term gratification always dominated long-term consequences. It was all a dream. All of us were chasing this dream. That's why we had high arrests rates for drug possession. On another front, overdose rates were proving everyday that we were pushing large volumes of high-grade heroin across the city. Out there in our world we all could agree on one thing. One man's loss is another man's gain!

People on the outside always ask us why we keep hustling since we know that trouble is the only outcome. Health officials and politicians try to come up with quick answers adding to the problems of using and selling. Well, that was their problem. Finding ways to keep making money without getting locked up was ours.

In the Nation

NEW YORK – Twenty-two airport and ground crew support workers were arrested and is said to have smuggled cocaine and heroin into the United States, several officials speaking on the conditions of anonymity said.

All suspects arrested in this sting have been employed or previously employed by a major airline at one of New York's busiest airports. Each are said to have stashed drugs aboard flights, hidden in luggage and cargo areas, into the United States and through security checkpoints avoiding detection.

Last week, local Drug Enforcement Agents confiscated and stored four boxes of cocaine weighing about 200 pounds. All evidence has been secured at police headquarters. Officials estimate its worth at $12 million.

Chapter 11

FAST MONEY

"I'll show you how to get this dough /
In large amounts— /
Until it's hard to count."

Jay-Z, "The Bounce"
The Blueprint 2

I couldn't be happier now that Raul finally figured out what I've been trying to tell him all along – he wasn't even close to being a suspect in that investigation. When I got to New York it was rainy and cold but not even that could stop the constant hustle bustle at the train station. Neither could the rain stop my hustle. You know how it is, people moving so fast they run you over and not even realize it. I could see Raul from a far off puffing hard on a cigarette; he looked like he could have smoked about a pack of cigarettes already in the short time he had been there waiting for me.

"What's up friend?" Raul asked when I finally made it through the crowd to our meeting spot.

"Just tryin' to hit it big like you, my brotha, just tryin' to hit it big," I answered.

We both laugh before giving each other a handshake.

"Well let's get down to business; I want this to be a quick turnaround for me today."

"This is for you," I said as I pulled a transformed CD case with his money from my black Comcast duffle bag I was carrying.

He didn't even open it 'cause our relationship had grown in trust like that. He just told me to toss it in the front seat of his metallic green Suburban. His heavy hand traveled straight into his White Castle bag of food when we jumped inside his truck. I looked around thinking to myself this is a perfect ride for someone like him.

"My friend I know I seemed paranoid—slowing things down, but I'm back now. I realize you were right; forget what Internal Affairs is doing. They're not looking at me. They don't even think I have access, so I am really not a suspect."

"That's what I've been telling you all along my brotha." *I reached for some of those White Castle fries that smelled so good when I first got in. I kept my eyes on what he was doing. I saw him push a button—and a secret section underneath the glove compartment appeared. He threw the CD case inside the compartment, and made it disappear while we were talking. At the touch of a button all that hard-earned money was gone.*

"I was a little spooked," he admitted, avoiding any eye contact with me and digging inside that greasy food bag. "But I'm back now and the timing of this meeting is perfect."

"Why," I asked as I helped myself to some more of his greasy fries that not only smelled but tasted really good.

"Because last week our drug unit busted an airport crew with somethin' like 200 kilos of cocaine—worth like $15 million or so. I went in just last night and copped!"

"No shit! Fifteen mill!" I said trying to control my excitement. "What have you got for me?"

"Well, 15 kilos for you, with two as a bonus if you will move it tonight, along with 8 kilos for Big Toney."

"Done," I said.

I could see the dollar signs float in front of my eyes. My crews would really be in business for a while now. One loss is our crews' gain. It was funny how stupid the people at the airport must've gotten. Police are really slow at this fast life—and they let the police catch them. Oh, well. What really matters is my Baltimore crew is getting fifteen fuckin' kilos.

I had to respond to him. "Just give me a few hours to hook up some reliable transportation and I will meet you back here. Then we can get the stuff and I will be out."

I was really going to be taking a risk, transporting that much stuff, however, I was always told that a scared man can't get money. I was determined and having that confidence had me growing in layers. Look at me. I was stacking bricks a thousand grams each—one on top of the other. My job was to make the product available, ensure top quality, and keep bargain prices. The truth was my crews made the money. They had the risky responsibility of flipping and showing me the money!

Being in big forced me to have attorneys at arms reach. Both attorneys I had on retainer told me at any point my freedom could be taken away for a long time. I knew that and it didn't scare me, but what I'd just learned was that Federal prosecutors had armed themselves with a tool that scared the shit out of me! Conspiracy was one! Back in 1988 Congress adopted a new death penalty for drug kingpins. That was the other! Society was fed up. I could tell what they weren't saying: they failed to mention that racial profiling and discrimination increased my chances of getting caught. They also stayed away from revealing to me that minorities, like me, too often received maximum punishment for those charges and were more likely than not to get a life sentence or the death penalty. The feds were making examples with gun and kingpin convictions and sure didn't need me.

No foolish chances could be taken since I was in a large conspiracy, and fit the kingpin statute including interstate transporting. I had to be careful in everything I did when violating the Harrison Narcotic Act.

What they did tell me was that in 1994 lawmakers had the nerve to concentrate on my drug activities when they expanded the federal death penalty to include kidnapping resulting in death. The streets were changing so all was fair in love and war. Anything was possible. I had no intentions of doing harm to anyone, but you never can tell in the streets. It was my priority to keep Tavon and Juvenile cool—with those wars on the street. I would be held responsible for my crews' activities since I was the head of what authorities, both FBI and DEA, would have no problems calling a major heroin and cocaine ring from New York to Baltimore.

For sure, I was looking at a sentence of Life for the quantities I transported across each state line starting from New York, into New Jersey, Philly, Delaware and then Maryland. One other thing I had to keep in mind was the two attorneys I trusted with my money and freedom didn't practice law on a federal level. So, I had to be really careful getting things carried by other people.

* * * * *

As Tavon and I cruised down Pennsylvania Avenue, I thought about how much he was proving himself to be real in this game. He's ever present when I get back in town and he and his crew been pushing everything in record time. We were bonding and building. The sick thing about our relationship was how his mother created it for her own gain.

"Tavon, you and Juvenile are tight as shit. Y'all are like two nickels in a dime, Yo."

"That's why I've been tellin' you Money. He's my one and only partner, man. You know what I mean? We've been through a lot since childhood. I can't remember a time when he and I haven't been there for each other," Tavon said as he looked out of my truck window.

"And what I am, kid?" I asked, feeling a bit jealous of the bond them two share. *Tavon always spoke so confident about Juvenile having his back.*

"Nah man, it ain't like that, you know what I mean. You my main man, Fast Money, but Juvenile is my brother. He was there when my back was against the wall. Man, you don't understand how much we been through from little boys to now being grown men. His mother used to feed me and keep me clean when P-Nut got so strung out on drugs. He has saved my life and will do anything for me. If I can count on anybody—it's him." Tavon said, looking like he was about to get a little sentimental.

"I feel that, Yo!"

My phone rang-like it does all the time. I was talking to the guy Bennie who had his own crew on Mount Street. I wanted Tavon to know who it was. That's why I called his name and mentioned some big numbers. I quoted those numbers to him because he needs my skills to tighten a bad package.

"Hear 'dat, Tay."

"What Money?"

"I'm so good with dis' shit that I cut other people's dope to make it better. The old-heads named me the 'cut expert.'"

"Oh, yea," he said with a hint of surprise.

"One day I see you stepping out on your own."

"Naw, Money," he said. "I'm with you until the end."

"Like I said, Kid. Listen to what I tell you! This shit won't last forever. When you are finally on your own, I'll help you, too."

He wanted to understand what I was saying. That's probably why he grew quiet trying to figure things out. I gave him a minute before telling him more of what he needed to understand.

"Everybody in this game gets some weak shit and so will you! And for the right price, I can even make your shit tighter!"

"I still don't see this coming to an end, but, just like you said, I'll look you up, Money."

He reclined the passenger seat as if he was being chauffeured around. As we passed Shake & Bake Family Fun Center, I noticed how Pennsylvania Avenue was busy as usual.

This was a good time to see and be seen cruising around in my Lexus truck. My cream sports utility vehicle turned heads. Because of my tinted windows, I saw them looking whenever I passed by but they couldn't really see me.

I glanced at him to make sure he was all right because he had gotten quiet again and seemed like just that quick he went in a reflective mood. As we pulled up at the stoplight, I saw a couple walking across the street with white plastic bags filled with little white boxes. The red trees on those boxes them gave them away. They were coming from where I should be going. That exhaust fan blew the smell of oriental food to all four corners of Pennsylvania Avenue. My taste buds cried out for some of that Chinese food.

"Yo man, let's go get some Chinese food, that stuff smell good as shit!" I said.

"I'm sittin' here thinking the same thing," Tavon said.

We both gave each other high fives and laughed. I pulled over to park after crossing Laurens Street. I tucked my jewelry in my shirt while watching a transaction go down right in front of the truck. It was business as usual on Pennsylvania Avenue.

"Raw out! Raw out! Shop open!" some young kid screamed out to anyone in hearing distance.

This kid could be no more than thirteen or fourteen years old. His hands covered his mouth so he could loudly echo what he was selling. He was dressed down in dusty black with a bright white T-shirt. He had a matching gang rag covering his face. Two other young hustlers were screaming by his side dressed just about the same way.

"Almost raw! Almost raw, y'all." *Signs of competition resounded from one side of the street to the other.*

"Shop open over here, shop open over here."

The action around that Chinese joint allowed me to see more of those Pennsylvania Avenue hustlers at work. I was seeing money and loving it! If it wasn't for the love of fast money, I wouldn't be in this powerful game, but I am. And it was time for me to show myself on these blocks, too. My time to spread out even further had come. A couple of familiar faces came over to shake my hand and talk for a minute.

Then I heard a female voice scream from a short distance.

"Fast Money! Fast Money!"

I looked around to see who was hollering my name so loudly, but couldn't really detect where the voice came from since the street was so busy and noisy.

"I'm over here. Right here," she said.

I looked across the street and saw a familiar looking car pulling over. It was the same Mercedes that impressed me some time ago. She threw on her hazard lights as she double-parked in the middle of the street. That's her. She was still acting like she was more than important as she ran across the street. You could see those expensive nails from a mile away. Tavon and I looked at each other as she came our way. We were probably both thinking the same thing. Damn! She is fine as shit!

"Money, where you been?" she asked as I stepped around the truck to hug her.

Our firm embrace brought back memories I wasn't even prepared to entertain. "I've been around, just not your side of town. You know how it is," I said in a tone that would give her no reason to think I was still interested in her.

"Money, you are sure looking good," she added after letting me go and taking a step back for a personal inventory of my looks.

"Stop playin' girl."

"I tried to call you a few months ago to see if you were still alive, but I couldn't catch up with you."

"Oh yeah, I'm a busy man Precious. You know what I do."

She looked pass me and focused on Tavon leaning on the front of the truck.

"And who is this, Money?" she asked.

"Dis' my man," I said while pointing.

"Damn, you sure look good," Precious said in a tone letting me know she was ready to work her pussy hustle on Tavon.

She scanned him up and down, and was already lusting after his pocket before I could even introduce her.

"This is Tavon. You met his mother, P-nut, but not him. This is my little right hand man. He knows already how to get things done down there on the Westside. This kid is going to blow up!"

"You're a cute little young thang'. Hi, baby. My name is Precious," she said as she hugged him long and firm enough to let Tavon feel her body against his.

"Anyway, Money, I gotta run. I just came down to pick up some money from a friend of mine, but I don't see him. Can I get a few dollars from you?" she asked.

"What'cha need?" I asked as I reached in my pocket.

"C'mon, Money. We go—way--better than that! Just give me whatever. You know how I am with paying bills?"

"Here. Just get off this *hot ass* strip," I said handing her a nice stack of twenty dollar bills. "Thanks, baby," she said hugging me again. "I gotta run. Don't forget to give me a call—let's meet up some time soon and bring Tavon with you!"

I looked at her like she was trying to steal something.

"Humph!" she said looking at him and licking her lips. "I should be gettin' money from his little paid ass, too."

If a woman can flirt with every part of her body, that's exactly what Precious did. As I glanced at Tavon, I could see how he'd been hypnotized by Precious that fast.

"Girl go on 'bout your business." *Those were my last words before she crossed the street putting on a show from behind for the both of us.*

Tavon and I both stared at her until she was gone and then at each other.

"Damn, Fast Money, that's Precious? Man, I've heard some stories about her, that chick is the bomb!"

"Yea, that's her ass, she's the bomb alright."

As we started towards the Chinese carryout, I could hear another hustle call. This time it was a female.

"Loose ones. Loose ones. Newports! Newports! Two for one dollar," she touted.

"Viagra! Viagra! Five dollars a pop, y'all. Take two of these and she—or he, however you float—will love you in the morning," one dude high off that shit shouted.

He marketed his pills through a catchy chant to anyone who wanted to improve their sexual performance and continued walking. As we entered through the bright red door of the takeout joint, we started up our conversation again where we left off while we were in the truck.

"Check this out, Tavon? I'm feeling what you're saying about Juvenile and all but he can't get you money like I can, can he?"

"Whatchu mean, Money?"

"You want one of these trucks, don't you? You even said you wanted a business, didn't you? I'm a show you what this game is all about. You just have to listen to me—and trust what I tell you."

"The first thing I'm telling you is to trust no one. This is no kid stuff now! You're dealing with the big times now. You have to start learning how to trust *nobody*. If you don't know how, you better practice--hear me? In this world it's all about you!" *I looked directly at him so he could see and feel how serious I was. He had to understand this in order to survive.*

"Blueprint! Blueprint! I got that raw Cocaine, y'all," announced a stranger who spoke for everyone to hear as he walked in and out of the carryout.

"Can I help you, Sir?" an Asian voice asked.

"Give me one big box of shrimp and rice, four wings with extra duck sauce, and two egg rolls—what you want, Tavon?"

"Get me the same thing, shrimp and rice, with extra shrimp and a Pepsi," he said.

Obviously still struck by Precious' performance, Tavon brought our conversation back to Precious as we waited to get our order.

"Damn, Money! Precious is a bomb!" he said.

"Yea, she's gonna always be like that."

"Is that still your gurl?" he asked.

"Naw. We still cool, but it's not like that," I told him. *I was thinking about her when he asked me that question. I learned quite a few things from her, but some things you have to let go.*

"You see where your mind is Tay?" I asked. "I'm trying to teach you how to get money like these dudes on Pennsylvania Avenue and more. This thing is about money, but you're thinking 'bout that trick."

"I'm hearing you," he said. "But some of my homies I trust with my life! How can I learn to do that crazy shit?"

"I'm a show you how to get this dough in large amounts until it hard to count! Just follow my lead. Watch how fast you start getting paid."

When I told him that, I looked him firmly in the face to let him know how serious all of this was. Life or death depended on lessons learned. I had to teach him. I sealed that session with some daps and a hug. That was our way of pledging our word.

As we ate and talked, he listened carefully. He should have—because I took lessons from his father. The streets made us family and I was committed to showing him how to get money in large amounts. I'd heard the same stories over and over while growing up in the streets. I wanted Tavon to show the talent of hustling like his father, but I didn't want him ending up spending the rest of his life in jail.

"Back in the day, your father Leroy was a big player on the gangster scene, did you know that? He was involved with a major organization out of New York. Not many could have done that in Big Apple back in those days. Legend has it that after plugging in with a black gangster name Frank Mathewson, Leroy became the Baltimore leg of a NY connection.

"Your family had rabbit fur coats with matching hats, suits and matching shoes, and imported outfits that set the trends. Tavon, they say you had Nike tennis shoes fresh off the shoe circuit before local stores had them to sell. Diamond jewelry and other luxuries came along with your father being a big drug dealer. He has always been my role model in the dope game, Leroy that is. I had heard so much about him—and in my own way learned much from him."

"Two for tens! Two for tens right here, y'all!" a touter bellowed out loudly into the airwaves as a police car patrolled the block. *Noise from passing cars made another distracting sound. That didn't matter because today in the hustle, like everyday, was business as usual. A man and woman team walked right by with money in hand.*

"Who got them two for tens? Y'all got dat' raw?" she asked.

"Naw, you better check with somebody else," Tavon replied nonchalantly. *Whoever they were, they were looking awful and obviously wanted that raw badly. Drugs had them on a fool's mission.*

"There are a couple of things the streets always gossiped about when it came to your father, Tay. Leroy made a lot of cocky mistakes being on top. He talked on telephones, spent crazy money on big cars and killed a few people.

"Your father was Baltimore's first in two categories. He was the first to really make big money out of this game. But he was also the first to receive the federal "Kingpin" charge in Baltimore. They say three of his key lieutenants snitched on him. He got paid one last time when Leroy's three friends got the federal courts to pay him sixty years for masterminding the biggest drug empire this city has ever known. Nobody, not even your mother, could forget the violence that went along with him," I said.

Top Officials ask for help

Baltimore's Top Cop is calling a community forum to discuss the ways in which his police force could help combat crime in certain areas of the city. Violence has increased in the last three weeks. There have been 11 murders and increasing reports of violent crimes. Commissioner Ned Morris is inviting all to come and support a better Baltimore.

Chapter 12

TAVON

"I done came up. /
Put my life on the line."

Jay-Z, "Coming Of Age"
Hard Knock Life Vol. 2
(feat. Memphis Bleek)

It didn't take me long to grow at all. Fast Money was my source and, like he told me, maybe I could be bigger than my father. I wanted that for myself, so I got on with him every time his connect put something in his possession. Money gave me lessons on trafficking back and forth—teaching me everything he could. With that, I never looked back.

His source was slowing down again, but Money didn't trip. He told us to use the money we had to get whatever we could to keep things going. He introduced to me to the Jamaican Posse. I know what he was trying to do. He wanted us to stay on with whatever so we could keep our spots on lockdown. Somebody would definitely try to take them over.

Prices for kilos on the streets were about $28,000 per brick. New York was selling theirs for around $23,000. The

Posse was selling kilos in Baltimore for around $25,000. Fast Money turned us on to some heavy hitters.

I must admit, my partner, Juvenile, wasn't getting half of what I was getting, but he was making out too. All he had to do was pay my crews—and the rest was his. I already told him that one day this whole operation would be his. He hustled hard banking on that. Every time I copped from the Posse, I would get J some weed. He loved going over to Butter's house in East Baltimore to get high at the end of the night. The weed they had was called Green. A regular ounce was going for eight hundred in the streets. They were selling theirs for $1200 and they had no problem moving that stuff because it was that good.

Ring! Ring!

Who the hell could this be calling me? I don't even feel like talking right now.

Ring! Ring!

As the phone rang continuously, I fumbled to find it while trying to keep my eyes on the road, and one hand on the steering wheel—Damn I really need to get a headset.

"Hello" I answered, almost out of breath from trying to figure out which pocket my phone was in.

"It took you long enough, where you at?"

"Hey, what's up? I just came back from the Avenue. I squared everything with Money, but he couldn't put us where we needed to be. The stuff he just brought back is finished already, and now he's in a holding pattern again. Anyway, I went to talk to our friends up Park Heights. I got squared with one *byrd* to flip. Everything else is ours. Plus, I got what you like."

"For real bro? You hooked a brother up with some of that good stuff?" he asked. "That's what I'm talking bout—you my main man Tay," he said before I could even answer him.

Juvenile was seeing money, the money I promised to show him. Lately we couldn't depend on Fast Money alone because his supplier had become so inconsistent. He wasn't coming through with too much of anything, especially cocaine. I kept seeing the Jamaican Posse to get some weight to keep us going because they had it all the time. I've never seen so much stuff in one place. Anyway, getting bricks from them would hold us, and our spots, until Fast Money got back on with his connect.

"Ay—Tavon! I just counted $31G's. That's 15-5 apiece," Juvenile said.

"It's all hood—and I'll take that!"

"Don't forget. We both have to do something for Trigger," Juvenile said sounding excited.

"I'm ready for that, too."

"I really wish he was here. All three of us would be running this shit right now. Let's send him a thousand between the two of us," Juvenile suggested.

I responded right away because Trigger was my homey, too, when he was on the streets. "No. Let's send him five hundred more. Make that fifteen. He should be straight with that."

"I'll take care of that by tomorrow, most definitely," he said.

"I miss Trigger. You know we came up in this game because our man put his life on the line for us. It's about time we get with that C.O. so we can send him two more balloons, too."

"For real, Yo. Trigger saved our lives," Juvenile said recalling what happened.

All of us shared the same story. Trigger was the dangerous one of the three who protected what little we had before meeting Fast Money. Our third partner got his nickname because he was a gun fanatic. He was responsible for our nickel and dime operation on Mount Street before he shot somebody for trying to take over our territory. Although he wasn't here in the flesh, we made sure he was well taken care of. Prison couldn't stop love—especially since he went there for saving our lives. The streets remembered Trigger as a die-hard soldier. Protecting us, his family, got him the time. Even in prison he was still fighting. This time he was fighting for his own life as a result of what he did. The bloodshed started in the streets, but didn't stop there.

CITY/COUNTY BLOTTER

INMATE STABBING AT JESSUP

An inmate serving time for an attempted murder at the Maryland House of Corrections suffered near fatal injuries to his neck and other parts of his body. Authorities said he was flown to the University of Maryland Shock Trauma Center.

Two homemade knives were found near his unconscious body in the Central Storeroom shower area of the prison. Medical authorities located within the institution removed a knife from his neck. Prison officials have placed two inmates into a highly secure segregation unit. The inmates were still wearing clothing covered with blood evidence while being questioned.

Preliminary intelligence gathered by the Internal Investigation Unit has revealed this incident was "in retaliation for the victim's criminal conviction." The victim was convicted of shooting and paralyzing a rival drug dealer on the streets. This was not the first incident of retaliation. Juan "Trigger" Bolden was being treated for major stab wounds and remains in critical condition.

Chapter 13

JUVENILE

"Only life of mine is a life of crime."
Jay-Z, "Money, Cash, Hoes"
Hard Knock Life Vol. 2
(feat. DMX)

"Speak," I said answering my cell phone. *After circling the block twice and not being able to find a parking space, I decided to park a little ways from the store. I was walking up North Avenue on a fool's mission. Returning for the first time to the sub shop where I shot Rabbit a couple months ago, I hadn't been back 'cause I wasn't trying to get snatched by the cops. But when my baby girl asked for a sub from this joint, I couldn't tell her no. I had a hard enough time trying to convince her that she couldn't come with me and I damn sure didn't tell her that I couldn't go there.*

"J, where you at?" Tavon asked. "I wanna show you something."

"It's so noisy out here I can hardly hear you. I'm on North Avenue, near the sub shop. I'm walking up to get Tiff a sub before I go over to Butter's house to get smoked up!"

"Man, you sure do like living on the edge," he said.

"You know me, anything for my baby girl."

"I know that's right. Look, wait for me at the corner of Poplar Grove and North. I'll be through in about five minutes."

"If you're that close, you might have to wait for me," I said before hanging up the phone.

I couldn't help wondering what Tavon had to show me. Lately we hadn't been able to get our hands on a lot of stuff to sell, so we were not out hustling much. What we did have, we had to make last until we could get back to moving heavy. Maybe he got some more work he wanted me to have. I didn't think that was what he wanted to see me about. I still had no idea what he needed me for, so I got the sub and drove up the block.

"Ggrrrrrwwww," I heard and recognized the sound as my stomach. *I laughed at the thought. Damn, I took a big sniff. The aroma of peppers, fried onions, steak and oils hit my empty stomach and it growled again. It wasn't just Tiffany's craving that sent me out on such a risky run because now my own stomach was crying out. I pulled up at the corner of North and Popular Grove expecting to see Tavon but he was nowhere to be found. Tavon is always late, I thought to myself and having this sandwich around on an empty stomach isn't helping much. As I settled in to wait on Tavon, I noticed a slick steel gray BMW convertible with tinted windows parked across the street. It was sweet and looked brand spanking new.*

I wanted to get out of the car to go take a closer look at this work of art but changed my mind when my stomach growled one more time. I couldn't resist Tiffany's sub any longer; I had to bite in. So I decided to admire from afar. I was only there for a few seconds when I saw the driver's door open and out stepped Tavon.

"Come on J," he yelled from across the street looking and sounding like a kid at Christmas.

"Yo, Tavon!" I said with a mouth full of food. "That joint's da' shit!"

"Yeah, it is. BMW M Roadster, 3.2L six-cylinder engine with heated seats, top of the line sound system and a ride that would impress all our competition."

He spoke as if he studied everything about the car just so he could recite it back to me. I walked around it, just looking, peeping in the door and taking it all in. I couldn't believe he went and got himself another ride like this. He must've bumped his damn head and forgotten about me.

"Come on. Let's show Tiffany before Jameel gets home from work. Wanna drive?" he asked handing me the keys. "Here. Take your keys."

I must have looked at him like he was crazy. "Take my what?" I asked.

"I'm not kidding. You have to drive this thing. How could I not share this with you? We are partners for life," he said hitting his chest.

I knew I would have let him drive my ride, but I also knew that he would have been the ONLY one and I probably would have waited until I had it for at least a day. But he didn't have to offer it again. I walked to the driver's side, grabbed the keys and got in.

I took a deep drag of the new car smell, rubbed my greasy hands on my clothes before I touched the leather steering wheel. I turned the radio to 92Q as soon as I sat in the driver's seat. Since the top was down I turned it up real loud because our street anthem song was on.

"Dis' is the Bossman. B'more—Stand up! Let's go. / This is the land and home of the—Ho! / This is the city where they rock them—Ho! / If you repping your city say—Ho! / Eastside-Ho! Westside—Ho!"

I pulled onto North Avenue heading for Hilton Parkway. I took Hilton to Edmondson and Edmondson down to Martin Luther King.

"Aren't we going to show Tiffany?" Tavon asked.

"Yeah. Just not right now."

"Well, then there is something I have to tell you."

"What's that?" I asked glancing over at him.

"Merry Christmas!"

"Huh?"

"This is my present to you, Hustler. I guess you can say Tiffany and I got it for you for Christmas."

"Man stop playin'." *I was sure I was hearing things.*

"You know you're my right hand man and without you we couldn't be doing all we do."

"This is unbelievable man! This is unbelievable!"

"Watch where you are going," he said. "We don't want to ruin your gift before she gets to see it. Now all we have to do is get *legit* licenses—not Age of Majority cards."

I drove out of the city, onto 95 South, pulled out into the fast lane and opened the car up. My head was reeling. This surprise had me dazed. After driving a few miles, going as fast as I dared for as long as I could, I looked over at Tavon again.

"How were you able to do this?" I asked.

"Fast Money hooked me up with a bonus. All that weight we been pushing for him, you know he had to do something special for me! Plus don't forget how much we're doing on our own in between. Money from both helped me to get you this. It's me and you against the world—don't forget that shit, J!" he said, extending a strong handshake to me.

"What about the rest of the crew?" I asked, at the same time trying to calculate how much of a bonus that could be.

"Everybody in our crew has a bonus coming. This is yours. What we have to figure out now is how to take care of Trigger."

"I'm telling you man, this is da' shit. I'm feeling this because you know we in this shit together for life!"

"I share all that I have with you man. You're the brother I never had."

"Well then, let's enjoy this thing," I told him.

"What about Tiffany?" he asked, remembering I had gone and gotten her something to eat.

"Tiffany may get to see it because I'll sneak up on them maybe today. But she will never get a chance to ride in it. Jameel doesn't want anything to do with this life and she definitely doesn't want it to touch Tiffany."

"You know what J? If I had a good woman like Jameel in love with me--and raising a beautiful daughter like Tiffany, I would go to them and never look back. I dreamed of having that kind of life all the time. My parents didn't have it, so I've never seen it. I don't know what it feels like or where to begin. But it's right in front of you."

"It's no good if I can't provide all they deserve. Having them means a lot, but I gotta do what I gotta do! You see what we do. That's the only way I know how to provide. Besides, Jameel ain't my wife. I'll tell you again like I told you before. The only wife of mine is a life of crime. The only way I can make it is to be married to the game we play."

"But Jameel doesn't let you give her anything now," Tavon said, "and you have plenty to give. If you had less, you would be wth them and you could actually help, even if it wasn't much."

"Now you sounding like Jameel. You ought to be a preacher."

"Maybe. You know she just might be right. I just want you to be happy man. I know why I am out here. I don't have anything besides chasing my father's legacy and trying to keep my mom together so she stays off the streets. But you have everything and you keep trading it for this crazy life of ours."

I didn't say anything for a while. Think about that...a crook preaching to a criminal. Tavon fiddled with the radio until he found some other hip-hop station playing Go-Go music. He figured out how to heat the seats and I kept driving through DC.

I knew Jameel loved me and was waiting for me to get it together. She didn't press me to change, but she didn't cross her line in the sand either. We both knew the boundaries of our relationship until I decide to leave this life. She never missed an opportunity to remind me that she and Tiffany were both praying for that day. But I had my own goals too. I wanted something first. I wanted to be the man.

I'm not hating or anything, but Tavon is the shit right now. Fast Money was grooming him, showing him the ropes, giving him the opportunities. He was on his way to blowing up and being just like his father. Even as a kid, he knew that it was his birthright, but it was my dream. Even though he's like my brother and shares everything with me, I'm still a step away from the top. I want to be on top-- just a tad bit more than I want Jameel and Tiffany right now. I know it's wrong to feel this way. Tavon trusts me with everything just like it was mine, but it's not the same as it being mine. I want what he has—and I'm gonna get it because I can run it better. Then I'll be giving him percentages.

"J, you've been awfully quiet," Tavon said bringing my jumbled thoughts to a halt. "Where we going?

I looked at the highway and saw that I was approaching the Washington Monument. Tiffany was going to be mad at me. I'm sure Jameel fed her something else by now.

"Back to Tiffany," I answered. "I hope she'll forgive me again for not showing up and having to eat food out of her momma's kitchen."

"Shit, I'd love to have something out of Jameel's kitchen right now. Homegirl knows how to throw down! "

Tavon spoke as if he could taste her cooking, just by talking about it. "I know, but kids never want what's cooked at home. They always want it from the greasy spoon down the block," I said in response.

"True dat."

As we came back into Baltimore, Tavon's phone rang. He didn't say who the caller was, but he talked like it was a booty call and asked me to drop him off. I left him at my parked car so he could get to where he was going.

I had to get to Tiffany. As I pulled up in front of Jameel's, I saw the ladies going in for her Bible Study group. I couldn't even knock on the door to say hello to Tiffany now. Jameel was serious about God and very focused on living right. That's why she limited my access to Tiffany and their space. She didn't want the life coming into her house and as much as she wanted us together, she wanted God more. She wanted that for me, too.

My priority right now is to do whatever, to get to the top of this game. I have to have the street life and style and I'm willing to do it all--for the love of fast money. After feeling disappointed that I couldn't see my ladies, I decided now was really a good time to go over to Butter's house to get high and celebrate.

Chapter 14

JAMEEL

"Don't wanna fight, /
Don't wanna fuss, /
You the mother of my baby..."
Jay-Z, "Soon You'll Understand"
The Dynasty

It was a beautiful Sunday afternoon and everyone was outside enjoying the weather after our first service. The kids were probably enjoying it the most. You could tell from the way they were running around, they couldn't wait for summer to get here.

"Tiffany, c'mon-baby. It's really time to go. We gotta go pick grandma up," I said, calling out to Tiffany trying to get her away from her friends so we could leave.

"Yes, ma'am. But are we coming back to the 4'o clock service, Ma?" she asked with concern.

"After we take Momma out to eat you can come back to see your Sunday school friends," I told her.

Pastor and his wife told me about a special place where I could take Momma out to eat without missing a lot of time from church on Sunday. Besides, this is the one Sunday a month I am free of serving dinners.

I had to treat my mother to something special this Sunday. She's been helping me with Tiffany ever since God gifted me with her. Those two together in my life helps me to define what beautiful is. And the blessings just keep on coming. Pastor's wife called there to make reservations for us ahead of time.

I pulled up in front of the house. "Tiffany, baby go inside and tell Momma Pearle I'm out here waiting. I don't mean to rush, but we have to travel all the way downtown and we have reservations for 1 o'clock."

It didn't take Momma long to come hurrying outside. She was hungry just like we were.

"Hey baby, how you been?" Momma asked, as she settled in the front seat and leaned over to hug me.

"Jameel, I heard a lot about this place where we are going. Have you eaten there before?"

"No, Momma. But I hear the food is good."

"Well, hurry up and get me there caus' I'm hungry," Momma said, rubbing her stomach. We all laughed at her silly expression.

I got downtown much quicker than I thought I would. There was not much traffic on the road on Sundays. When we passed Martin Luther King Boulevard, I knew we were close because the directions said it was located near Maryland General Hospital. The State building was on one side and the hospital on the other. Tiffany was amazed as the light rail passed by while we sat at the red light on Read Street right off of Howard Street. Just like Pastor said, right across from Diva's beauty salon there was a small lot where we could park.

"Momma, where are we now?" Tiffany asked, as we got out the car and started walking towards the restaurant.

"I think Pastor said they call this area Mount Vernon," I said before looking inside the beauty salon we were passing by. "He said this whole block—all the way down the street—is called Antique Row."

"Did you know that, Ma?"

"Child, I haven't been down this way in years. I'd forgotten what down here looks like."

We walked far enough to see the restaurant's burgundy awnings, but the shops on the block looked so unique we decided to walk the block a little despite our growling stomachs.

"Tiff. Each building holds a lot of history, especially the historic *Eubie Blake Center* right here." *I couldn't resist grabbing the shiny brass rail like I owned it.*

"Momma, look at that hospital over there," she said pointing directly across the street. "Look how big it is."

"This is far enough, now. Let's do what we came down here to do," Momma said in a stern voice.

I glanced down at my watch and realized we were running out of time. We headed back down the street so we could be there on time for our reservations.

As we entered the double glass doors to the restaurant, the sounds of gospel met us inside. You could here Kirk Franklin's distinct voice.

"Put your hands together—and Stomp! / All the people say—Stomp! / I promise to stomp, the whole stomp—nothing but the stomp*!"*

My head just naturally started bouncing to the beat as I looked around and saw the employees adding the finishing touches to the setup.

The entranceway was alive with color from the magnificent artwork. The first oil painting looking at me was Ray Charles, and then B.B. King.

The smells of the honeydews, strawberries, pineapple, cherries, cantaloupe, and mangos forced my head to turn to look for the fruit. The fruit bowl looked so good I wanted to walk right over and stuff myself.

As we stepped further inside, a life-size painting of Cab Calloway looked down on us from a vibrant oil canvas painting, beckoning us to come in and be a part of the action. And then I smelled it. Not the fruits this time, but the food! Talk about home cooking--this stuff smelled like one of Momma's Thanksgiving dinners. The closest thing to me was fish, basil, garlic, barbecue, chicken and lemon. It all smelled so good I didn't know where to start. Rumor had it that stars coming from out-of-town would make this their first stop. Now this is the kind of classy African American restaurant we really needed in this city.

Chafing dishes sparkled from a good cleaning--just like the tongs displayed in front of them. All these things were sitting on top of snowy, white tablecloths. The buffet was laid out in style.

Fresh flowers added a special touch. I reached over and smelt the display near the dining entrance. This place really made you feel like you were at home.

"Finally," Momma said with a sound of relief. "Somebody in Baltimore has stepped out on faith to create a beautiful place where everybody can eat in style. Now this is classy."

"I know that's right, Momma."

Wicker baskets played the role of beds to crab legs and steamed shrimp. People were standing in line waiting to be served at an omelet and waffle station.

"I'll have a waffle and omelet with cheese, onions, green peppers. I want this on two plates for me and my husband," I overheard someone say as we walked by.

The chef catered to each individual, one at a time. It sure smelled like somebody could cook up some southern foods.

"Grandma, it's an all-you-can-eat Sunday brunch," Tiffany announced before being greeted.

"Good afternoon. And welcome to Downtown Southern Blues where we feature an all day brunch for $24.95 and children, ages twelve and under, like she is, are half priced. I am your host for the day. Do you have reservations, ma'am?" the manager asked with a pleasant smile.

"Yes. It's Ms. Jackson for one o'clock."

"One moment, please, Ms. Jackson, while I check the guest book."

"Thank you."

"Ahh, here we are," he said, after highlighting my name. "Please, follow me to your table for three. And how are you, young lady?"

Tiffany responded right away, "I'm fine. Thank you."

We were seated at a table for four, but the host removed the extra setting. Yellow chairs made their second floor seating area stand out. Each table was arranged beautifully. Silverware sat on each side of a folded white napkin. Everything, especially the colors, complimented the warm feel of the place. I couldn't believe the details of the artwork on the walls. I sat there in amazement before hearing my daughter speak.

"Momma, why do we have two forks," Tiffany asked.

"One fork is for salad. The other is for eating your main meal."

Tiffany and I talked while we waited for instructions. I had to explain what she was seeing for the first time. Momma, on the other hand, knew what to do. She was already leaving to serve herself when our server came to tell us what to do. It's almost as if she'd been here before.

It didn't take long for us to fill our plates with whatever we desired. I took some shrimp, a couple crab legs for starters, and some catfish. Tiffany had waffle with strawberries and whipped cream on top.

Back at the table we had an opportunity to talk—like we try to do every Sunday after church.

"Jameel, I've been meaning to talk to you for a while. You have to slow down some," Momma said calmly in her start-up tone.

"Momma, please. Let's not have that conversation right now. Can we just eat?"

Momma reached over closer to whisper. "Your health is my concern. You never slow down. You're working at the Post Office full time, going to night school at Coppin State University, being a good mother to Tiffany, and taking care of everything at the church."

I watched her every move as she finished putting homemade peach butter on her hot roll. I knew she wasn't finished her I have a dream speech.

"Baby, you're doing too much—and you have to slow down, at least long enough for you to settle down."

"Momma, lets not start with the settle down lecture again, I've told you and Juvenile I'm not having that street stuff in our lives. The streets are killing people everyday—and I don't want to be a part of it. I've seen my share of funerals. We are not going to be a part of it. Until her father gets his life together, we will never have a chance to settle down."

"I know you keep saying that baby, but sometimes you have to take the good with the bad."

"Come on, Ma. We're here to have fun. This is just my way of saying thanks for all the love you have given Tiffany and me. From the very first day she was born you've help me so much. This is just my way of saying thanks."

"Now Jameel you know I'll give my life for any one of my children and for my grandbaby. Whatever I do, I do it from the heart—you don't have to worry about making anything up to me."

"I know that, Momma."

"But as I was saying, ain't nothing wrong with that boy. He will eventually get himself together and you should help him. You are the first one to agree that behind every strong man is a strong woman. I was always behind your father--bless his soul. He wasn't an angel, but he took care of his family. You loved your father. Nobody could tell you that he did any wrong — even though he did. And Dorian wants to take care of you and Tiffany, but you won't let him," she said, sounding almost like she was sent to plead Dorian's case.

I remained silent for a moment. I tried to focus on my food and my response to what she believed should be right in my life. Everybody who'd ever been to the brunch brags about the food. Now I could see why!

"We'll never agree, Momma," I told her after I got done cracking my last crab leg. "I really don't understand. On one hand, you say you're proud of my life. Then, you turn around and say I have to get it together so we can be with Dorian. I agree we all love him, but he chooses to live life in the streets and not with his family. I'm not having that. God wants me to have more; I deserve more. Tiffany deserves more. And I don't understand why you condone that stuff."

"Well baby, you wouldn't have to work so hard if you'd allow him to help—is all I'm saying. That boy helps me out every time he gets a chance. That's all I'm going to say about it."

"Ma, I can't believe you taking that blood money!" I said.

"You don't see me killing myself to pay bills do you?" she asked.

We ate in silence until it was time for us to get dessert. It was time to get out of there and go back to church. Tifanny wanted to walk down the street to see the Eubie Blake Center again. Not too long after that we pulled off from the parking lot and headed back to church.

As we pulled up in front of the church Tiffany started screaming. "Momma! Momma! There's my Daddy right there," she said, as she quickly jumped out the car and ran over to her father to hug him.

I love the way she loves her father. That girl thinks the world of him. They both enjoy love like it was meant to be between a father and his daughter. I miss him not being a part of what we started together. They both looked at me as if I was missing something.

"Hello, son in law," Momma said quickly, as he made her way over to him.

"Hey, Ms. Pearl," he said, as he reached out and hugged her.

"How you been Dorian? Boy, I fell behind a little bit this month again so do something to help your mother-in-law out."

"I got something for you before I leave Ms. Pearl--don't worry about it. As a matter of fact, here it is right here." Dorian reached in his pocket and handed her the money he came up with.

I couldn't believe Momma could stand in front of my face, right in front of the church, and take money from Dorian like that. She knows how I feel about that money.

"You are just such a lifesaver," she said, as she hugged him again. "Thank you so much."

"Hey, Jameel," he said as he reached out to hug me. "What's up, baby?"

"Hello, Dorian, please don't hey baby me. Tiffany, could you go inside while I talk to your father, please?"

"But Momma, I want to talk to Daddy."

"Tiffany, go inside, please. You'll see him after I talk with him, Okay?"

"Go ahead, baby. Listen to what your mother is saying" he said to her.

"I started to call you this morning, Jameel," he said. "I wanted to get with you and Tiffany and go to church and go with your mother to get something to eat. Honestly, I did, but time got away from me."

"Let's not get into that conversation again, Dorian!"

"C'mon Jameel—I don't wanna fight nor fuss with you—you're the mother of my baby. We shouldn't be going through these changes anyway. What we should be talking about is getting our family back together."

"That's not what I wanted to talk to you," I replied. "Besides, that will all happen when you decide it's time for a change in your heart. Anyway, I wanted to tell you that Tiffany has a few things coming up at school and church. She has a program this coming Friday at school and one Sunday at the church. You know she'll want to see you there."

"Jameel, I promised Tavon already that I would be holding things down for him on Friday, but I might be able to make Sunday. I know you don't like to hear this, but things are finally coming together for us."

"So now the streets are more important than your daughter. You can't even spare enough time to see her perform? What is wrong with you? The bad part about all this is that Tiffany loves you so much and you can't even give her a little of your time!

"Dorian, every time I see you, you keep saying the same thing. When are you going to get your life together and come out of the streets?"

"Jameel, I'm gonna get it together, but I'm trying to make some things happen first. Just trust me on this! Why you always gotta be fussing at me?"

"You know what Dorian, I'm done trying. I don't want you around until you decide it's time to change. As much as it hurts, we can't have you around us like that. It hurts every time I see you. Everybody knows what you are doing, but they make me feel like I'm the bad person because I don't want that around us. Momma is one of your main cheerleaders!"

"That's because they know we should be together, but you keep acting crazy Jameel. I'm getting it together baby, but it has to be on my time," he said, reaching into his pocket. "Here, baby, this is for you and Tiffany. This--"

"This nothing, Dorian! I'm sorry, but I told you time and time again that she can't have this money. We don't want it—stop trying to give it to us. None of that money can replace your time. That's what we need—you! Plus, I'm not my mother or one of your cheerleaders. Goodbye!"

I should have just taken the money to burn it up—just to show him how serious I am. I looked at him, I know, with sadness in my eyes. He was just such a young talent. Like Pastor says in his sermons, there are too many like him that are going to waste in the streets.

"But Jameel, you don't understand. Can I at least see my daughter? I just want to spend some time with Tiffany like you do!"

"Tiffany doesn't need that in her life Dorian."

"Jameel why you always try to *dis'* me in front of my daughter? All I want to do is give my daughter the things I couldn't have when I was growing up. I want better for her Jameel, and for you too—if you let me, but you just don't understand that!"

Without an answer I turned and walked away. He chose the streets over us, his family. And I can't keep explaining that it is him we need and not that money. I couldn't get through to him and all we did was go back and forth on the same conversations.

As I walked towards the church to get Tiffany, I couldn't help but think about all the things I've been hearing about him and Tavon. It hurts me so much because I'm close to both of them, we all grew up together and all of us have been friends for so long. Tavon is Tiffany's godfather, but what they're doing is dangerous and its wrong and I refuse to be a part of it.

Lord knows I've shed enough tears for Dorian. I never know whether he'll be the one featured on the 11 o'clock news or not. One thing I couldn't do was to let him see me cry. I wanted to cry even more as I looked up and saw Tiffany through the window crying and waiving goodbye to him. Whenever he leaves we never know whether it will be our last time seeing Dorian or not. It hurts me to see my daughter in so much pain each time this happens, but I can't give up—no matter what people think. I can't be a drug dealer's girl and neither will our daughter get caught up in that crazy lifestyle. All I can do is just keep on praying.

Community News
West Baltimore

Community Improvement Association

The Director of the Responsible Black Family Alliance Group has sponsored a program created by ex-drug dealers in efforts of getting others off the streets and into the world of work.

"Hustler's Anonymous clearly allows an outlet for men and women who want to turn their lives around. We've never had a program for recovery from the streets unless we used drugs ourselves. But we find that hustling, selling drugs on the streets, is just as addictive," said Greg Washman. "As Director of this program I saw the need for change. If you wanted help to get away from life on the streets there was no immediate help, but we've changed that."

The Mayor's Office of Employment Development has taken notice of the effectiveness of this unique program. Many young adults in this program have changed because of the amnesty this program offers as well as counseling, and employment opportunities. "I've never had a real job, but this program (Hustler's Anonymous) has helped me to overcome that," said Tidy Rogers.

Researchers are monitoring the attempts of one hundred ex-dealers who have said no to the streets and yes to a better life. "Our interest is to change lives. And if other interested family members, community group associations, or businesses have any ideas, they can contact our office." Mr. Washman said.

Chapter 15

FAST MONEY

"There are 36 ounces in a ki[lo] /
You do the addition... /
I was moving byrds like an Oriole fitted."
Jay-Z, "What They Gonna Do"
The Blueprint 2
(Feat. Sean Paul)

Business had picked up back for me again and everything was booming. I hate to say it, but it was becoming too much for me to handle. I have so many things to do and not enough time to do it. I have money I need to strap and stash in my holding locations and I need to get some product ready to go out. I've really been neglecting putting my money in the right places for some time now. I know I shouldn't do it, but I needed help so I decided to ask Tavon and Juvenile to help me out. After all, it was time for them to get another lesson anyway. Before now they only knew how to handle the end product but today I'll hip them to the tricks of cutting heroin to make it the best.

It was time to put something fresh on the streets like every two or three days. Raul's packages made me a magician. I would make drugs disappear and money would appear like magic. As we got comfortable in the kitchen, we wasted no time getting started.

"Hand me those two bags right there, J. Grab the spoons and sifters out of the drawer, Tavon. See, this is the way you mix this stuff, but you have to use these in the right order," I told him after laying everything out on the table.

I was serious about showing them what needed to be done. "Pay attention—both of y'all. See, you have to make sure you keep two separate brands of dope on hand. One has to be more potent. See this pile right here? This is ours. It only has a little bit of cutt on it."

"Money, why do you have two types?" asked Juvenile.

"I just told you. One is for us and the other is for those hustlers buying from us. See this right here. This white stuff right here is quinine. And this is mannitol. You use both of these to cut the raw and break it down for the streets to sell. There are 36 ounces in a kilo—something y'all have been calling *byrds*. If you put this quinine and mannitol on top, we'll be moving byrds—or whatever you want to call them--like an Orioles fitted cap."

"Oh, so that's how you do it!" Tavon said, nodding his head in amazement as if he were learning to solve an algebraic expression.

"See, my hustle, on the wholesale level, is to break down the potency and increase the amount. Once you spoon your mix, you have to use these sifters to strain it together. Put this little bit on this pile. These will be the sample-testers we pass out today," I explained. "Now, here," I said. *I handed them the bags and the spoon and put them in the driver's seat.* "You two try it like I showed you."

Having a consistent supply or just knowing somebody who could get what was needed on demand will get you paid in the street. It's unbelievable how this white substance makes a poor man feel great and create thousandaire possibilities in the minds of everybody taking that chance.

This was a new aspect of the business for him to be involved in. No longer a small timer, Tavon was now all the way in. They were both so attentive when we have our little teaching sessions.

I watched, as they both worked together as any corporate America team would, for a common goal. As a matter-of-fact they were doing it better because there was no power struggle going on in this boardroom. I could see that Tavon needed answers to something else he was dying to ask. After he had filled a bunch of Ziploc Baggies with 30 grams, he looked at me.

"How many of those things do you go through a day?" he asked.

"Too many to count!" I answered vaguely, not wanting to show my hand totally.

"I'm just saying Money, between me and Juvenile alone we go through at least 10 but when you add your other crews to that you are really doing this thing big time man," he said, still trying to dig for exact figures.

"Do the math son, do the math." I smiled because he was determined to figure it out. "Let's just put it this way, the more they pump, the more they get. And you know what, as soon as we hit them with this, Son, we have to start gettin' ready for the next time we re-them up."

I still had money to count for Raul and I needed to get this done because I was due in New York in two days. I decided to let Tavon in on another aspect of this business.

"Yo, Juvenile. You got this man, 'cause I need to go count out some cash upstairs."

"Most definitely, Money. I got this. Go handle your business my man," Juvenile said, looking like a kid around a bunch of Halloween candy.

"Tavon, lets go take care of some other business upstairs. This way, you'll know this business from start to finish. *The only other skill he needed to know now was how to count and stack large sums of money. Today was as good a time as any to school him on the whole operation. He would be the one I would introduce to Raul when I retire—or something else happens.*

Back in my upstairs room, I opened the wall safe while Tavon watched. He helped me carry the money into a small room I had set up just for counting. I dumped all the cash on the floor after locking the door. It was okay having Juvenile downstairs getting the bags together for distribution. Even though he was high off that weed and Hennessy, his hands would help speed up the process.

Nobody really knew I kept most of my money and drugs at Precious' girlfriend's house. Pretty was my real partner, somebody who I could trust with my life traveling back and forth. I tried to keep that on the down low. Nobody else needed to know what I was doing and how.

"Tavon, make sure you don't mix the money from the different bags, because you wanna make sure each crew turn in the right amount of money.

"Oh, OK."

"The first thing we have to do is to count each bag and just check it with the little piece of paper inside the bag showing how much is supposed to be in it and how much dope that crew got," I said, sounding like I was teaching an accounts class.

"When we're finished," I continued, "we have to sort the money by denominations and then we can count and strap for a grand total."

"You gotta do all of that with all of this?" he asked, looking at all the money we were sitting in midst of.

"Yea, that's why I always told you to keep each bill with it's own kind, now you see how much easier it would be to count."

We sat silently sorting bills in stacks. I glanced over at Tavon a few times and noticed him looking at the stacks as they grew higher and higher. For a minute, I thought about his mom and her role in all of this. I still find it hard to believe that a mother would put her child out there like that but then I thought, who I am to cast judgment on anyone.

"Do I use these to strap now?" he asked, pointing to money straps in the container on the desk.

"No. Everything will be easy now from here on out. Just grab that counting machine over there on the shelf over the desk."

"What's this Fast Money?"

"Just sit back and check this out," I told him. "See now that we have it all sorted, a few buttons on this machine will get it all done for us. Just take up a stack of bills and set it in this slot on top and the machine will automatically count it for you. It stops when it gets to 100 bills. Then, you can start strapping using the strap with the correct amount of money on it."

"Are you serious? Is this thing that good?"

"Yea, this is the technology age son–the less manual labor you do the easier life gets, and the more time you have to do other things."

"Yo, this shit is tight. This is un-fucking-believable! This is where I'm trying to get to Money–the big time."

"It does take a minute to get it all counted by crew and sorted out. But, a slow grind is a sure one. This is what the game is all about—us lovin' this fast money."

When we were finally done and added it all together, even I was a bit surprised. It was over a quarter of a mil, $263,048 to be exact. I didn't share the total with him. My way of bragging was to have him total it himself. As he watched the calculator tape got longer and longer the smile on his face got wider and wider.

"Yo, Money, I ain't n-e-v-e-r seen so much cash in all my life, much less to be holding it. Man I'm ready to go back out, cause I'm gonna get mine!" Tavon said, as he got up from the desk looking like a man with a plan.

In the beginning, Tavon wasn't trying to be a monster and Juvenile was only a little crazy. But when runners got out of line, or people tried to step to them, something had to be done. They learned early on to play the game the right way. That's the only way to get respect from the streets. That was key.

Baltimore City Police Department

Internal Memo

A West Baltimore woman was arrested after our district narcotics officers investigated reports of a well-known drug dealer frequenting her house on Pulaski Street.

Drug enforcement agents and undercover detectives had been investigating several open-air drug markets for three months and gathered intelligence through informants. Several callers revealed the suspect's relationship to this homeowner and his whereabouts. At 9:18 p.m. last night narcotics officers received a warrant to search the premises of Pretty Jenifer, 33. She was arrested after tactical officers confiscated two loaded handguns, more than *$280,000 in cash*, 6 kilos of crack cocaine and approximately 2 pounds of heroin, some already packaged in cellophane bags with it's color coded brand name ready for street sales. This investigation is continuing.

Chapter 16

TAVON

"So to death do us, /
I'm never breaking my bond."
Jay-Z, "Coming of Age (Da Sequel)"
Hard Knock Life Vol. 2

I still had to do what I had to do since police raided Fast Money's stash house and got all that cash. They even got some of the drugs Juvenile and I helped him bag up. Apart from the cash, everything else he had was in that house! He thought it was a secret, but everybody knew he had Pretty trafficking and holding for him at her house. She talked too much. All you had to do was give that broad some weed and money. You'll hear everybody's business. Now, Fast Money is scared to even come out until nighttime.

Things kept going for me since I made some moves with the Jamaican Posse on a regular basis now. They were the best we had locally. I had no problems working with the weight I was getting through them. I bought a new truck in no time as a treat to myself. The first thing I want to do is to get it detailed to custom fit my style, so I made me an early morning appointment at this new detailing shop on Reisterstown Road. It didn't take them long to hook me up with a nice tint and them slick-ass rims I always wanted.

Today, Juvenile and I are gonna hang with one of our friends from school, Carl. We hadn't seen him in a while but we always talk to him. He did pretty good for himself since he was the only one of us with a career. He was now a FBI agent. On my way down Reisterstown Road my stomach communicated to my brain. I was definitely feeling Lexington Market. I had to get some of that Lake Trout fish and a fresh bag of UTZ potato chips I've been craving like a pregnant woman lately. I checked my watch and saw I had more than enough time to take care of my body, get my usual haircut and still be at the range on time. I better call Juvenile and remind him because he can get a little carried away. He has no concept of time.

"Yo, Tay, what's up?"

"Don't forget we are suppose to meet Homeboy at the spot today at three o'clock. Let them runners do their thing for a minute. We're gonna have some fun today. Yo, check this out! He finally got his hands on two of those new 50 calibers we been talking about gettin', so you know it's on. I can't wait to get one of those five-shots in my hand."

"He got two of them, right?" Juvenile asked in excitement.

"Yea, J."

"Count me in man. I'll be there--you know I've been tryin' to handle that shit."

"Just make sure you're on time and be ready to bet it all!" I said.

All of us knew the end result. It happens every time we get together. I'm the one always ending up being the loser.

"I'll see you when I get there and just have my money ready," he replied, laughing hysterically at my false confidence.

"J, you heard from Fast Money today?

"No, I tried to hit him up on the cell to see if he got anything worth having, but he didn't answer. I think he's still out of it."

I was in and out of that market in no time. After getting my fish, it was haircut time. I drove around to my Howard Street appointment. I'm always on time with no problem. It should be like that with everybody, but it's not. Home wasn't too far away, so after I left the barbershop I popped in for a quick shower and put on some relaxed gear and headed out. I'm always there early. It's something about going to that gun range that excites me every time we meet up.

Carl kept looking at his watch as we stood talking in the parking lot. "Where is that slow ass Juvenile at? It's almost 3:30pm, Tavon."

I was listening to automatic guns rattling off. Usually, in the city, when we hear gunshots it's time to run. But here in the county, at them fancy gun ranges, this is shit legal, no need to take cover. Just hearing all those high- powered weapons got my adrenaline pumping. I was ready!

"He had to change cars," I said in Juvenile's defense. *Carl hates to stand around waiting.* "What he drives when he's out on the strip is just for work purposes only. You know what I mean! Ain't nothin' changed from school Carl. His ass is still slow!"

We both laughed as we remembered how it was back in the day. "We may as well go ahead and get started," I said.

"OK, here is your ID," he said handing me my new identity.

"I don't know why you're rushing, Tay. Juvenile beats your ass and takes your money every time, since we've been coming here."

"Just go ahead and get our lanes, so I can show both of y'all what I can do! I'll wait for J while you get the lanes."

"Here," he said, as he handed me Juvenile's new ID. "Just give them to Dean at the front desk when you go in."

As I watched Carl walked across the parking lot with the black duffel bag in hand. I thought about back-in-the-day when we were growing up.

We always had Carl as a silent part of our team. We've known him forever. Some things in life don't change. To my partners, my word is my bond. I'll never break that. And I am in this with them until death.

Carl never did get caught up in the game, he always talk about getting out of the hellhole we grew up in. Now, he could identify himself with status, FBI status that is. He had his credentials and was a part of the bureau, but his love for his homies began way before his interviews, exams and training as an agent in Quantico, Virginia. A few times I went up there to pick him up for his weekends at home. He was the one responsible for our membership in this elite gun club. I don't know where he got the alias name of Melvin Crenshaw, but that worked for me. Juvenile had one, too. Members in this gun club had to undergo thorough background checks in order to get in and all firearms had to be legally registered. Carl handled all of that. It took only a few more minutes for Juvenile to come driving in the parking lot like a mad man.

"Juvenile, yo' ass is always slow—smelling like a shipload of weed! You'd be late for your damn funeral if you could. C'mon and take this whipping like a man. Carl already has everything ready to go."

"Well, what you waiting for. Let's do this," he said acting hyper like a 2 year-old kid that just went on a candy binge. "I spoke to Fast Money, but I'll tell you what he said later when we get done."

We found our lanes as soon as we stepped out of the lobby area. We stood right behind Carl as he took the loaded weapons, fresh targets and ammo in our lanes.

Juvenile noticed right away. "Damn! That thing is big—and it's fresh out the box!"

He was bubbling over with excitement. I know the weed had a little to do with that too. "Let's get ready to rumble!!!" I shouted. "How much on this since we both don't know how to use this thing?"

"Let's bet a thousand. And I'm going first this time," Juvenile said, as he stepped in front of us sticking out his chest.

He seemed ready to claim victory. I watched Juvenile as he positioned his body. It was true that he won most of the bets at the range when we went. He had a perfect aim at body shots. All I could do was admire his skills as he popped that cannon like an expert. The range on the targets went as far as 50 yards.

"Go ahead! Pull your target in, Tavon. We'll see who's going to walk away with a thousand dollars!" Juvenile said as soon as I finished my turn.

I knew he had hit the marks, but I wanted to fight him to the end. "The evidence is right in front of your face, J."

J was already pressing the button to bring the used targets in. We all gathered around to check each target to choose a winner.

"A hole is a hole. Damn! Carl, can you believe this? He won again." *I knew I had to pay, but we never exchange money at the range.*

The loser also pays for the meals after we're finished and that's when the winner gets paid. Running his mouth and counting my money had me heated most times, but it was all in fun practicing with those guns.

The county helped us prepare for the life the city had waiting for us. Everybody knew that the streets only respected those who were ready for war at any time, at any place. But the winner had to be ready.

We decided to go to this seafood restaurant downtown. We wanted to go to a place where we could chill out and do some catching up with Carl because we hadn't seen him in a while. Juvenile couldn't wait to show off. He started as soon as the waiter came to our table with the menus.

"Give me two of the most expensive seafood dishes that you have—he's paying for all of this," he said pointing at me and talking a little too loudly for the environment we were in. "Waiter, if you want, you can get yourself one of those expensive dishes as well."

"Here we have *the Extravaganza*—which is Salmon, Catfish, and Crabmeat. All three are layered—one on top of the other—and also topped with a Cajun southern soul imperial sauce. This is $28.95," the waiter said.

"Well, give me two of those," Juvenile said.

"I think I'll have one myself since I'm not paying either," Carl said.

"Well, I am paying, so give me a crab dip and a order of Buffalo wings to start."

As we waited on our meals, we played catch up on each other's lives for the past year.

"So what's been up with you lately, Carl?" I asked.

"I'm just hanging in there man, just barely hanging," he said. "I've really been going through some shit at work that kind a has me feeling a little low lately, but apart from that I'm doing good."

"Oh yea, they been giving you a hard time? Do I need to get some ass kicked for you homeboy?" I asked.

"No I'm cool, I'm just frustrated with how much your race determines how far you can reach in a job like mine. Check this out, y'all. Most black agents definitely feel the sting of racism at some point throughout their career. We just had a guy with 15 years of experience who trained an inexperienced white officer with less field time and no real experience. Guess what happened to him?" Carl asked us.

"What?" Juvenile asked.

"After he trained this guy, the white guy was hired as his supervisor and his personal performance rating, which was always above average, is now just average. Can you imagine that shit?"

"That's why I ain't never working for nobody," Juvenile said.

"Damn." I said. *From his tone, I could tell Carl was feeling frustrated.*

"Man, I'm determined to straighten that out in my case in court. It's just that those class action lawsuits take so long. But I'll be all right cause I still have my homeboys!"

"You got that right!" I said. That was always Carl. He was a fighter. We all laughed and gave each other high fives.

City Police Request New Tools to Combat Crime

Top Baltimore officials brought their request for new technologies in their war on drugs before the Baltimore City Council today. Many Council Members requested more details from Baltimore's Top Cop before voting to approve more than $400,000 in funding for surveillance and wire tap equipment.

"Tools to fight crime have to be just as advanced as drug dealers and their power to purchase more sophisticated gadgets. We just showed the community how much money is involved when we arrested a female suspect with more than $280,000," said the Mayor. "We have to become just as advanced and much smarter drug dealers. We are fighting a war and we're going to win with City Council's support." The Mayor of Baltimore City, the State's Attorney's Office, and State Troopers were on hand to testify and show support for police and their aim to purchase new technology in the *war on drugs.*

Chapter 17

JUVENILE

"Turn a[n] 8 to an ounce."

Jay-Z, "The Bounce"
The Blueprint 2

Here today, gone tomorrow. This truth applies to everything in life, especially in the streets. We had to be careful because the streets were watching. Fast Money was now in hiding since they raided his stash house and took the owner of the house in custody. Almost everything he had was in there. The streets had this one rule that you never lay your head where you holding your drugs—or keep drugs and money in the same place. Fast Money had slipped. This time he really hurt himself.

Tavon was making sure he and I were okay. Nothing was going on without us knowing about it first in the streets. I hadn't heard from him all day and was feeling a bit concerned about my partner when my cell phone rang.

"Yo. What's up?"

"How long before you get here, Tay?" I asked.

"We're on, hustler, slow down, man!"

"What?" I asked, in offense to his comments.

I'd been waiting for him to get this thing going for two days —and he had a nerve to make a statement like that. I must have been tense because, for that split second, I started thinking how he had changed somewhat. First of all, who was he talking to like that? Second of all, I'm the one always in the background waiting for him to make the call. Yet, I'm the one making all the money on these dangerous streets. It was still always clear that Fast Money thought Tavon was in charge. And now Tay's acting like that shit.

"I'm just joking. Stop being so soft! I'll be there in about 5 minutes. Have everything ready to go," he said with a sneaky laugh as the cell phone started breaking up.

He made it to me in no time.

"J, you have everything ready man?" Tavon asked as he entered the apartment.

"Yea, I got more than enough vials." *We had been using our own money more often, so we decided to double the amount this time. I was more than ready. I had the scale all set and the cutt material was already measured out. My new deck of cards I got this morning will help me to mix everything together. Now, all Tavon had to do was tell me what to put on the new package.*

"This is going to be on a three and a half. Watch me— I'm getting to be a master at this. I'll turn these 8 grams into an ounce and turn the dope game out. I'm gonna put these ounces on a four," he told me pointing to another pile.

I emptied everything on the glass table from my duffle bag. I started grinding the cutt materials through the cooking-size sifter, but my mind was still full of those crazy thoughts I had just experienced. I knew how to do it, but he always took the lead. There have been times that being second in line got me upset, but he is in charge—and I have to respect that. That's all I kept thinking to myself.

It didn't take him long before he started pushing piles of stuff in front of me. I have to admit that he learned the game well. He was following Money and imitating all the stories we heard about his father growing up. I was checking him out as he pushed different piles of stuff my way.

While watching him I could smell those chemicals in the air. I had the vials lined up on one table. Other smells like the fresh trash bag sitting next to the table had my nose on alert. I couldn't see it but the dust from the powders filled the room because it was all over the table. I could even see white powder in his nose hairs.

"You want me to start putting the vials together, Tay?"

"Make up about forty samples. Yea, make about forty testers to pass out down Westside and about six g-packs for work. When you make the first five thousand from the first five g-packs then come back here to the table. I want you to put all the rest of these ounces on a five," he said, pointing to the black bag. "By then most of the junkies will be so high they can't feel it anyway. Once we get this stuff on the table together we can start passing out testers down the spot."

"Alright. I'll take care of that when it's time, Tay. But what's this "we" shit?"

"I'm going down the spot with you tonight. Yea, that's right, hustler. I still know how to work the blocks. I *ain't* never too big to stand beside you. We are going to the top or we'll go broke trying."

I was putting things together like clockwork. My mind raced a thousand miles a minute, part of me was feeling guilty because I was just dogging Tavon out in my head, but I couldn't shake the feeling that he was just going out there to check up on me. I might be sounding paranoid, but I'm the one that run the streets so why all of a sudden he's coming out now. I like my partner's help, but I couldn't let it go that it was more to it than him just sharing the weight. I had to say something.

"Aaay, Tavon. I was thinking of how big we are getting without even getting shit from Fast Money."

"Yea, I think about that myself—especially when I buy from the Jamaican Posse and some of our homeboy's in town. The prices are higher by a couple thousand, but we still make out. At least we don't have to pay for NY hotel and traveling."

"Why don't we just step all the way out on our own since it's like that already?" I asked. "We can make so much more money doing it that way. We only would have to answer to each other and no middle man."

I had to say that to him since everybody looks at me as the little partner. I wanted him to know that I was doing some thinking too. I wanted to be on his level and work that side of the business. Plus, it's my turn to shine.

"I feel that. That's why I hooked up with a New York boy. He has a consistent source up there. He said that his people are blood family. Still, man, I feel like I owe Fast Money. He started me in this game and gave me my first spot and he turned me on to *the Posse*. That's why I still pay him even though he fell off. He put us where we are, J."

I didn't say anything to that, but it irked me that paying Fast Money was another decision Tavon made without consulting me. Partners talk and decide stuff together and he made the connections by himself and was spending money without my having a say. He wasn't treating me like a partner. No matter what I said, he wasn't seeing it. I mean, I always got my share and really he was paying Fast Money from his pocket, not ours, but he was not handling me right. I am his partner, not his employee. We have got to get this straight.

We finished doing the bundles in silence, and packed some up in my cabinets and the rest in the bag we use for transport. We were nearly half way to one of our 24-hour spot before either of us spoke, I guess we were in deep thought from our conversation.

"You know they saying Pretty is out on bail," Tavon said.

"No she ain't! She ain't got no bail! And if she did have a bail, word on the street is that Fast Money don't have enough to get her out either."

"They saying some crazy shit about her, too." *The streets have news sources, too. One thing is right about every street newsbreak. There is some kind of truth to every rumor. It may not be precise, but a hint of truth can be found in each one.*

"Damn, I'm wish he was able to get her ass outta there because she's gonna break under pressure and tell everything," Tavon said with a sound of concern.

"Maybe, but it may be too late."

"I hope not—for Fast Money's sake."

"In a minute we'll be on our own, J. I'm feeling what you're saying about giving Fast Money 'loyalty cash.' We could be keeping all that for ourselves. We don't owe him, for real."

I pulled out a blunt to smoke while taking some short sips of Hennessy because now he was sounding like he had some sense.

"That's what I been saying all along. He can't just get one hit and get scared. He gotta take it like a man and keep going. Falling is a part of this game. He wanna be 'kept' and I ain't into that shit! He shouldn't have had all that shit in that house."

"Well, I'll be hooking up with Jose shortly," Tavon said. "He's the guy I wanted to introduce you to the other day when he was in town."

"That's what I'm talking about," I said after taking a long hit of that good weed. "When am I going to meet him?"

"Let me get in first to see how things are going to be done when I start going up New York. Then I'll introduce you. You probably don't need to meet him anyway. I can handle that part. You just make sure we have the cutt material and the workers are paid. I'll do the rest with the money and connects."

We jumped out of Tavon's truck on Franklintown Road and started setting things up right away. This was our biggest moneymaking shop so far and the one I treated like a newborn baby. We called the rest of our crew into the house. Tonight just happened to be payday for them, so we had them help Tavon and me start before letting them go early.

We had them give out free testers to anxious addicts who were praying for this time to come. We do it every time we bring a new package to the streets.

Before long it was me and my partner holding the streets down without the rest of the crew. This is the way we started this operation, so tonight would be just like old times. The addicts gave us rave reviews on how good the stuff was. From that point, it was on!

"Damn, J. you got me running, boy!"

"That's how it is out here now on a Friday night at this spot," I told him.

"I know, I know, but damn! How many g-packs have we sold already?"

"Only four."

"What you mean—only four? That's close to four grand in less than three hours," he said counting some of the money he had in his hands.

"Man, you haven't been out here in a while. Sometimes we do more than that."

"I see now."

Another crowd was forming as we held down the streets. "Tay, we need more and it's your turn. Here, take the gun with you. There are a couple guys out here who seem to be waiting for the crowd to come."

"Alright!" he said, taking the gun from my pocket. "We shouldn't have let them dudes go tonight. We should've paid them extra to do this shit."

"You going to get the stash or what?"

"Alright, I'm going. Give me the money you've got." *He checked his pockets and pulled out the key.* "I'll be back."

I surveyed the area and realized how ideal this spot is. Franklintown Road is a narrow one-way street with houses on both sides in spots. A corner like this had its advantages. We worked out of old houses and hoopty cars and could spot police damn near a mile away. Narcotics cops couldn't swarm in and take this part of Baltimore City back. With this positioning and block-watchers informing us about large police stings, we were pretty safe down here. For added protection, we usually post lookouts on strategic corners, but everybody was gone.

It's funny how all the addicts cleared out just about the same time. The street looked as if nothing was going on when it really was. I leaned on the wall and waited for Tavon to come back with the stuff that would get the action started again.

I noticed the same two guys walking up to me looking behind them and over their shoulders like they lost something. "I got those two for one specials. 911! 911! How many y'all trying to get?"

"Bitch! You know what this is," the tall guy said as he hit me with a solid punch to my face. "Where the fuckin' money at muthafucker!"

Now after all the money Tavon and I made tonight, this shit has to jump off! It was a night forus like old times. My worst nightmare was unfolding before my eyes. That's why I couldn't believe this shit was happening.

My heart stopped—as if it was skipping several beats in my chest. There was pounding inside my head. I couldn't take in any air. It was almost like watching it happen in slow motion—like one of those Spike Lee movies. The world was spinning while I stood there not believing this shit was happening to me.

"Search his bitch ass, G," his partner said. "These whores think they all that! Get that fuckin' money from this muthafucka and then shoot his ass!"

I glanced up as he spoke and saw him pointing a shiny magnum at me.

"Aww, c'mon, Man. I ain't got no money. What? What!" *I took a few steps back as I responded to see if I could run, but they snatched me.*

Tavon was back at the house. He should be back any second now. He saw how hot the streets are tonight! He's rushing back, I know, with more stuff and the gun. He wouldn't be in there talking on the phone like he usually does. Not tonight! Sometimes he talks to people like he's running for President of the United States, especially when he's talking to that girl he has. Not tonight, he wouldn't do that tonight.

I felt one of the guys pulling on my pockets; my hands were in a surrender position. He poked the gun in my face. I was shaking and couldn't stop! He put the gun to my head and slid his large arm around my neck. I felt the barrel of the gun grind against my temple. I said a quick prayer. 'If I get away from this, I promise I'll will change God and give you my life—like Jameel told me! I promise, please.' *I could feel my knees shaking like crazy. This shit wasn't fun I thought to myself and then suddenly I heard the noise of a speeding car pull up.*

He released my neck. A quick flash from the impact of his hand to my face made me see stars. Everything stopped as I fell like a tall tree landing parallel to the ground. The other guy still pawed at my pockets, tearing them off, in search of money. The only real thing I could figure out was the taste of blood inside my mouth.

The next punch, which came from boots to the back of my head, had me praying for relief. They started yanking on my body. These fools were trying to kidnap me inside a car. This couldn't be happening. It was either a dream or Tavon was coming to save me from being kidnapped. He had to be coming right now! It was no way he would let me get snatched and treated like this.

Newsbrief

Several top brass law enforcement officials are under investigation for crimes ranging from accepting bribes, misuse of authority, interfering with a federal investigation and money laundering. Federal authorities have uncovered cases of cover-up now that witnesses have come forward. "Our Mayor is committed to public safety and has placed each alleged enforcement official on administrative leave pending the outcome of a federal investigation," the Mayor's spokesperson said at a news conference this morning.

More on this late-breaking story as it unfolds.

Chapter 18

TAVON

"It was all a dream."
Jay-Z, "A Dream"
The Blueprint 2

I was feeling good because I still liked working the streets. I knew every business needed a person doing the deals and behind the scenes stuff, and I was glad that was my part. I liked it and I was good at it, but there were times I really missed being on the streets.

I had to get back out there to see what was happening. This money we made had to be stacked first. It's easier to arrange as we make it. As I sorted, I picked up my cell and dialed my new friend. She didn't answer. I'm not worried about it, but Juvenile is not going to like my new female friend. I decided to get back to her sometime later—like tonight-–and went back out to see what was happening.

I opened the door and started down the steps. I was still stashing drugs in my pants. As I looked up, I saw Juvenile's hands in the air. We play about a lot of things, but never something as serious as this. Damn, there was a gun at my partner's temple. Then I saw the unthinkable. He smashed Juvenile in the face as hard as he could.

"Oh! Shit!" I said and dropped the stash near the steps. *Then I took a few steps and dropped real low beside the old hoopty car we keep parked there for cover.*

I pulled the gun, glad that it hadn't been on Juvenile. They had to have gotten the drop on him, which means it wouldn't have done him any good. If he'd known what they were up to, gun or not, at least one of them would be really hurting right now. Juvenile was not a man to be played with.

I gripped that 9-millimeter like a catcher would an old glove. I could hear Juvenile saying, "*Aww*, c'mon, Man. I ain't got no money. What—what!"

Out of nowhere, the other guy knocked him off his feet. *I had to bite my tongue to keep from yelling out. I was full of rage over what those guys were doing to my boy. It was like a bad dream.*

I started creeping around a car in front of the stash house because both their backs were in that direction. Juvenile caught my eye between the one guy's legs as the other searched the ground for a stash he couldn't find. As I watched, I was praying their greedy asses didn't give up before I had a chance to handle Juvenile's payback for him. I got closer as they tried to drag him to this old Crown Victoria with heavily tinted windows.

J was not about to let them go like that. Once he knew I was coming, he started pleading to the guy with the gun. I don't know what he was saying, but it kept them distracted until I got off the first shot.

I ran down on them. The guy with the gun was closest. My first shot, at pretty much point-blank range, took the back of his head off. Blood and brains splattered on his partner and gushed out of his skull.

The car pulled off! I didn't give the other guy a chance to react to what was happening. I popped him two times from behind with body shots. I grabbed Juvenile's arm to help him up and we both ran through the alley. I couldn't believe what just happened.

I found myself in shock because they tried to kidnap Juvenile and then to think I was only out there for money and something like this could happen. Damn! I was just in the middle of what could have been a triple homicide if the driver of that car hadn't pulled off. But I love my man Juvenile. I always have since we were kids, I would never have hesitated to sacrifice myself for him. He'd do the same thing for me. So, now as a soldier on the streets, I did what I had to do in order to save his ass.

DEAD BY MURDER THIS YEAR
BALTIMORE CITY

Two men were shot Saturday night near Westside Shopping Center. They were approached by two armed suspects on South Franklintown Road and apparently robbed of their valuables. Both victims were shot before both gunmen fled through the alley.

Police found a large caliber handgun. They are investigating this as a drug related incident since drugs were found not far from the scene.

Michael "Big Head" Emerson, 26, was pronounced dead on the scene apparently from one critical gunshot wound to his head. Evan "Philly" Baxter, 29, was shot several times and was rushed to St. Agnes Hospital where he was listed in critical condition.

This is homicide number 257 of the year compared to 254 this time last year. Police said they know of no suspects or motive. Anyone with information is asked to call authorities.

Chapter 19

JAMEEL

"Never been afraid to say what's on my mind..."
Jay-Z, "Renegade"
The Blueprint

My brothers are always trying to tell me about the things that go on in the streets, but I don't really listen unless it's about someone close to me. I was fighting against my brother's blasting music trying to get a nap on my mother's couch. I must have been really tired because somehow, despite the noise, I was able to get an hour in. I woke up to what I think is the same song with the same beat over and over again. I lay there tossing a little before I started listening to the lyrics.

"Lucifer, Son of the morning. I'm gonna chase you out of earth. Lucifer, Lucifer, Son of the morning. I'm from the murder capital. Where we murder for capital. Lord forgive him. He got those dark forces in him. But he also got a righteous cause for sinning."

In a state of being asleep and wake, I had to say a quick prayer for whoever sang that song because from the lyrics you could tell that the devil was trying to play with my idle mind. I got up and walked by Fruity's bedroom door. I could hear him talking on the phone, sounding like a deaf man trying to hear himself over that loud music.

"Flubber you ain't gonna believe this," he said.

"I heard Juvenile and his crew blew his brains out, Yo!"

I couldn't believe what I just heard. I took a step backwards to the room door just to make sure I was hearing correctly.

"What was that Fruity?" I said. "What did you say about Dorian?" *I couldn't control myself and I know I sounded a little anxious.*

"Sis, I didn't see you were standing there," Fruity said, looking startled by my presence. "I don't know how true it is Jameel, but I heard he was in some shooting on Franklintown Road and one dude is dead and one is in Shock Trauma refusing to die. Those boys don't play down in that area," Fruity said, as he paced back and forth using his hand to imitate shooting a gun and laughing as if someone had done an act of kindness.

"Did he do it? Did he do it?" *The look on my face must have given my thoughts and feelings away because Fruity put the phone down and held me around my waist as I tried to sit on the bed to regain my composure. I could hear Flubber in the phone screaming for Fruity to pick it up. My head started throbbing, instantly, and my stomach suddenly got sick.*

"Alright, man—damn. Hold on for her," I heard Fruity say before handing me the phone.

"Hey Sis."

"Yeah," I answered. I was trying hard to not seem upset. I even faked a phony smile.

"Don't listen to your big head brother 'cause he don't even know whether Juvenile is in it or not. He just talks too much sometimes," Flubber said.

I know he was just trying to make me feel good.

"But somebody was shot and killed down there!" I said forcefully. "You know how I feel every time that happens out there on the streets. Y'all have to get yourselves together and get off those streets. God is trying to tell all of us something, especially both of y'all. Momma raised us better. That's why she brought us up in the church!"

"C'mon, Sis. Don't start that church stuff again."

I was feeling so scared for Dorian but I had to let them know they were all God's children. I knew he realized he had no choice but to listen. "Talk all you want Flubber but mark my word. Nothing good ever comes out of something crazy like this. God loves you and Fruity. And y'all need to get off those streets."

"But Jameel," he tried to say before I cut him short.

"I gotta go now!" *I was trying my best to get off the phone before I broke down in front of my brothers.*

"Jameel, don't worry, we're OK and I'm quite sure Juvenile wasn't involved in something like that," Fruity said.

Him trying to sound reassuring and calm wasn't working this time. I stormed out of the room so quickly that I felt like I was in a trance. I know Dorian is out on the streets but I just can't believe he would be involved in something like that. I sat back down on the couch for what seemed like forever before I got up and called Dorian.

Ring! Ring! Ring! Ring!

"Yea, who dis'?" Dorian asked when he did finally answer.

"Dorian, it's Jameel, are you OK? Why you take so long to answer the phone?" *I spoke with my words and questions running into each other.*

"Oh, hey! Slow down baby. I just got outta the shower," he said in a softer voice that sounded like him.

Hearing his voice after so long made me remember the reason why I love Dorian so much. He was always such a gentleman. In a way I felt so relieved after I heard his voice."

"Are you and Tiffany OK?"

"Did you hear about that shooting out on Franklintown Road?" He could sense something was wrong from the tone of my voice.

"What happened? What you talking about now, Jameel?"

"I heard was two people got shot and one died down there where you hang at all the time. That's why I'm calling. You need to get off them streets—you and Tavon."

"Jameel, stop listening to people. Ain't nothin' going on out here in the streets. And me and Tavon are alright."

"Dorian, don't lie to me!"

"I have more shit—I mean stuff-- to do besides killing myself or anybody else in these streets. Why would I get involved in something crazy?"

I had to believe what he was saying since I had no information to contradict him. I've never been afraid to say to him what is on my mind—at any given time of day--but the streets were really changing him. I pressed the conversation, hoping that I could get some more information out of him without him being mad at me, but he wasn't having it.

"Dorian," I said, "I just called to see if you were okay. I'm not accusing you of anything. I pray for your strength and I want you, Tavon, and my brothers off the street before something crazy happens. I can't handle a three in the morning phone call telling me something happened to one of y'all. What would I tell our daughter? I don't know what I would do! That's all, Dorian. I'm scared!"

"I know, Jameel, but that rumor ain't true!"

Too many tears started running down my face. I could no longer speak and cried through the phone.

"Baby, I'm OK, everything is just fine," Dorian said.

He pleaded for me to understand. Through my pain I was able to communicate my truth. "Dorian, I can't handle this."

"Jameel, I really have to go now!" he said and hung up the phone.

Chapter 20

JUVENILE

"Can't Knock the Hustle."
Jay-Z, "Can't Knock the Hustle"
Reasonable Doubt

It was still pretty early for me to be up, but I guess I'd had enough sleep 'cause I've been lying here for what seem like hours not being able to go back to sleep. My conversation with Jameel a few nights ago was weighing heavy on my mind. There wasn't a rush this morning since Tavon was outta town and I've really been laying low off the streets. I'm just letting my boys do the work and bring the money in. That stick-up shit kind a have me jumpy and paranoid. I had no place to be and nothing really to do. Now that Tavon started going up to New York to cop I might as well start getting used to lazy days like this.

As I crawled out of bed, I began to feel the effects of last night's splurge. Last night I had that weed from the Jamaican posse! Damn. That's about the best I've had so far. I didn't even know when my workers left last night because I was so blunted. But now I'm hungry like I haven't eaten in two weeks.

I staggered into the living room with my eyes half open but woke up very quickly when the smell in the area hit me, or I should say literally slapped me in my face. The living room was a mess, not to mention the kitchen. The microwave door was wide open and the inside looked filthy. Half empty cereal boxes were all over the counter along with what seemed like all the half –eaten food I've had for the past 30 days. A half-eaten bag of Oreo cookies, dirty cups, plates and bowls took up almost all the space on my already small dining table. The room had a sour, rotting smell because of a variety of spills. I opened the cabinet door under the sink and pulled out a can of air freshener and sprayed. After a few seconds I took a deep breath; now it smelled like fresh cut flowers. I really couldn't believe how rundown my apartment looked but then again, I'm never home.

I put the can away and thought briefly about washing dishes "It's my day off," I said out loud to myself. "I ain't washing dishes or doing any cleaning today."

I looked at the rest of the room. The trashcan in the corner by the back door was over full, and in a semi-circle around it on the floor were plastic two liter Pepsi empties and Heineken beer bottles. The layer of dust on the floor was turning black especially in the corner because of the buildup. This place really needs a good sweeping. It's time for me to pay somebody to clean this shit up.

But for once I could see through the glass table—sitting under what used to be a window before I covered it to keep people from looking through from the outside. Usually my table is covered with white powdery residue. Today, everything we have left is already bagged up and ready for pickup.

I opened the refrigerator only to find out that it wasn't in any better shape than the rest of the room. An empty soda bottle and an outdated milk carton looked lonely on the top shelf. Two boxes of leftovers were on the bottom. I grabbed the soda bottle and tossed it towards the trash. Of course, I scored a three pointer as the tumbling trash knocked over the other empties, which clanged and crashed against each other and the floor. It made the empty silence of my place all the more deafening.

Breakfast this morning was gonna have to be a choice between some hot wings that looked as if they would make my nose run, a big bag of Doritos or the Colonel's. It wasn't hard choosing. I grabbed the KFC box and pushed the door shut. I pushed the trash from the front of the microwave and shoved the box in. My mind must have wandered off a bit because I jumped when I heard the beep-beep--letting me know the microwave had stopped.

I got my honey barbeque wings out of the microwave and sat at the only table in the kitchen that had some space for my morning meal. What if Jameel was right about me getting out of this game before it's too late, I thought as I poured some Doritos onto my paper plate. I ate some of those stinky treats before tearing my wings apart like a hungry animal. I was really hungry.

I quickly dismissed those crazy thoughts of Jameel's warning out of my mind and thought about what my agenda would be for today. I decided to go back to my room that looked much better and just lay around and wait for Tavon to call.

As I lay there looking up at the ceiling, I had so many mixed thoughts running through my mind about Tavon in New York and about Jameel and Tiffany. I must have dozed off a little because I was awakened by the telephone ringing which I thought was only ringing in my dream. I just knew I had picked up the phone but it just kept on ringing. Turns out I'd picked up the phone in the dream, but not my cell phone which seemed like it had been ringing forever. I jumped up and snatched it from the nightstand and quickly answered it without even checking out the number first.

"Hello," I said in a groggy tone, still half a sleep.

"Yo, did you get that shit I left you last night?" the voice asked on the other end of the phone.

I sat up and shook my head, rubbing at my eyes. I wasn't sure who was on the phone. I took a second to get myself together before responding.

"Who dis?"

"Dis Tay, man, what's wrong with you?"

"Oh it's you! I was sleeping that's why. I never caught your voice."

"So, sleepy-head! Did you get it?"

"I ain't get nothing. What are you talking about?"

I didn't know Tavon was back already. It pissed me off a little. I always wanted to know every move he made, to be in on everything going on, even if I couldn't be there. I glanced over at the clock and realized it was 3:00pm. I had slept almost all day.

"Yo, I left work inside the safe last night. You wasn't in there, but I thought you would know I'd been there because I rushed out and left the safe open. I got back last night," he said.

"Wait a minute," I said hopping off the bed and going to the safe. "Let me check."

Everything was like he said when I walked inside the room. Now I was really awake. "Yea, it's there. I got it, Tay. Damn, boy!"

"Damn boy, what?"

"You made it happen, didn't you? Dat's what!"

He really was making it happen. When we were with Fast Money, he always tried to tell Tavon what to look for. Seems Tay learned the lessons well. I wish I'd had that same opportunity to get prepared first hand like that. But we could all see Tavon's potential. I keep waiting, though, trying to be patient until I get my chance to be out front like that. I know I can do it. I just have to seize the chance.

"J man, you won't believe how many different races of people are in the game up there," he said sounding excited. "Spanish, Cubans, Jamaicans, Nigerians, Black and Italians are all doing dis' shit. They got crazy loads of whatever a person has the money to buy. This time when I copped, a dude from D.C. was buying fifteen bricks from my man's connect when I was there getting ours. It seems like they are getting that shit off the boats. So, the hundred grand we decided to start with doesn't compare to what some of those dudes were spending. They got their shit tight, J. You can't knock the hustle up there. They even have armed dudes searching you before you get inside. That shit was just like in the movies."

"For real?"

"Yea man you gotta see this setup."

"Damn, Tay! We are gonna blow up in no time!"

"You told me a while ago that we should've been on our own. I couldn't understand when Fast Money told me that shit, but now I understand."

"Fuck Fast Money. He's history! You should've listened to me—I'm your partner!"

I never forgot when Money was trying to split Tavon and me apart.

"I know but everything happens in time and this is the right time. Anyway, I tried my hand with this dude I like named Jose. There are so many games up there I only took the chance to spend sixteen rather than risk everything we had. This kid seems as if he's cool but I still wanted to start with him kinda slow—testing the waters, you feel me?"

"I feel you, Tay."

"What I did was buy those *200 bundles* I gave you last night for sixteen thousand. This kid Jose is deep into knowing all the right people. Whenever I get him down here you'll meet him. You never know when you might have to go up there, too."

"I'm gonna call Outlaw," I said while I looked around for some clean clothes. *All I could think about was getting to work. No water or soap was necessary. I had to make up for the loss time this morning.* "I can put him out there to get some testers started."

"I'll call you back in an hour," he said. "Outlaw should be back in by then. Let me know what the junkies are saying about it."

A few minutes had passed since I called Outlaw. I was still trying to bag as many testers as I could put together like Tavon told me before Outlaw swung by to pick me up. I'd be right there to make sure he'd put it out there real quick.

I thought more about what he had said about his new source in the Big Apple. Numbers were jumping around in my head. I was trying to figure out how much to front the crews.

"Ring! Ring! – Ring! Ring!"

The loud sound of the phone ringing interrupted my calculations. I checked the caller ID and saw it was Tavon calling back.

"What's up Tay?" I asked. "Outlaw left about twenty minutes ago. He's on the way to pick me up."

"Hey, I was figuring what we could make out of this for starters. We paid eighty dollars a bundle. We can front it to the crews for a hundred and fifty a pack, especially down South Bal'more."

"Yea, I'm one step ahead of you my brother. I've already got it all figured out. We might be able to go even a bit higher than that. We'll decide that once Outlaw lets us know what people are saying."

"He had more of that shit and told me if I wanted anything else—no matter the time-just call him."

"Well if this is any good, he won't have to worry about that! We will be doing a whole lot a business with him as long as he can keep the supply up."

"Let me just ask you this before I get off the phone because I know you tryin' to do your thing at the table. Did you see the bag with the stampers? Jose told me to use those to put different stamps on different bags even though it's the same. Each shop will have a different brand. This will keep a lot of people out of our business," he told me.

I looked and listened at the same time. He had a good idea. "I like the one called D.O.A. for where I am. I'll do that for us down there. I'll put *Suicide* and *Lethal Weapon* down on Mount Street and the rest I'll spread out."

"That sounds like a good plan."

"Hold up Tay, I got another call coming in on my other cell phone."

"Who's that, J?"

"This is Outlaw right here on the other phone, Tay. Let me get outta here so I can make this happen."

"A'right call me as soon as you hear something!"

I raced down to the steps. Outlaw was waiting in the car like a running back for my hand-off. That was one of his good qualities. He was always on time.

He drove like he was rushing me to the hospital. Westside is not that far from my place. When we got there he raced off down the street. He had some of our regular old-heads on standby already.

I waited around while he handled his business. While standing still I became lost in my thoughts. Everything was running through my brain.

I looked to the other side of our block. I remember playing as a kid around drug dealing. I hated seeing those little kids play in the alleys we worked in. I could still see what happened to me the other day. Crime scene chalk was still on the streets. Damn!

I could hear Outlaw's favorite touter make another tester call from the alley. Fiends knew our routine. It's a sad sight seeing those addicts run down to the trashy alleyways where the children play in search of another dose of liquid dreams.

I label that older generation like I do Tavon's mother. That's why I feel sorry for Tavon when it comes to P-Nut. She was just out here the other day begging to suck one of our worker's off—in exchange for a bag of dope belonging to her son. I really have no respect for that older crowd. P-Nut's generation are all "used-to-bes." They can still recover and start all over again. Some of them do. But, the majority of them are still getting high, like a bunch of dope fiends, hoping to relive yesteryear's highs.

Just around the other corner stands the younger generation. I shake my head all the time when I see them doing anything and everything to get one more blast. Young addicts, those around my age, are following the same footsteps. Our breed of hustlers are the ones who sell all day, making somebody else thousands, only to receive something to eat, two bags of dope at the close of business and twenty dollars.

I had another funny thought. No matter how high they become, it's never like the first time. But they keep chasing and I keep taking cold advantage of that shit! That's why I only drink, smoke as much weed as I can, and mind my own business.

Outlaw called me down the street a few minutes later with the results. Before I could even get into my conversation with Outlaw I heard my phone beep. It was Tavon. I decided not to answer it until I was finished, but Tavon was not giving up. He hit me on my two-way.

"Hold on Outlaw. Let me get this phone. Main man is on the other end."

"What's up, Tay?"

"Did you hear from Outlaw yet?" he screamed in excitement.

"He's right here now! Yo, if your impatient ass would give me a chance! I'm trying to hear what he got to say!"

"Ask him what did they rate it on a scale of 1-10?"

"Hold on man, give me a minute to talk to the man, stop sounding all jumpy and shit!" I said in a joking way, but really I was getting a bit annoyed.

"Outlaw, what are they saying on a scale of 1-10?"

"They're screaming a 9 ½, Yo. They want more of this shit. You should see how everybody is running for it! J, they love it! All the junkies are saying it's the best thing out here!"

"Did you hear that Tay? Speak loud enough so Tavon can hear you on the two-way. "

"No, what did he say?"

"We're getting a 91/2!

"Word!" he shouted, laughing like he had hit the mega million-dollar lotto.

"Damn, right! When it's on, it's on. And competition can't knock the hustle because our product speaks for itself!"

"Man, that kid Jose kept his word about how good that stuff is. I can't wait to get back up there! We're gonna get rich with him!" Tavon said.

"I hear that!" I said.

"Yo, Outlaw. Give me your car keys. I'll be back here in 10 minutes."

"I'll be waiting along with everybody else," he yelled, "so make it quick."

"Yo Tay, let me take care of this and then I'll hit you back up in a minute."

I needed to concentrate on driving and other things. The last thing you want to do when you live a life like mine is to give the police any reason to pull you over.

Things started really growing for us on the streets. Jose could get Tavon whatever our money called for. Tavon could purchase a kilo of cocaine in Baltimore from a reliable dealer for about $30,000. At best, he could get two kilos here for no less that $55,000. To anyone in Baltimore trying to make a dollar that sounds like a good hustle. But taking chances to go see Jose, we could get close to two and half for $52,500.

We were buying from Jose almost every week now, sometimes even twice per week!

Baltimore City News

Christian ministers taking over the streets
Drugs are public enemy number one!

Drug advocates, treatment centers and court officials all agree with religious leaders that our city has a problem. They also agree that Baltimore's drug pandemic is number one on the list of public health threats and should be dealt with more effectively. Medical reports to the General Assembly yesterday showed that annual projections of drug overdose and abuse will increase dramatically.

Local Law Enforcement officials contacted for this release said that there has been an increase in the amount and quality of drugs and they are preparing to wage a new war on drugs campaign with FBI and DEA officials.

Christian ministers are not taking no for an answer. They have presented City Council with a funding proposal and steps which they intend to combat this problem. "We are not only praying our way through the streets where the devil is taking over, but we are taking action. All church leaders and members in the area are asked to get involved," one local pastor said.

Chapter 21

Jameel

"Mommy where daddy went?"
Jay-Z, "Where Have You Been"
The Dynasty

Tiffany and I spend a lot of time in church at all types of activities. This way of living has become my way to escape the evils that surround us in the city. Pastor expects his mature flock to step up and make God's love real.

This morning we got there shortly after the doors were opened for Sunday morning service. I was working in the central kitchen this week, so both of us had a few things to carry from the car. I had cooked a few dishes last night and wanted to get started on a few others before service started.

The side door was open that leads to the church hall and kitchen. It was right near the parking lot, so we didn't have to carry our things far. After we unpacked the car, Tiffany knew exactly what to do to help. She began putting Sunday school materials on the tables for the children and adult classes. Then she put out the folding chairs.

I always sang and prayed while I worked. On mornings like this, I can belt out a hymn at the top of my lungs. "Jesus loves me, this I know..." That's one of Tiffany's favorites. I sang as I watered the steam tables, made sure the silverware was shiny and set the temperature timers. I emptied the containers of food I brought into the warmers and went back to the kitchen to get a few more dishes started. I looked up from the counter and saw Tiffany walking towards me as I poured the brown sugar on the candied yams. She had one of those looks letting me know a question was coming at me that needed my undivided attention.

Tiffany never fails to take advantage of the opportunity to talk with me about whatever is on her mind. I was proud of that. She put down the Bible study books I'd asked her to place on the tables and grabbed me for a big hug.

"Mommy can I ask you a question?"

Whenever she started like that, I knew it was going to be on the subject I really didn't want to talk about—something to do with her father and us being a family. It's not that I didn't want to talk to her, I did. It's just that she was so young and I had to hide the complete truth from her when we talked. The thought of telling my baby the truth about Dorian was as painful for me as the half-truth I shared every time this came up. But I want her to come to me. I want to know what she is thinking. So, I wrapped her in my arms and kissed her forehead. My discomfort was not her problem so I encouraged her to share with me.

"Sure, baby. You can ask me anything you want."

"Where's daddy at? Why doesn't he come to be with me sometimes?" she asked. *She was looking at me with really sad eyes.*

"Baby, your daddy has to get his life together. And we have to help him. He'll be with us one day. Right now he thinks other things, things in the streets, are more important, but that's not right. I'm sure daddy misses his baby—just like you're missing him. He'll be with us one day. That's why we have to keep on praying," I said, realizing that my answer wouldn't hold her for long.

"Can we go and get him and bring him to church today?"

"I would love to go and get him and your uncles sweetie, but we can't make them come. They have to come on their own."

I could see the long stream of tears flowing down her face, so I reached into my pocket book and got some tissue to wipe her face. I really hate to see Tiffany hurt like this when there is really nothing I can do about it.

"I'll tell you what we can do," I said, trying desperately to give her some hope. "Today we're going up to devotional prayer together and send up a special prayer for your Daddy. Is that okay, baby?"

"Yes, ma'm," she said reluctantly. *I could hear the disappointment in her voice*. "But I want him to come and be with us today."

"I don't think your father is coming today, but we can recite those words you recite to God every night." *Tiffany misses her father so much. I only hope he realizes this one day soon.* "We'll call him when we get home to invite him to service with us next Sunday, okay? Now hand me the aluminum foil—right there--so I can wrap this food." *I was trying to move away from the subject.*

"Ma, can we write Daddy's name on a sheet of paper together this time?"

"Sure we can, so Pastor knows we want a special prayer of love for Daddy. So, when the ushers pass the basket, we'll put your Daddy's name in. Okay?"

Our church service includes a special ritual. Our ushers pass around a basket at the beginning of the service. This basket isn't for financial offerings. It's for the names of loved ones we invest our thoughts of love in and ask a special prayer for.

"Yeeah for Daddy!"

That made her happy. I can't take it when all she wants is her father and he doesn't want to be around. He misses her homework and school activities. When I try to tell him how this makes Tiffany feel, how it makes me feel, he acts as if he just can't make the time. He is so far away from us he doesn't know what is going on in our lives everyday. He doesn't even know about our concert out-of-town tomorrow.

All evening long I replayed the conversation Tiffany and I had this morning in my head as I gathered things for our trip. I don't like using the word, but I hate when that happens to my child. She doesn't deserve to feel abandoned or unloved. I know Dorian loves her, but his only way of showing it is buying things. I don't want anything in my house that's brought with money from the streets. The phone rang and interrupted my personal thoughts. As I picked up the phone I could hear my mother talking before I could even say hello.

"Gurl, why haven't you called me back yet? You know I was waitin' to see if you needed a ride to the airport. I couldn't go to sleep until I heard from you."

"Sorry momma, but I forgot. I called and made arrangements for a BWI shuttle to pick us up," I said as I tried to balance the cordless phone on my shoulder and pack our bags at the same time.

"Okay, what time are they coming to pick you up?"

"At 4:30 tomorrow morning. We should be at the airport around 5:30a.m. The plane leaves at 7:00a.m and we should arrive in Atlanta in no time."

"I still can't believe our church choir is making a CD," momma said. "Hiring Brother Andre as the music director was the best thing Pastor has done so far. Plus, I want to go back to that restaurant downtown when you get back—so we can celebrate!"

"Momma, I won't believe it's real until we get on that plane and into the recording studio. I know one thing, though. I'm gonna sing my heart out on my two lead songs. And yes—we can go back to Downtown Southern Blues to celebrate when we get back!"

"I wanted to speak to Tiffany before y'all left," Momma said. "Don't wake her up now. Have her call me in the morning because she has been talking about that food ever since we went."

"I will."

"I bet she was too excited to go to sleep."

"I love you and have a good night, Momma. Tiffany will call you in the morning."

"Goodnight."

There's one thing I love about performing. It allows me to show my daughter different parts of the United States. I can show her that the world is bigger than the tragedies and pitfalls surrounding us in the city. I never knew more than West Baltimore while growing up until I started reading more. Neither did her father. It was hard making it through, but I did it. I chose life through my beliefs and it carries me through. Now I watch my child experiencing life like I never did before. That little girl is my heart and soul. She has the potential of achieving so much more than we did.

Tiffany loved BWI airport, watching the planes land, unload, refuel, being sprayed, and rise up again. She knew it would be her turn next to board the "Big Bird" and fly away to a new place. Each time we flew it was the same way. When we finally got settled in our seats after takeoff, she'd takeout her pencil and paper and start writing. Every time it would be a letter to her father.

Dear Daddy,

I am on the airplane. The world seems small from high up in the sky. Giant buildings look like sticks and big trees look like green spots. And the people are so tiny that I can't see them. This is the part where my tummy feels sick, but Mommy and the lady on the plane makes sure I have my pillow and TV headphones to make me feel better. I'm looking out the window now for you. I wonder where you are down there? Do you think we can take a family trip like this together? Daddy, I miss you.

Love, Tiffany

Chapter 22

TAVON

"I'm new in town. /
I don't know my way around. /
[They] got that soft white /
That's sure to come back brown."
Jay-Z, "1-900-Hustler"
The Dynasty

I called up New York to set something up with Jose. "Yo, B. What's happening up there?"

"Shit is real cool up here. What about you down there T-Nice?"

"My game is tight. That's why I'm calling you."

"Ain't nothing change! Step off early and call me from the spot when you are in Midtown," he said.

"I'll be there, B."

Jose and I made our plans quickly but very precise. I would book my room at whichever one of the exclusive midtown hotels we both agreed on and waited for him to touch base with me. I had heard so much about these hotels from Fast Money and I really liked them myself.

It was early when I boarded the Metro-liner at Penn Station in Baltimore the next morning. I smiled as I sat with my trusted female traveling partner! It's funny how everything is falling in perfect place.

My friend purchased our tickets separately, but, in the end, we both traveled in the same car.

"Baby, you got the tickets? I asked, as we walked through the train station.

"Yea, it's right here in the side of my pocket book," she said in her usual soft-spoken, sexy voice.

We'd been several times before together. But I couldn't believe it when we went the first time. She said that was her first experience with a hustler going across the state line to cop. I thought to myself, there ain't no way no one ever used her pretty ass before and she'd been with so many other high rollers! Regardless of what she said she sure as hell was gonna earn the money she got from me. I ain't no fool. I know what happened between her and Fast Money, although he didn't tell me.

We got to New York in no time. I headed across the street to find a payphone so I could contact Jose. I must have passed at least twenty payphones inside the station but Jose always said it wasn't safe to use any of those. Jose picked up on the first ring as always.

"Yo, B. I'm here. I got my favorite, Kid. I'm doing 603," I said, using our coded way of communicating with each other.

"Get settled and call me right back, you got two, right?" Jose asked.

He sounded a little like he was in a hurry.

"I know the routine. Handle your end; I got mine."

Now that's a good businessman I thought. We rode along in the cab we took to the Marriott hotel. That's how he is--always ready to go!

I put my new friend in room 713 and I stayed in my room 603 with the money, transacting all business. All she would see when it was time to go was the final bags packed. She would never know what to do or how it was done. She knew whatever she was given to bring back was her responsibility to get it from point A to Baltimore.

I sat in my hotel room counting out some shopping money while I waited for Jose to come over to pick the money up. Every time we're in New York, we always go on a shopping spree while we wait for our product. As I was about to put away the money, I heard a familiar knock on the door. I peeped out just to make sure anyway.

"Hey, Jose! What's up, Man. How you been?" I asked, as he and one of his female runners walked in the door.

"What you got for me, my friend?"

"This is the deal, Amigo," he said putting his arm around my shoulder as if to whisper a secret. "I got the deal of a lifetime for you on the coke. If you want dope I'll have to check with some people. But for now listen to this!"

"I'm listening."

"They got that soft white that's sure to come back brown, B. That shit's going for $16,000 Uptown. That I can get real quick," he said with a lot of energy. "Then they got high quality bricks going for more."

"Is that all they got?"

"You said you wanted to go big this time. I made the connections. I can get whatever you want, B," he said. "Don't back out on this because these kids are getting it big—and I can get it from them at any time."

I pondered for a minute on what to get and how much. I decided to go big.

"I'll get you a deal. You know I always hook you up."

"OK, get me—uuhhmmm--six for ninety thousand. Do that and we got a deal!"

"I got you! Don't I hook you up every time you come!"

I pulled the money out of the bag and stacked the bundles so it was easier to count. Jose signaled to his girl to check the money and she got up right away and started counting.

"Yo! This will put me on *Cash Money Street*! Pull this off and I'll be set for life!" I said.

"For you, my man, I'll do whatever to get you wherever you're tryin' to go. Now listen. It won't take long to do this deal so don't go anywhere. I have somebody else waiting too. I'll get him first and get right back to you," he said. "B. Keep riding with me and you going straight to the top!"

He said everything I expected to hear before I gave him the cash. I was thinking how this transaction would be right on time for the streets because it was early Thursday. If we made this happen real fast--like he said--I could be on my way early Friday. This was perfect timing.

"My man. I'll be right back. Listen out for my phone call. I'll hit them real quick and swing right back to you," Jose said before doing his usual handshake hug.

"Alright, I'll be here."

I lay flat on my back on the luxurious sheets on my king-size bed staring at the ceiling still in disbelief about how big this purchase was gonna make us. I couldn't help but think about how easy that transaction was. It was perfect! What were Fast Money and my father talking about? This was some easy hustling. One more phone call and I'm on my way. Those kilos would be all mine! I'll give Jose about $4,000 and a piece of what I bought. All I had on my mind since they left was the sweet deal that was going to change both our lives.

Now, all I had to do was call Juvenile back home to set up my return, but before that I had to check on my girl on the floor above me.

Ring! Ring!

"Hello," she answered in her sexy voice.

"Baby, you answered kind of quick? The phone didn't ring."

"Yes it did—stop playing."

"Don't tell me you were sitting by the phone waiting on big papa to call?"

"You know I was, for real. Is it time to go shopping yet?"

"Well not quite. If you wanna come down we can get some other stuff started."

"Just give me five minutes big papa; let me get myself together."

I really had to laugh out loud as I hung up the phone because this chick was off the hook. While I waited for her to come over I made my next phone call.

"Ayy, J," I said, as soon as I heard an open line on his end.

"Hey what's up? You sound like you in a hurry."

"Nah man just make sure you have some help with you at the spot tomorrow night because you gonna need it."

"You don't worry about nothing! I got this! Just get that stuff to me kid--besides, I already have Nikki right here with me."

"You are the man J. You the man!"

We've been following in Fast Money's footsteps and have started having a few cutt girls strip down to their underwear before breaking our products down. This prevented stealing but best of all making them have sex with each other wasn't bad at all after business.

"Tay, you know how I do Nikki, but check this out. They put the slugger on somebody down the way on Catherine Street—somethin' terrible. So don't go down there until you talk to me. It wasn't our beef, but Homicide police are running crazy."

"Listen to me clearly," I told him. "I should be 6 at 5, hear me?"

He could understand that I would be bringing about six kilos around 5 o'clock tomorrow. Just as I hung up from Juvenile, I heard another coded knock on my door.

"Girl what took you so long?" I asked my friend jokingly. "Big papa been waiting on you baby."

"You seem to be in a good mood baby, but I can make you feel even better."

"As a matter a fact I am in a good mood–things are going so good here–this is gonna be the big one baby. So you betta come on over here and come take care of your big papa because now all we have to do is wait."

"I love the sound of that," she said, as she unbuttoned her shirt revealing the juiciest looking titties a man could ever want.

With my friend working her magic on me, I threw myself back on the bed. Everything was falling in place. All I had to do now was wait.

Police Blotter

Man's beating death ruled a homicide

A twenty-one year-old man was fatally beaten last night. Police are searching for more leads after investigating initial eyewitness accounts. Intelligence sources confirmed that the victim, Dave Gordon, was involved in a dispute about the sale of drugs. This feud ended with him being attacked by several assailants with metal objects causing trauma to his head and body. Concerned residents were able to call paramedics and police. "Before ambulatory services arrived, Mr. Gordon collapsed into shock and was pronounced dead at the Maryland Shock Trauma Unit," said spokesperson Glenallen Finke.

Chapter 23

FAST MONEY

"It's a hard knock life—for us... /
Instead of kisses [now] /
[I] get kicked..."

Jay-Z, "Hard Knock Life"
Hard Knock Life Vol. 2

The party was jumping in the background. People were all around, eating, drinking, and dancing. The music was really loud, or it seemed loud to me. I couldn't help thinking about how much of a shadow of my last Platinum party this one was, and being more than a little bit disappointed about that. I let some old friends use my name and the Platinum title to promote this party. It's not like I'm getting any money to do this. Actually, it's not my party at all—I'm just acting like I'm still on top. I find all this hard to believe. Like almost overnight things changed for the worse, but my plan is to get back on top—right away.

I spun around on my bar seat and looked into the action in the room. At the last party I looked out at a sea of hustlers and their ladies, dressed to the teeth. This time, as I looked out, what I saw the most of was the still well stocked food tables across the room. I turned back and watched the bartenders fixing drinks for folks along the bar. One thing for sure, people were definitely drinking. I kinda wished it were my cash bar. Tonight I would be walking away with a few bucks.

I lifted my glass. "Get me another one," I said to the bartender. *He hadn't known how to make a masturbating butterfly, but he was a quick study. By my third one, he was a seasoned pro. I should probably stop, but being a little numb was the only thing really keeping me going.*

While I was waiting for the bartender's next effort, I slipped off to the bathroom. I'd just gotten comfortable again at the bar when I felt a friendly hug surrounding me.

"Hey Fast Money," the voice said behind me.

My fourth drink was placed on the bar. I picked it up and sipped as I turned around. "Black Face! Good to see ya' man. What's been happening?"

"Nothing much. Just keeping my head low--flyin' under the radar, you know! I see you are still flying high?"

"Yea, right! If you don't have something good to say don't cuss me out politely."

"Polite? Man this is a sweet party. You have to be doing okay because you look like a million bucks. And look at you. You put on another bash like this. I know you're waiting for one of those beautiful honeys to come and scoop you up."

"Naw, I'm hangin' out by myself. I just had to get out for a minute to think," I yelled over the music.

"I've been hearing things, but I didn't believe it. Then I heard you had something to do with this party."

"This ain't my party. I wish I had the money to still throw one. It would be better than this, though. This party is all right, but not like the parties I threw."

Black Face put his hand on my shoulder and held me firmly. "Calm down man. What's up wit' you?"

"Man, everything is all wrong! Between you and me—I had to pawn all my jewelry just to get Pretty a big lawyer who is still trying to get her a bail before she tells it all. Every time I hear from her she's talking crazy about turning me in--as expected.

"I'm just keeping my head above water. The last time I had a party, I was frontin' to make a rep. I was trying to get the people who already saw me as a man on the way up to believe I was at the top of my game. And it worked for a minute."

I paused for a moment before pointing around the room. "Look around. You should see why I'm saying this shit is different! Who isn't here?"

"I don't understand, Fast Money. Hustlers I know are here. The ladies are here. Everybody's here! The place is full. Whatchutalkin'bout?"

"It's not like last time," I said. *I downed my glass and addressed the bartender.* "Get me another one!"

I saw Black Face look at me and realize that I was sounding a little strange. He couldn't understand. I guess the alcohol was making me crazier than normal because I just wanted him to get it. I want him to see what I was seeing.

"Precious isn't here. Neither is Big Toney. I haven't heard from him, although that's not so odd because we weren't really friends. It might not even be safe for us to talk really." *I stopped talking again. Then I looked at Black Face.* "There's nobody from my old crews with me because my shit is dry and my money's gone. Shit is all wrong! Not only can't I have a party, but I can't get my homies to hang wit' me 'cause I can't pay. Not even just to hang out. What kinda life is that?"

"Well," he said, "I do know about Big Toney and your crews, but I'm glad Precious skipped this one. I was really worried when y'all hooked up and I was so glad when you stopped seeing her. She was no good . . ."

I cut him off. "She was everything you said, but if this was the place to pick up a new hustler, she would be here and you know she would. But of course, aside from this not being the happening spot, she already has a new hustler, Tavon! And picture this. He has her going back and forth to New York!"

"No way, man."

"Oh yeah, they haven't gone public yet, but I know it's going on. Tavon started seeing this secret "woman" right after Precious made a pass at him a while ago--in front of me at that! He asked me if we were still seeing each other. I told him we were long over. I even told him she was trouble, but that she wasn't my trouble anymore.

"This whole thing is a hard knock life; the ins-and-outs, the ups-and-downs. I can't stand this life sometimes man. Big Toney and Outlaw are both dealing with Tavon now. That's how bad we had fallen off. Big Toney didn't mind working for that young kid, but I did!

"When I am supposed to get kisses—it's just my luck I get kicked by the very people who say they love me. Now that's the part of the game that I don't want to accept. But money sure as hell make people do funny things. I see that now!"

Black Face was still listening to me, I guess. The room was spinning and I could hear a voice over what sounded like music.

"Well, for Precious it is just like that. I wouldn't expect her to be around you now," Black Face said. "But Tavon, I know him. It's not like that with him. If he's not here, there is a reason, a good reason.

"You're doing all that fuckin' crying! My ass is the one out on a two hundred and fifty thousand dollar bail for a drug charge, not you! My probation officer already issued a retake warrant to lock me up. They've been to my mother's house twice, kicking her door in-- looking to lock my black ass up again because I violated Johnson's probation! I went in front of him one time for an old drug charge. This new charge violated the main condition of my probation. And you think shit is rough for you? I should be the one crying and getting' fucked up at the same time! At least you don't have the police on your ass!"

I had to respond. "Man, I ain't trying to hear that shit! That probation shit is your problem. That's how the game goes—you knew that shit! What I'm saying is Tavon and Juvenile took the crews they were running for me and moved out on their own! Now that's some fucked up shit right there!" *I stopped talking and drained my glass. The liquor hit me hard. I turned to the bartender.* "Gi-mee-a-nutta-one."

"You sure about that Fast Money? Cause you look like you're startin' to feel it right about now."

The bartender spoke up. "Perhaps I can get you a coffee first and you can have some food. Then we can come back to the liquor. Do you take your coffee black?" he asked.

"No! Hell no!" I yelled, shrugging Black Face's hand off my shoulder.

Out of the corner of my eye, I saw Black Face put a hand up to the bartender, signaling him to back off. I had to tell both of them what I wanted.

"I don't want coffee and I don't want food. I want another drink. I want to forget." *I spun back to the bar. I thought I could feel myself floating, but wasn't sure.* "Another masturbating butterfly, dammit!" I said before falling off of my stool.

"Fast Money!" *I knew it had to be Black Face picking me up and screaming at the same time.* "You sound like a lot is going on with you but you can't melt down here man. You have too much to lose and the money ain't the only thing. If you say something you shouldn't, in here, tonight, it could cost you your freedom. One more drink and then I will get you home. Bet?"

I didn't want to go. I just wanted to drown in the liquor I was drinking and float away. But, Black face was there again, watching my back and keeping me focused. I can count on him. "Bet," I said, wrapping my hands around the tumbler one last time.

Chapter 24

Juvenile

"It's a hard knock life, for us... /
Instead of treated... /
We get tricked!"
Jay-Z "Hard Knock Life"
Hard Knock Life Vol. 2

"Hey, J. I'm still waitin'. I haven't heard anything either way," Tavon said when he called me from New York.

"You haven't!" *He sounded really anxious and I was running out of patience waiting for him to get back. This is the break we've been waiting for.*

"He may have called, but I was in a deep sleep. I was tired as shit! This running is burning me out!"

"That's how I felt yesterday when you called, so I know the feeling."

"I hope I didn't miss his call. He told me before he left he had to go take care of something else. Maybe that's why he's so behind in his schedule," Tavon sighed heavily.

I could feel the tension through the phone. He was grasping for any excuse to hold onto hope.

"It's ten o'clock at night. I was scheduled to be there at 5 with six crazy ones earlier today. You feel me? I'm calling all the numbers Jose gave me."

"This deal is everything to us now."

"Yea, it will definitely put us where we want to be. Plus, I got a big surprise that will make your pockets even fatter."

"Man, where the fuck is he?" I wondered. *I was hoping he didn't get knocked with all that money. I could hear Tavon counting the money he had on hand. He'd only expected to be there overnight. The hotel charges for a few days must have been wearing into his pocket.*

Throughout the night I had to call Tavon back myself a few times—and the phone rang straight through to his room.

"Jose?"

"Naw Tay, it's me. He hasn't called back yet?" I asked.

"No, I keep calling all the numbers he gave me but I still haven't heard from him yet. I'm trying to stay off the phone, hoping he'll call me back."

"OK call me as soon as you hear something."

"I will."

After what seemed like forever, I decided to call Tavon because I couldn't stand the wait any longer. He answered the phone on the first ring.

"You still haven't heard anything?" I asked.

"Nah and those numbers that worked so well before," he said and took a deep breath, "have no answer. Absolutely no answer at all--they just ring, and ring, but no one answers."

He sounded like he was ready to cry.

"Well Tay, people step out sometimes." *I was trying to give him encouragement I didn't feel. I had a sick feeling that it was really too late, that we had blown our $90,000 sure thing on too big a risk.*

"Do you really think so J?" he asked. "Every time I called any of the numbers before somebody answered. If Jose wasn't there, somebody would take a message. This just doesn't feel right to me."

"Well, it is sort of strange, but what can we do?"

I didn't know what the answer was. Should he just come back? Ninety percent of me believed we'd been tricked out of the money. There was a part of me that was not ready to lose that much money, but each day he stayed, we lost even more. At this point the only thing we can do is hold onto hope and continue waiting...

"Look J, I'm going to get off the line in case Jose is trying to call," he said in a passive tone.

"Okay, Just keep me posted."

Saturday night came in a hurry. Tavon was as edgy as a cat afloat on a straw mat. He was chewing his nails so hard I could hear it through the phone.

"J," he said during our eighteenth conversation that night, "I'm down to the last couple dollars, enough to get home, but not much extra. I mean, if I leave we lose 90 gran' for sure, but it may already be gone and each day I stay we lose more. What do you want me to do?"

"I ain't there man. You have to make that decision."

I could tell he wasn't crazy about my response. He didn't want to be the one to decide to abandon that much of our hard earned money and neither did I. With that much money on the line, he had to answer his own questions.

I know Tavon. My man has a good heart. If he could have found out if Jose got arrested, he would've definitely helped him out on bail. He decided to wait another day because his man, Jose, wouldn't trick him like that. They both had treated each other too good.

Each transaction was done to perfection so many times before, but never this big. Tavon couldn't make sense of it all since there was never a phone call from Jose – although his hotel number was still working fine.

He had to give up since Sunday night was well into giving up it's right to claim the day. With no product of equal value, and an unbearable loss in his hustle, he was forced to start the process of recovery early Monday morning.

He called me a couple times from his cell phone, when there was a signal, on his way back on the Trailways bus. It took him forever to get from New York to our Baltimore station on Fayette Street. Since he wasn't bringing anything with him, I met them at the station.

Chapter 25

PRECIOUS

"And if your man got you baggin' up-- /
It could be worse. /
Just put a little in the baggie— /
Put a little in the purse."

Jay-Z, "Show You How"
The Blueprint 2

"Mam, we have the new spring line of clothing from all the major designers over here. As a matter of fact, the sale starts today," the saleslady said to me with a smile that seemed practiced.

I really liked seeing summer hats on display mannequins. Everything was color coordinated. Linen pieces and color schemes got me ready for the warm weather. All that makes it even more inviting to spend money at Lord & Taylor. There were so many designers—I really didn't know where to start.

Flowers and pastel colors filled the room. I started flipping through some Prada skirt sets when my cell phone went off. I forwarded all my calls to my cell phone. That's why I looked at the caller ID and realized right away who it was. I pressed one when the recording gave me the option, so I could speak to the caller.

"Hey, Pretty. What's up, gurl? I know something is up since you're calling me!"

"Gurl, I still got my ass in this deep shit. You know I'm over here with no fuckin' bail and Fast Money can't do shit about it because I had everything."

"I heard that he's been getting things together for you, so you can get a bail."

"Well, he ain't moving fast enough because some federal investigators came over here with pictures of me and him getting off the train here and in NY. They were asking me questions about him. They're trying to get information on his ass and some stuff about NY."

"They did?"

"Yea, gurl and I'm scared as shit. They gave me all this information to contact them if I feel like talking. They had pictures of you and him at his house and showed me pictures of guys I've seen around—nobody I really know, though. They were saying Fast Money dealt with all of them, and if I could provide them information then they'll let me go."

"Don't go for it. That's one of the first things Dollar taught me. They're always trying to trap somebody. Don't let it be you."

"I'm trying, but…"

"They act like we don't watch those police shows on television. We know our rights—and don't tell them nothing."

"Money did get me a new lawyer. He was over here telling me he could get me out on bail, but it takes time."

"Shit's gonna work out, Pretty. Trust me on this one." *I had never been in her situation, so I tried to share words of comfort. She needed it because she wasn't getting out anytime soon. That's what Tavon told me. She has to sit for a minute until Money can sort things out. I know one thing: It couldn't be me!*

"Let's talk about something else on this phone, gurl."

"You keeping your spirits up?"

"As best I can, Precious."

"I know how tough that could be over there."

"I can handle myself, but Fast Money gonna have to do something—and do it quick because I can't keep staying over here. They offered me a deal and my ass is about to go crazy about it."

"I can imagine."

"No! You can never imagine this shit. Trust me! Imagine crying yourself to sleep all the time. Imagine trying to sleep on these cold ass floors day-in and day-out. This is crazy and I gotta do what I gotta do to get outta here."

"You need me to send you something?"

"Yea! Help his ass with that money, if you got some!"

"Alright, I got somebody I can talk to about some money to help out."

"Gurl, this shit wasn't worth it. Once I'm outta this, I ain't messing with no more hustlers in the game! I'm telling you it just ain't worth it. You should've heard how they kicked my door down and started tearing shit up. They came in there like wild animals throwing me on the floor. Now they come over here, one by one, acting like I'm their best friend."

"Pretty, don't let them fool you because you're smarter than they are."

"Let's change the subject for real this time, Precious," she said with a serious voice. "I heard that you been getting with Tavon--the dude that worked for Fast Money."

"And so?"

"Ain't you something? You just don't care, do you? You knock 'em all down!" she said snapping her fingers so loud I could hear it over the phone.

"I'm gonna work it as long as I can. Plus, I was finished with Fast Money's ass a while ago. When the money dries up so does the luv. Anyway, as long as they're gonna pay me, then—oh, well! And to answer your question—no, I don't care. It doesn't matter who it is. I do them all!" I said bragging as I walked toward the hot, new Donna Karan fall line.

"I heard Tavon lost a lot of money in New York the other day and they say he's still messed up—losing all that money. He's the talk of the jail. Word is, Juvenile is taking over—with his sexy self. Now that's a project, but I'll get him in my arms yet! Watch me—when I get out!" Pretty said.

"Listen to who's talking. Didn't you just say you ain't gettin' with no more hustlers. And what about Joe Lewis and Ronnie B? You been doing both of them and you're saying something 'bout me? You have some nerve! That's your bail money."

"Go ahead! Do you—Precious!" she said laughing.

"But I'm gonna work Tay and mold him—like I did all the others, Pretty. Hold on one second." *The cell phone slipped out of my hand because of the way I held the clothes. As I tried to pick up the clothes and not lose my call, the sales lady who has been secretly, or so she thought, following me around rushed over to help me.*

"Let me get that for you mam," she said giving her phony smile.

"Oh, thanks. I need to try them on."

"Come this way to our dressing room."

"Let me know if I can get anything else for you," she said as she unlocked the door.

"This will be all for now," I said, returning her phony smile.

"Oh gurl I'm back. Sorry about that, I had to deal with this heffa who been following me around ever since I came in this store. You know how it is when we come into these malls where they don't think we belong."

"Yea gurl, they always acting like somebody wanna steal something," Pretty said.

"Like I was saying before, he'll be back out there. And I'll be right beside him setting up shop. If I am going to be in his life, he has to do something to take care of me, Gurl. I don't come cheap."

"I know that's right! I'll have to work on that Juvenile when I get out because my ass is broke. Gurl, I lied just a minute ago about that hustler thing."

"You still crazy—even over there. What's up with Fast Money?"

"Fast Money used the rest of his jewelry and money trying to get my black ass out on bail. Now he's gonna have to pay my lawyer and some other shit. You know they're talking about some illegal search and seizure because they didn't have a warrant with my address on it," Pretty said before my signal started fading. *As my signal came back, I could hear a female voice screaming in the background.*

"Who's screaming at you to get off the phone?" I asked because somebody was being rude-as-I-don't-know-what.

"Precious, gurl, I gotta go—I gotta get off the phone. I'll try to call you whenever we come out again for rec. This crazy C.O. is making me get off the phone. I'll call you back."

"Alright, gurl. Bye."

After we hung up, my conversation with Pretty took me into deep thought about Tavon and his new situation after we hung up. I could see his future when I first laid eyes on him. So, from the beginning, I was determined to get next to him.

It was somewhat a secret, I thought, that I was traveling to and from New York with him. I carried his money up and brought the drugs back. That seemed easy. I didn't know I would like the business side of the game. Anyway, he and I promised to keep our fling and everything that went along with me getting money from him secret—ever since he and I hooked up after meeting through Fast Money on Pennsylvania Avenue. Everything between us had to be secret because too many people enjoyed my business and the men I deal with.

It seemed like my job out here in these streets. I was the self-appointed chaser who makes stars out of those up-and-

coming hustlers. Tavon was my newest project. And now I am right beside him.

It's the same ole' hustle. My looks caught his attention. Traveling with him all those times brought him closer into my web. He is kind of different though. We have some real good conversations about our lives. We shared our life's dreams with each other. For the first time someone cared enough to listen to me when I talk about the real person I've always wanted to become. Now I think he's feeling something for me

I ain't gonna lie. I don't believe in love or love at first sight, but I'm feeling something for him, too. Now, that's some bullshit because I've come too far to start letting my guards down for some cute young hustler.

Tavon was looking out for me before he was taken for all that money the last time we were in New York. I've been telling him that I knew somebody who could help him get back on his feet. Although, it wasn't his feet he needed to get back on, it was his heart that needed tightening up. He needed to get up off his ass and stop feeling sorry for himself. It's almost two months now and he hardly ever goes anywhere. I'm starting to feel flustered in that house with him. Bills have to be paid and things still have to get done. Life didn't stop because Tavon supposedly quit. I guess he was still in his imaginary state of retirement when he finally introduced me to his partner Juvenile. We actually met by accident because I've been spending so much time at Tavon's house. I'm glad he has Juvenile as a partner because he needs somebody like him right now. Somebody who can brush off the bad luck and keep moving.

The last time I gave Tavon one of my speeches Juvenile was there to back me up.

"Tavon, how long are you going to let this break you down? You've kept it real so far and you gonna let this stop you? You still gotta make things happen! Forget that shit that happened with Jose. He ain't nothing!

"All that was suppose to do is teach you a lesson making you better at your game. That's how the game goes. I keep telling you I got a sure connect—and you ain't even taking advantage of that!"

"What's up with you, Tay? We need all the help we can get man–so let's do this thing. Ain't nothing ever stop us before. So don't let this little setback stop us now, my brother," Juvenile told him.

He refused my offers in the beginning. However, I could see his interests was still there because he talked everything over with Juvenile. It didn't take Tavon long to ask me to put Juvenile on with Darryl. Getting stuff from the Posse couldn't put us where we needed to be. It helped for what it was worth, but that wasn't big enough.

I made the call right away. All it eventually took for Juvenile to get on with the little money they had left was for me to get in contact with Darryl. Some of us call him Dee for short. He was one of my friends from Baltimore who made things happen in Brooklyn. He had cousins from BK who took the opportunity to meet supply with demand, so he moved there.

I went into the bedroom to call Darryl so no one could hear my conversation. Juvenile was waiting to pick up the phone in the dining room whenever I gave him the signal.

"Hey, Dee," I said flirting with him as usual.

""Who's dis?" he asked in a rough, but firm tone.

"You know who it is. You *betta* stop playing! You ain't been gone dat' long, Dee."

"You took long enough. I knew your ass would be calling me."

"Hey, Baby."

"You ready for me now, Precious? I can Western Union you money to get up here—right now!"

"I'm always ready for what we talked about, but this is business. I told you about the dude I'm with now. His partner Juvenile needs to see you like that. He's somebody you would want to meet."

"Oh, yea."

"I'm telling you, Baby. He and his man are like that. I'll be there to introduce him to you, if that's what you want. You can get rich with this team."

"Can I see you then? We can sneak off like we always do. I'll take care of him later."

"We'll have time to do whatever when I see you. I've been crazy thinking about you, too, but this dude is thorough. He's just like you—somebody I can work with," I said in a sexy, but serious whisper. *Talking to him like that gets him every time.*

"If this shit don't work out—Im gonna make you pay! Now put his ass on the phone."

"Hold on. Let me get him now."

"J pick up the phone," I yelled down the steps. *After I introduced them I listened to their conversation for a second before I hung up.*

"Man, I've been hearing a lot about you--Word. And I'm definitely trying to get up with you in the Apple," Juvenile said.

It didn't take long before Juvenile and I were doing the same thing I did for Tavon! It was to my advantage to connect Juvenile and Darryl. Getting involved in the business carrying for Tavon was one thing. Making this connection work gets me money—whether Tavon wants to be involved or not. Getting a chance to hook up with Dee also has its benefits. Homeboy is always sweatin' this sexy ass.

I was doing something with Tavon that went even better with Juvenile. Tavon started me to bagging the products up. He would sit there with me to make sure everything was being done right. Juvenile was a little more relaxed. He was always doing something so most times I would break that stuff down for transport by myself. It never failed. That weed and Hennessy had him outta control. He'd take a nap on the couch or start falling asleep at the table. And then it would be time for me to make the fair exchange: A whole lot in the baggie for them--and just enough in my purse for me. Momma ain't raise no fool. This girl knows how to work it!

I guess from the side I've always hustled. It didn't matter whether it was people, places, or things. I always get my way. And I was determined to be right beside both Juvenile and Tavon when they set up shop around town. Before long we were going back and forth almost every three days.

Chapter 26

JAMEEL

*"I look in the eyes of our, our kid, /
this little life we made together. /
I'm trying..."*

Jay-Z, "Soon You'll Understand"
The Dynasty

I usually pick Tiffany up from school as soon as I get off at the Post Office. It's a straight shot from there to the school. Most of the times, when I arrive she's playing with her friend, LaBria, but today things seemed different. She was sitting on a bench by herself. When we made eye contact, she started crying and running in my direction.

"Mommy, Mommy, this mean boy in my class named Jermaine, who always picks on me, said something mean about my daddy," she said with tears streaming down her face.

"Who's Jermaine?"

"His other name is Smurf."

"What happened baby? Did he put his hands on you?"

"No, Mommy, but Smurf said that he heard his father saying he would kidnap my father and kill him for the money he's hiding in our house."

To see my baby shaking in tears got me so frightened. I couldn't believe what I was hearing. You know kids only repeat what they hear their parents say. I couldn't say anything for a minute, I just held her. "Tiffany, now you listen to me--nobody is going to do anything to you, your father or anybody else in our family. It's just not going to happen."

I hugged her with one arm while wiping her tears and runny nose with my hand. I had to explain to her that whatever her father was doing in the streets was wrong so she could understand why he couldn't be here with us.

"But I don't want my daddy to die!"

"And he won't, baby, neither will we! I promise you that, Tiffany. So stop crying!"

My baby girl loves me dearly, but she really loves her father. Both of them were on my mind all the way home. That love is my envy. She even talks about him in Bible study class. At this point, all she wants is to spend time with him. That's why she'd always take the phone to her room so she could speak with him privately. At the end of their conversations, Tiffany would always say her special prayers. Dorian said little when Tiffany took over that part of the phone call. Actually, he looked forward to that. Somebody had to be praying for him. He didn't pray himself.

I took my baby home for a quiet evening of homework and playing a couple games before the night ended. I couldn't help but to gaze in the eyes of this beautiful life Dorian and I made together as I finished getting her ready for bed. I'm trying the best I can with her, but she needs her father too. All evening I tried to call my mother and her father so I could talk about what happened to her today and it was just my luck—my mom wasn't at home and Dorian changed his number—again—without telling us. I tied her hair up and was on my way out of her room when I turned around and reminded her to pray.

"Tiffany," I said, "Don't forget to pray before you go to sleep."

"Yes Mommy, I know."

Tiffany usually invites me to pray with her, but she did it on her own tonight. As I stepped away from her door I could hear her saying her prayers. Listening to her ask God about her father again really upset me.

It's almost as if a cloud of sadness surrounded me and zapped my energy. I was trying to get her father off my mind, but listening to her changed that. When I talk to my friends about what I'm going through, I have to make sure she isn't around. My adult opinion is not hers to hear when it comes to him. Conflicts have to stay out of the ears of our children. It's respect for my daughter. Tonight I would really have something to tell him if he had answered that phone. They always say the Lord knows best.

When something is heavy on my mind I can't sleep. A sea of tears flowed down my face as I thought more of what my daughter prayed for. Thoughts of Dorian being out on those streets ran through me. It's a shame he won't take time out for his daughter and the needs she has growing up. He's never there for her. It would be easy for me to take what her father wants to give instead of himself, but money isn't everything. I know hate is a strong word—Lord forgive me--but sometimes I have to use it. I hate that he doesn't want to be here with us.

It was smart of me to insure his life. Anything could happen to him out there. At least I do have a legitimate means of putting him away. Lord knows—he's not even thinking about that. Just thinking about that whole ordeal makes me upset with him. Sometimes I wake up during the middle of the night with a gut feeling that something is terribly wrong. I worry about whether I'd ever see him alive or be in his company again.

In the wee hours of the morning I have paged him--with no response. After paging him I would wait by the phone, checking the line, calling again and again. It is constant pain wondering whether a 3 o'clock in the morning phone call would tell me he was gone. Never knowing if the next will be collect from Baltimore City Detention Center worries me sick. I resorted to prayer, held on to hope and writing...

Think About Us

By: Jameel

It's so much happening in the world
Sometimes it scares me…
I know that you are a part of *"that life."*
Baby, wise up and be careful.

I know you say you do what you have to
Because this seems the easiest way to survive,
But in that life the odds are stacked
And the stakes are too damn high!!

I know the money is good
And when you give, I won't take…
Because our lives shared are more important
And if we work together, somehow I know we'll make it.

It is you I love
And if I could, I'd steal you away…
Away from the world's hostility
And the dangers you sometimes have to face.

I hope this is just a phase
That you are going through,
I don't want you to let our dreams go…
Without us spending the rest of our lives with you!

You are my life and my committed love.
Help me to make our chances better
By letting go of *"the game"*
And showing me your love!

Chapter 27

JUVENILE

"Stick to the Script.../
We cop, we flip, we re-up—/
And get back on our ship..."

Jay-Z, Stick to the Script
The Dynasty

It took a while but we did bounce back. Making that move outta town with Precious was the reason we blew up in different parts of the city again. But now she is acting like the First Lady. It's kinda funny how she's all up under Tavon when we're in Baltimore and when we are in New York it's a different story. Dee sure is getting his money's worth, but so am I.

She told us how old dudes like Fast Money were constantly calling her trying to cut our throats. He was asking her to put him in contact with Darryl even before we hooked up. While counting money at the table Precious started talking about it.

"Y'all that damn Fast Money just keep on calling me trying to get me to put him in contact with Dee. I'm through with his sorry ass and he should know it because each time we talk I end up hanging up on him. I told him that the feds were showing his pictures to Pretty. Every since then he acts like he doesn't know what to say on the telephone!"

I scratched my head out of habit before telling her his truth. "Money is out there now smoking that weed like there's no tomorrow. Plus he's gambling all his money away or whatever he has left. That's why I only give him money every now and then. He's still cool with me—but I'd like to see him back on his feet."

"I keep telling you J, the more you give him, the more he wants. That's why I cut him off. Plus he's hot with the feds!" Tavon said.

"All he keeps saying is what he's done for us. That's why I really hang up on him—because all he does is hate and put our business in the streets—or to whoever is listening in on the phone! I hate that shit because he knows better!" Precious said sucking her teeth.

"For real?" Tavon asked.

"Yea, and somebody needs to talk to him because it's getting out of hand. He just kept screaming into the phone."

"What else was he saying, Precious?"

"He was like, Precious, I asked you a long fuckin' time ago to hook me up with Darryl, but you won't give me the time of day. It wasn't like that when I was on top! Even before the first-fuckin'--ring, you would be picking up the phone. Now, bitch, things are so different, but I'll be back on top one day. When I am—don't fuckin' call me! None-a-y'all. I knew I should've put Juvenile on from the very beginning! Tay ain't shit either. He of all people should be worshiping me. His motha brought him to me like a little punk begging me to take him on. And now he wanna act like he don't know me. He was even talking about Outlaw being two-faced because he was working for you!"

I could see Precious playing Tavon. I know she was exaggerating and he was feeding into it.

"That fool's asking for trouble," Tavon said. "I'll talk to him when I see his ass again."

"Hey, Tavon. If I open up, what time are you coming down so I can leave?" I asked to change the subject.

"Precious and I are going to finish up in here. We have one thing to take care of and then I'll be ready. Just call me ahead of time--I'll be right there."

That's right. Tavon was back with me. He finally decided Precious and I were right about what happened up in New York. It was Jose's loss, not his.

"You have to stick to the script, Tay. A scared hustler can't get money. I need you. Man, you got me out there doing it all by myself."

The last time we talked I told him the truth. "Precious is hustling with me, but that's not you. You are my man. Darryl wanted to deal with you from the beginning—know what I'm sayin'--because he heard about you working for Fast Money. I need you to cop from Upstate. I'll be here making sure things get flipped here. That's the only way this shit is going to work on a big scale!"

Finances exploded again for us. Tavon wanted others to feel it too. First, he purchased a diamond pendant and an Italian link chain for his mother. He had a Manhattan jeweler make her an eye-catching diamond horseshoe piece. Pave' diamonds dressed the borders while a beautiful horse head accented the center with more diamonds underneath. A lucky charm for his mother was special since she had been through so much out there getting high. She still used, but he really wanted that charm to represent hope for her recovery and a better life for both of them. It was his hope Kamila would treasure it as a reminder of how he treasured her.

Then, he did something even bigger. For more than 40 G's he purchased a Mercedes in Virginia. Homeboy even put Latrell Sprewell rims on it. Damn, it looked good as those rims spun while the car stood still. That alone cost another 10 grand.

I must admit that Tavon knew how things happened in the Big Apple. He was better at transporting large amounts across the state lines back into Baltimore. He and I still took turns because this had to be done right. Tavon was still better at handling business.

Every time we went up, copped, and made it back safely we'd pay Precious forty-five hundred plus expenses. That was her reward for stuffing raw heroin in her body cavities and carrying cocaine by the kilos. We didn't know whether she was putting some of that heroin inside her vagina or not. I watched her when it was my turn to travel back and forth. I know it was all about that dollar and I respected her on the streets for that, even though I didn't want to trust her.

Chapter 28

JUVENILE

"If you with us, /
throw the diamond up one time."
Jay-Z, "Diamond is Forever"
The Blueprint 2

It was close to three in the morning when we finally got a chance to count the money we'd collected these last couple of days. We cleared my apartment table of sandwich bags, vials and cards.

We pulled the bags off the floor and placed the contents on the table. My glass table was filled with money, a counting machine and rubber bands. It was time to go to New York again, but this time we were going large. The three of us sat around the table checking counts behind each other. After what seemed like forever, we finally got to the end. I guess it took so long because we were talking and counting at the same time.

"What's your count, Tavon?"

"I came up with $118,700. What'd you get?"

"Man, I keep coming up with $119 even."

"Precious, what did you get?"

"I just put those things in ten thousand dollars stacks. I didn't count like you did, Juvenile," she answered shrugging her shoulders as if she didn't care. "That stuff is too hard to count, anyway, because it sometimes sticks together. Plus, I'm hungry."

"Well, take your hungry-ass in the kitchen then!" I said.

"Whatchu got up in here?"

"Go see for yourself—I ain't your butler."

As she stepped out of the room, Tavon peeped to make sure she was gone. With the look of a happy child on his face, he pulled something out of his pocket. He put both price tag and product before my eyes.

"Check this shit out! J, whatchu think?"

"That's phat!" I answered. "Now, that rock is huge."

He hid it back in his pocket and tiptoed into the kitchen so she couldn't hear him coming. I was still holding money in my hand when he walked to the kitchen to speak to her.

"What you doing scratching in your pockets. You itching, Tavon?" she asked while holding a bowl of cereal.

"No, I'm trying to get something—if it would ever come out."

"What is it?"

"Yo, Precious--I know you think I don't take you serious. I do wanna show you how serious I am about you. I think I should have done this a couple months ago, but here you are," he said extending his hand toward her.

"Whatchu talking about Tavon?" Precious asked while looking directly at the blue velvet ring box in his hand.

"Here. This is for you. You hung in there with me when I was down. Now that I'm up I wanted you to feel it."

"Oh-my-goodness. Tavon, I know you didn't--but this is—Oh-my-goodness!" she said jumping up and down like a kid who just got their favorite candy. "Thank you, baby! Thank you! This is gorgeous! You're the best baby!"

Tavon had her ring finger frozen with ice. That was my cue to walk away from him, her and the unsettled money. I just couldn't believe my eyes. "Yo, that's nice," I said with a straight face. But I have to roll and leave y'all two lovebirds alone. Don't forget about relieving me so I can get that other stuff done, tonight."

"If you with me, Boo, throw the diamond up one time," Tavon said, as I went through the door. He had the nerve to try to rap like he was Jay-Z in an offbeat tone. I couldn't believe I was walking out of my own apartment in anger!

I jumped into my car and immediately pulled out my cell phone. When things start bothering me in the streets I have one good friend I depend on to just listen to what I have to say. I called him because he taught me a lot—even though he didn't like me in the beginning.

"Yo, Fast Money—man you ain't gonna believe what your man just did!"

"Man, what did he do this time—buy a yacht?"

"I can't believe he did that shit. He bought her one of those expensive platinum rings! That shit has two heart shaped diamonds, I know, weighing about two carats. Man that piece cost about twenty g's!"

"Are you for real? He could've given me twenty thousand to get back on my feet! I mean, help a soldier out, you know what I'm saying J?"

"Check this out Money, they were talking about how bad you're doing again—and how you keep calling Precious trying to get hooked up with Dee. That *ho'* got Tavon all caught up and believing everything she says about you."

"She got some nerve—I wish I would've known that she would carry that shit. I hear that she's even stuffing it, J."

"I told you that shit."

"He knows that I need help. I borrow money from you and should be getting some from him so I can get my game right, again. But he's buying all that stuff—and I'm suppose to be his man—so he says."

"I got a few dollars for you now, Money, but I got a few things to take care of first."

"She's gonna run his ass in the ground just like she tried with me. With all of the money she's seeing, Tavon is thinking she's impressed. Her other lovers, especially her ex-husband, exposed her to so much more."

I was a little shocked he said that over the phone. I tried to stay on the same conversation about Tavon. "Man, I'm his partner. And you—You taught us the game and he won't even let me help you like I want to. He's showin' love to everybody besides me and you."

"I would be hot with his ass, too," he said.

"All I want is a barbershop and hair salon. That will get me out of this game, so I can be with my daughter. But, no! He decides to spend money on shit like that. Money, that's crazy since I'm the one who has been there for him."

"What time can we get together so I can get that money?" he asked. "I wanna go to the bar to shoot some dice. I'm tryin' to make a dollar out of fifteen cents here. I feel lucky-as-I-don't-know-what! Plus, I still have to pay some heavy dollars to Pretty's lawyer before she goes to court."

"I know you don't come out until night time, so call me about nine tonight."

"I'm out, Yo!"

"Alright. One."

In the Nation

New York -- New York City Police suffered public embarrassment when it had to arrest one of its own. Internal Affairs division has been investigating the disappearance of confiscated drugs in large amounts from highly secured evidence lockers at local precincts.

Complaints from Manhattan's District Attorney's Office initiated the investigation after several judges dismissed dozens of cases after police failed to produce drug evidence in high profile cases. Raul Rodriquez, 39, of Brooklyn, was arrested and charged with stealing millions of dollars worth of high quality heroin, marijuana, ecstasy, cocaine and Oxycontin.

Authorities are continuing their investigation to determine whether other NYPD personnel are involved. Mr. Rodriguez is cooperating *fully* with authorities. More arrests are expected in other east coast cities.

Chapter 29

PRECIOUS

"Mommy, why you playing with me?"
*Jay-Z, Jigga that N***A*
The Blueprint

Some months had passed and Tavon and I were still together. He did give me this phat piece of ice a few months ago to display how much money he was making. That was growing old too.

I get bored fast and having another man who wants to marry me is having that effect. Tavon was hard to get in the beginning. Now he does whatever I tell him—and that's taking the fun out of what we share. To be truthful, I'm getting bored with him and Amtrak.

Tavon was preoccupied in his world of toys. Spending, trying to impress, has become his whole life. If you really want to know the truth, I'm no longer impressed.

That's why I'm glad I always have one sometimes two on the side. Don't be frowning up your face – a girl has to do what a girl has to do. You know that. Talk about forbidden love--the sex I was having with him was so strong that the condoms were breaking. I'm probably like most men. I want what I can't have. He wanted me just like I did him. We were never supposed to share that side, but we did. And whenever we had the chance to get together it was like magic!

He's in the game, too. Tavon had gotten so caught up in money now, to me, he had become a different person. Sometimes I am happy, but that isn't happening too often. We no longer have our little talks that means so much to me. And lately, I've been feeling some terrible abdominal cramps that make me wanna curl up like a ball. My new friend is the one I've been sharing that with. He's been telling me to go to the doctor after we were together one day and the cramps started but I still have not gone yet. My conversations with him were getting deeper about his child and what he wanted out of life. One thing he wanted were some businesses so he could get out of the life.

My body was still going through changes, but now that I know why, I'm happy because that's what I wanted. Tavon wanted no children, but I did. I was thinking if I got pregnant I no longer had to travel to and from—and he could stop using those smelly condoms. That's why I was putting pinholes in condoms in the house. I was lonely and always going through changes. I don't know whether I was lonely for excitement or just longed for more of Tavon and wouldn't admit it. You know right now I really don't know what I want.

Traveling to New York was special this time. This time, my new friend and I took the trip. I took some sexy overnight wear because of how I was feeling. Right after we checked in, I went to my room and got started with my routine. I dropped my bags and got straight into the shower. We always booked two rooms even though we both end up staying in one. That arrangement suits me fine because sometimes I wanna accommodate Dee without my friend knowing.

I had a new red thong set and Teddy I was dying to show off. He needed some time to get stuff ready for Dee later this evening so I left him counting out money.

I came out still wet from the shower and decided to get dressed and take a trip down the hall to his room.

"Who is it?" he said after I knocked lightly on the door.

"It's me, just open the door," I said.

"What are you up to girl?"

"Can I talk to you?"

"Yea, Precious. Just let me finish doing this and I'll be with you in minute."

I went in and sat on the bed allowing the split from my long dress to open over my left leg to show him just enough. I wanted to see how he responded. I know the scent from my Victoria Secret's lotion was beginning to get to him because he started drawing up his nose as if he liked what he smelled.

"Girl, what you got on? Oh my goodness--look at those legs! Come on and show Big Papa what you got under there?"

I stood there and posed for him—showing off what he like most. He was looking fine as ever because he had no shirt on and his jeans zipper was open showing his underwear.

"You don't look too bad yourself Big Papa," I said, while I was twisting my way across the room to him. *Every good sex session has started like this.*

"You put that on for me?"

"Maybe? What you think since it's only us two up in here?"

"C'mon, Mommy. Why you playing with me? Bring that sweet thing over here."

"I wanna talk to you first."

"C'mon. I wanna feel you in my arms."

I went over to him and lay my body on top of his before kissing him all over. We'd done this several times before. I know what he likes. And it didn't take long to have him ready for pillow talk.

"You know I talk to you about everything."

"I know that," he said rubbing my hips.

"I went to the clinic the other day and took some tests. Remember? You dropped me off that day."

"Yea, I remember."

"Well, I was trying to see if I was pregnant."

"A-N-D?" he said looking surprised.

"A-N-D, I am!"

"What—by who?" he asked in suspicion.

"Don't act crazy—you know it ain't yours. But this is the other thing I wanted to talk to you about. My body is going through more changes than that and I'm scared for my baby. I have this discharge, so they did some other tests."

"You alright?"

"Yea, I guess. But they are supposed to be calling me with the results. Anyway, I feel better with you knowing just in case something is wrong since the condom broke last week."

"You know you can talk to me about anything," he said in a calm voice although still preoccupied.

I started to respond to him with a hug—but the room started spinning. Nature forced me to run back into the bathroom to give up the contents of my stomach. I could feel his arms around me as my mouth gave way to how I was feeling.

"Damn, you alright?" he asked.

I stood over the sink to wash my mouth, but couldn't. I had enough energy to tell him what to do. "Just sit me over on the bed so I can get myself together. I just needed to lay my body down for a minute."

I quickly fell asleep. I don't know how long I'd been out of it when I heard the phone ring. I could hear him responding to the caller.

"Stashfinder did what?" he screamed.

There was a pause as the caller relayed more information.

"Got-damn, Tavon! He shot him without him having a gun! Yo, that police is going down for that shit. I'm tired of his ass anyway, but, Yo—he's going down! All that because Troy and his crew wouldn't get down with him."

There was another short pause before he spoke to the caller again.

"She should be in her room, Tavon or she might have stepped out to get a bite to eat downstairs. You know Precious is a social butterfly," he said as he signaled to me to go to my room. "Tay, give her some more time and call her back man."

I was feeling a little better so I crept out of the room closing the door quietly behind me so it wouldn't make any noise. I knew exactly who Juvenile was talking to. I rushed to my room lay there waiting for Tavon to call me. It has been about five to seven minutes before the phone rang.

"Hello", I said sounding sleepy.

"Hey, baby!"

"I expected you to call me some hours ago Tavon. I miss you already."

"I tried to call you a few times but I didn't get any answer."

"For real, you know what, I must have been knocked out and didn't hear the phone. I was feeling so tired when I got in, so I took a shower and went straight in the bed."

"Are you OK?"

"Yea, I'm just tired."

"Precious a lot a' crazy shit is going on down here. Stashfinder shot Troy—that's the police I was telling you about that keeps following us in that unmarked car. Some more stuff is going on. But this is what I wanted to tell you. The hospital called twice today on the answering machine, but you were already gone."

"They did?" I asked, hoping that they wouldn't have left any messages. "I'll call them back when I get home. It's no big deal. I just went and did my annual check up, that's all."

"Well you take care and I'll see you when you get back."

I called the clinic the minute I arrived home the next day.

"East Baltimore Medical Center how may I help you?

"Yes, mam. My name is Precious Jenkins and I'm returning a call to Nurse Patricia Davis.

"Hold on one second, please."

"Hi, Ms. Jenkins. This is Nurse Davis. How are you today mam?"

I really wasn't in the mood for chitchat today. "I'm not sure, I'm waiting to hear from you."

"Well, she said, your test results came back abnormal so we need you to come back to the clinic ASAP so the doctor can discuss it with you. Can you be here by eleven?"

I stared into the receiver as if she was talking to a ghost.

"Ms. Jenkins, are you there? Hello?"

"Oh—I'm sorry, Nurse Davis—my mind was somewhere else. Yes, mam. I'll be there by eleven."

My heart started beating faster. I was already afraid, and this didn't sound too good. As scared as I felt, I started flashing back right to all my partners in the last month or so. The last time I got with Dee, we started out without a condom but then he did get up and put one on. And J, he always uses a condom. This wasn't getting any easier so I got up, grabbed my keys and headed for the truck. The traffic downtown was not making it any easier for me. Right now I wish there wasn't so much construction going on in the city. About 15 minutes after I got there and registered, a nurse came out and called me inside.

I sat in the room in a complete daze listening to the doctor telling me why I had a heavy discharge. I couldn't believe it.

Chapter 30

TAVON

"Mo' Money, More Problems /
Gotta move carefully."
Jay-Z, "Heart of the City"
The Blueprint

"What the fuck is this shit you talking about, Precious?"

"Tavon, please—just listen sometimes!"

"I hear what you sayin', but I ain't trying to hear that shit because I ain't doin' nothing!"

"I'm taking antibiotics now, Tavon. It's not that serious."

"How in the hell did it happen then? How did we get it then—answer that!"

"I mean, syphilis is curable, Tavon. Women can get stuff like that from using the toilet or wiping wrong. But that's neither here nor there--all you have to do is go to the doctors!"

"You do that shit to me and then talk shit!" I screamed at the top of my voice. "You don't get syphilis from using the bathroom, Precious. I'm the one who looks out for you and you do something like this shit? You must've bumped your damn head! Who you think you're playing with!"

"Here. The nurse told me to give you this information. All you have to do is call so you can get treated since you're my only partner."

"Well, who the hell you fuckin', Precious—cause' there had to be a somebody else for us to get this shit. I ain't fuckin' nobody else! So who is it?"

I know I didn't step outside of our situation even though I had opportunities all the time. I really didn't have time. It took too much time struggling to maintain freedom from Baltimore City cops, and all that other stuff that comes with traveling back and forth. That's a full-time commitment. I just didn't have time. That's why I was taking the news so hard.

I had to get out of the house before I did something real crazy. The more money I get, the more problems I have.

"You know what Precious. I'm getting the fuck outta here because right now my mind is not straight and I might do something that I regret."

I could feel her eyes looking at me as I walked to the door, opened it and slammed it behind me. I needed to be able to speed. I got in my truck and head for interstate 95.

As I drove through the city to get onto the highway, I couldn't get my mind off my situation. I more than likely have a sexually transmitted disease. I ain't never have nothing like this in my life because I've always been careful up until now. Now, I even have to move carefully with my own girl. I never really thought she would be messing around. The only other times she was away from me was when she goes to New York with Juvenile to cop when I have other things to do.

Just as I was about to get on the interstate I realized I shouldn't be running away from this shit. She had to answer for what she was into, not me. I decided to go back home to get to the bottom of this because I didn't understand. Plus, I remembered Juvenile was supposed to meet me at my house, so I slammed on my brakes and pulled off to the side. Luckily for me, no one was too close so I was able to reverse and get back on the street.

When I called her on the phone I could tell she was on the line with somebody else. I could hear her sniffling in attempts of recovering from our earlier argument.

"I'm on my fuckin' way home. If Juvenile gets there before I do then tell him to wait."

When I got there she was sitting in the living room in the chair with her legs pulled up to her chin rocking like a scared little child.

"Tavon, please, listen?"

"I don't wanna hear that bullshit. Who you messing' with? Who is it?"

I watched her start crying. She was hurting so bad inside her body was shaking. I heard the front door open up just as I was about to smack the shit outta her.

"Yo, Tavon. I'm not in your business, but that ain't called for homey!" Juvenile said.

"What she's doing ain't right, man. This trick been messin' around on me, Yo—and she keep lying to me."

While I was screaming I heard Precious start to gag. She tried to run, but I grabbed her. I watched as she grabbed her stomach and started throwing up something that looked like blood except it was black. That's when I realized she was really sick. I put my arms around her to prevent her from falling. Juvenile was right beside me holding the both of us. She ran to the bathroom. I could still hear her coughing and throwing up.

"Tay, go see what up with her, man. You hear that shit?"

"Man, fuck that trick!" I said still not being able to get over what Precious did.

Juvenile ran toward the bathroom. I followed behind him. Precious was curled up on the floor in her own vomit.

"Yo, J. Take her to the hospital," I screamed. "Do something—call 911! Look at all that blood!" *I was too angry to deal with this shit. I didn't care what the hell was happening.*

Later, I got a call from Juvenile. He called me from the hospital to tell me Precious loss our baby.

Chapter 31

JUVENILE

"He don't need [her] /
So he treats [her] like he treats [her] /
Better him than me— /
She don't agree with him..."

Jay-Z, "*Excuse me Miss*"
The Blueprint 2

Tavon was trying his best not to pay Precious any attention. The only thing between them two now was distance--at least that's what he was saying. When he talked about her he had nothing good to say. He blamed her for what they were going through. He was hurting, but he never voiced it. He had become a father who lost his child because of a disease.

He always left a lot of money in the house. Before this, he allowed her to get whatever she wanted. He didn't question that. But now she had to ask for everything. He would decide what she'd get and how much and where she'd go—for how long. His trust was gone. That's why she called me now for everything because she didn't agree with how he treated her.

She had actually become a mother. This was the first time she was pregnant. Her hurt was losing the soul she had finally created in her womb. I could see the pain in her eyes. It wasn't like she had loss something you can get back. Plus, she still wanted to love the man who helped her create it.

I was feeling sorry for both of them. Actually, I got soft toward Precious before this happened. I got to know her in a different light because we took the time to talk. I couldn't believe how good that woman's heart was. It was too hard for her to hold onto her emotions and him at the same time. She started telling me how her body was there with him at night, but her mind was on the other side of town. Better him than me because I wouldn't let a beautiful woman like that get away from me.

She'd done so much for us and I couldn't just walk away from that without showing some support. I knew how it felt to lose money or jewelry, but not a child. Precious' miscarriage made me think about my own family. I couldn't imagine losing my daughter. Tiffany is everything to me and I want to get my life together so I can be a part of hers. Not only does my daughter deserve that. Jameel shouldn't be doing everything on her own, so I have to get my life right.

Seems like every time I go to Tavon's house they are always arguing. I don't know why Precious doesn't go to her house. It ain't like she don't have one of her own – that she owns! As I pulled up in front of the house I heard them going at it again.

"Precious, who did you get this from?"

"I took my own money and bought this, Tavon."

"You expect me to believe you used your own money to buy a Rolex tennis bracelet? You don't spend your money for shit!"

"Tavon, please."

"Don't Tavon me! I don't need you! That's why I treat you like I treat you!"

"I don't agree with how you treat me. And, then again, I ain't going through this shit about me messing around! I didn't do that shit the first time. And I know I'm not doing that shit now!"

"You doin' something—because I don't give you enough loot to just up and buy something expensive like this! Where da' fuck did it come from?" he said.

As I stood outside the door I could hear her scream. It sounded like he slapped her. This time I didn't feel like being a part of this so I drove off.

POLICE BLOTTER

OFFICER INDICTED AND ARRESTED

A city police officer accused of planting drugs, lying under oath, and forcefully taking money from the pockets of suspected dealers was indicted on several federal charges including civil rights violations.

Officer Barry "Stashfinder" Crupt, 38, has been assigned to Baltimore City Police Department for 8 years. More than 57 separate civil complaints were lodged against him by African American male residents, but never fully investigated by city officials. Federal officials have charged him with 19 separate racketeering and civil rights violations.

Officer Crupt, who is also African American, became the subject of federal investigation after shooting and paralyzing an unarmed, suspected dealer who refused to join his operation. Court documents revealed Crupt is also being investigated by the DEA in other cases for taking illegal drugs for personal gain and extorting rival dealers into his operation. He is being held without bail at the Baltimore City Detention Center in protective custody. He is cooperating and willing to testify against his superior officers, including Baltimore's Top Cop, about other illegal operations.

Chapter 32

FAST MONEY

"I ain't goin' no where. /
They gotta deal with me!"
Jay-Z, What They Gonna Do
The Blueprint 2

I was trying real hard to get back on my feet. Nobody would really help me and it's usually that way when you're down and out. My bills were piling up on me and Pretty was still in that no bail situation. I finally contacted, Harlem Reds, an old friend in New York who was traveling between D.C. and Virginia. I had done some things with him in my past, but lost contact after that. He had called me up to see what I was into. I took the opportunity to invite him down. I was hoping this would be the break I was looking for to getting back on my feet.

He had something big to sell in D.C. and would be in the area. I had two days to get some money together. I scraped up enough money to buy a half-a-kilo which also included selling a watch. That was a small amount compared to what I had done before. I called him to let him know exactly what I was working with.

I started putting some things in motion. I called my man Rock. He was always looking for opportunities to make money.

"Yo, Rock. It's about to happen, so get right because I'll be at you, first!"

"Is it gonna be today, tomorrow—what?"

"Today, man. You in?"

"Is this coming from out of state?" he asked.

I could hear his cell phone ringing in the background. Somebody must've been pressing him because he showed immediate anger when he answered the phone.

"Hold on—hold on!" he said to be before covering up the phone.

I could still hear him.

"Yea, what you doing calling me like dis'!" he said to the cell phone caller.

Then there was a moment of silence before he spoke again. I didn't want to listen because I had to make this deal happen, but I needed Rock and his money.

"Yea, this is #519. I just called!" he said before a brief pause. "I can't right now."

I was thinking forty things at one time. His numbers and response had me wondering, but it only took a second for me to focus back on meeting my man from outta town.

"Yo! I'm back," he said. "So you said this was coming from outta town?"

"Yea, I'm getting ready to make this happen in a minute."

"Call me when you get right!" he said before we hung up.

I jumped in my car and thought how lucky Rock has been in the streets. In our crowd he has survived being arrested by police's like Stashfinder and always has money to spend. He was any smart hustler's go-to-man and probably was included on a lot of deals in our hood requiring a quick turnover. That's why I called him in the first place.

Reds and I met out Route 40 in Ellicott City. That wasn't far from my apartment, so I had the money counted already. I was already at the meeting spot when he pulled up. I got out with my bag in hand. When I hugged him, we made the exchange.

"Hey, man. Reds, I'm so glad to see yo' ass!"

"You looking good, Money."

"C'mon and give me a million. I know you have it."

"Boy, I've been doing this nonstop ever since we were together. I'm tired as shit now, B."

"And I'm trying to get tired of having so much money again—like you!"

"It ain't easy being me, but somebody gotta do it."

"That's 14 G's in the bag," I told him.

"That's more than a half a kilo. You knew I was gonna give you something to help out. You my man, Fast Money, but yo' shit sounds rough, B."

"I feel that! I'm glad we got together. Man, shit has been hard as hell. I think this is my breaking point—and I'll be on my way back to the top. I got a situation to deal with because one of my houses got knocked off. I got a broad over the jail with no bail and I have to finish paying the lawyer some heavy ass fees."

"Man, fuck a hustle—I wanna be a lawyer, B. They make all the cash, not us!"

"I'm a change my career, too. We'll be the dream team from Harlem and B-City."

"Man, I would've been got to you. You know that! *We are one for life*."

"Man, all I can say is now they gonna deal with me. Now that I've got you--I'm going hard again!" I said as I hugged him. *I had to show him some love because he was putting me where I needed to be. That doesn't happen often.*

"Oh, yea?"

"Oh, yea, I was down for a while. Now, with you, I ain't going no where!"

"I got mad luv for you, but where the hell can I go to get some sleep before I travel back up?" he asked.

"The best hotels are downtown."

"I'm not trying to make it all the way downtown. One of these spots will be good enough for what I'm trying to do."

"You can go to my place—that's not really far from here."

"Naw, that's alright. I'm gonna travel down here until I see a spot. "

"Alright. Then I'll follow you to make sure you get settled before I leave."

I was finally feeling good, like my old self. I turned my sound system up as loud as it would go. I had one of my favorite club music CD's playing: "H & H in the house. Oh! My God! Yale Heights in the house. Oh! My God! 41st in the house. Oh! My God." I let him get in front. He was looking for a place to lay his head, not me. So, it was his choice. I wouldn't want to be in one of those places with all that money. Anything can happen.

We came close to passing the Westgate Motel when he pulled over all of a sudden. I almost hit him in the rear. We backed into the entrance and parked. He went inside to register while I stayed inside my car making phone calls.

It didn't take him long to get his room keys. Honestly, I was tired myself from a sleepless night before. I couldn't sleep knowing my life was about to change and I'd be back on top! I still had to go to the Korean store downtown for vials. I whipped around the back of the motel so he could find his room. We pulled up. I was barely out of the car to help him when he waved his hands and told me to go.

"Go do what you have to. I'm okay, B. I'll get a few hours before I take off. Just give me a call when you're ready and we'll take it from there. Maybe next time you can come up," he said.

"Alright, Reds. I got your numbers, now. I know how to reach you. Later."

I was about to in get my car when a car parked at the far end of the parking lot caught my eye. A Mercedes sat parked on an angle. This four door S600 had gold trim around the body that complimented those Sprewell rims. I knew one day I would finally catch up with Tavon's ass. It was a female with long hair in the car that he was with.

I hated to disturb him, but he would just have to get his young ass out of the front seat or put whoever was with him out for a minute so we could talk. He'd been saying some shit about me on the streets that I didn't appreciate.

That is Precious. I know her red ass a mile away. That was her in the passenger seat. I walked closer. Tavon still dressed expensive. He and Juvenile dressed damn near the same. Part of his leather hat matched those bright cream leather seats with the purple Mercedes sign at the headrest. He had this habit of turning his hats around backwards. He wasn't a kisser, but I couldn't tell. He was putting his tongue down her stomach. His tongue passion showed because of how he was moving his head.

I tapped on the window kinda hard—just to play with him a little. The way he and Precious were kissing they should've stayed inside the motel. That Ravens hat turned away real fast. And Precious jumped because I startled them.

Damn! That wasn't Tay.

"Yo! What the fuck y'all doin'?"

Precious quickly pulled away. She sunk down in the passenger seat while trying to pull her clothes together real quick.

"What da' fuck you doing, Money!" J said through the small crack in the window. "You scared the shit outta me!"

"No! What da fuck y'all doing in Tavon's whip like this?" *Although I didn't put anything pass Precious, I still couldn't believe she was fucking both of them. I had a KY Jelly strategy and was immediately thinking how I could take cold advantage of all three of them to get back on top.*

As I turned and walked away from the car with my head low and hands up in the air expressing confusion, I was trying to think of the best way to make this work for me. J jumped out and rushed behind me trying to explain.

"Check dis' out Fast Money," he said, in a low tone of voice. "We were just playin' around, bullshitting, and things just happened. You know, Tavon is my man—and I wouldn't do him like that, but he ain't treatin' her right man. You know how we do, real men anyway."

"What you mean by *real men*?"

"I'm just saying—I'm on some *keep-it-real* shit. You saw what you saw. I can't take that from you, but what would it take?"

"What da fuck you mean, *what would it take*?"

"I'm saying, what would it take to keep all this between us? I don't want this to go no further than us three. C'mon, man. I got mad luv for you because you taught me what I know but--" he said before I cut him off.

"Juvenile, you know I'm bigger than how you been treatin' me! I'm a hustler! And you say I taught you the game, but you treat me like some worker on the streets. You give me a few hundred here and there, but I'm the fuckin' man. Now *whatchu* can do for me is front me a quarter kilo and a few dollars."

"A quarter kilo?" he repeated. He sounded surprised that I would ask for so much.

"Yea, you don't think I'm worth that--*now*?" I asked him not really expecting an answer. "Take it or leave it man cause this is some shit I know Tay would wanna hear. I know his reaction when he hears his main man is—I don't even *wanna* say it. Man you better put out or else..."

I left him standing with his two hands in his pockets trying to keep himself warm from the brisk wind that was blowing into the night.

I walked back to the car to see Precious still sitting there looking like she'd seen a ghost. "So what you got to say for yourself Precious?" I asked looking directly in her face.

She had the car window up and I motioned to her to roll the window down.

"Whatchu want Fast Money?" she said sounding very irritated.

"My, my, my Precious. If I were you, I would lose the attitude so we can get straight to the point. You were the first one to say that Fast Money slowed up cause I cut you off. You even told Pretty some shit about how broke I was and how you stopped messing with me."

"It ain't what you think!" she said without trying to control her anger. "Plus, you don't remember! You cut me off!"

Another car was pulling up beside us with four people inside. She rolled the windows back up as I stepped out of the way so the car could park. She wasn't exposing herself anymore than she had to. I tapped on the window again. Juvenile got back in the car and rolled the window down on the passenger side.

"I'm telling both of y'all. Tavon doesn't have to know a thing. All this is between us. Ain't dat' right, Precious?"

"My mouth is closed," she said looking at Juvenile.

"Precious. Now, when do I meet Dee? I've been asking you for a long time."

"I can do that for you with no problem," she said.

"Now, we all making sense here," I said smiling inside.

"I feel that, Fast Money," J said with this fake smile.

"I think it can happen almost right away, can't it?" I asked. I had her eating out of my hand.

"So, Juvenile. Can we get that stuff we spoke about right away too?"

"All you gotta do is follow me man—and we can take care of that right now."

Police Blotter

Home Invasion

A West Baltimore man was seriously injured last night in his home in what police suspect was a drug robbery. Darnell "Big Toney" Carson, 26, of the 2300 of Eutaw Place was found shot by a live-in girlfriend. Authorities were called to investigate "shots fired" by at least two armed attackers.

The gunmen entered through an unlocked rear entrance and robbed the victim of money and unknown valuables before shooting him in the upper body. He remains hospitalized in serious but guarded condition.

Federal authorities have taken custody of Darnell "Big Toney" Carson because he was also wanted on federal charges of conspiracy to sell confiscated drugs stolen from New York City Police evidence lockers. Officials are seeking the apprehension of another high-ranking co-conspirator involved in this large drug network. The investigation is continuing.

Chapter 33

FAST MONEY

"Your career has come to an end /
It's only so long fake thugs can pretend"

Jay-Z, "Takeover"
The Blueprint 2

I hadn't contacted Tavon in a while, but I knew how. We had our share of differences. I said some foul stuff about him to Precious because of how he treated me. He responded to that by sending me threatening messages because of Precious—and what she was saying. Tavon handled his business on the streets. Juvenile kept me up on that, so I knew his history. I didn't think for one minute that he would do what he said. He was just mad because Precious was trying to fuel that shit.

I know I would be the last person he'd want to hear from after I got that half a kilo from Juvenile, but telling him how his man was sticking him in his back and sleeping with his girl was important. First things were first, though. I had a whole brick in the trunk that was all mine.

As soon as I got my stuff stashed away I decided to use my contact to get to Tavon. P-Nut would call him for me right away since I was the one who helped her family out.

"Hello," she said, sounding high as a kite.

"What's up, Babe?"

"Who dis'?"

"Hey, P-Nut—this is Fast Money."

"Hey, baby boy! Things ain't the same without you being out here."

"I hear that, but that's not what I'm calling for."

"What's happening with you? You ready? Boy I can work that ass of yours for anything you got. You know I been tryin' to give you some for the longest time now."

"Come on P-Nut, you know that's not how we roll. Listen I need to get to Tavon for some important shit that's going on."

"Is he in trouble?"

"Naw, but he could be. Shit's been going wrong between us, but he needs to call me right away. Dis' shit is life and death."

P-Nut was from the old school. She knew business even in her addiction. Tavon called me right back.

"You crazy for calling me. You talking all that shit about me and now you got something important to talk to me about."

"Man, this shit is real—and you need to know what's happening."

"Money, if you trying to borrow something why don't you go to where you've been going. Didn't you tell Precious that J is your man—and all?"

"You know it gotta be something important for me to call your ass! It shouldn't be like this, but Tay you've been acting crazy about shit that ain't real!"

"I'm real—what da' fuck you talking about?"

"I'm talking about what's going on right under your fuckin' nose! Just meet me so your ass can find out what I'm talking about."

"Meet me downtown at our old spot around 8 o'clock."

I was speeding down Pratt Street in my old, gold Lexus Coupe a few hours later. I was feeling good because I finally got back on—not like I used to, but I had to start somewhere. I wasn't feeling sorry for Tavon because Precious was his problem.

My CD player cranked Baltimore's dealer's anthem real loud. "North and Long--pull your guns out! Pull your guns out. E.A.—pull your guns out! Pull your guns out. Hollins and P—pull your guns out! Pull your guns out. Westside—pull your guns out! Pull your guns out..."

My cell phone rang. "Yea?"

"Yo, dis' me, Rock. What's up?"

"I'm gonna get to you as soon as I leave from downtown."

"Where you at down there?"

"Right now I'm getting ready to meet somebody down by Trailways. Why?"

"I was just asking so I'll know how long you gonna be, that's all?"

"It won't be that long. Give me a half hour. I'm trying to get that money."

"Alright, are you driving your gold Lexus?" he asked.

"Yea."

"Alright. I'll holler then."

I turned the CD player off and hit the first preset channel I had programmed in my system.

"92Q love dedication. Who do you want to send a love dedication to?" the radio announcer said.

"Do I have to say names," the caller softly asked.

"No, sweetheart. Just send your dedication."

"Okay. The man who is my life and my daughter's inspiration loves your radio station. That's why I'm calling."

"We love hearing that here at 92Q."

"I want to send a love dedication to the initials D.C., but his friends call him J. We just want you to know if you're listening that home is here with us. Where you are in life now is not meant for you and it won't last. We pray for the day when your life will be changed and love for us as a family will be complete. Tiffany and I send this love knowing…God can't fail."

"Thank you," the radio announcer said. "I just want to say to D.C. if he's listening that sounds like true love to me. You better go home J."

Now that was deep I thought to myself as I made a left off of Baltimore Street onto Park Avenue. When I pulled up on Fayette Street he was already at the location. He was leaning against his vehicle on the passenger's side with a beer in one hand and a McDonald's sandwich in the other. He was impatiently waiting to hear what was so important. I could see that look in his eyes.

I turned my music down, shut my lights off and got out.

"You call me with all that important information shit—and you late?"

"I don't care how late I am—you would want to hear this shit!"

"Just so you know," he said, "I called my lawyer already to tell him that somethin' might be going down. So what's up?"

"Man there's no need for that. That's not how I do business." *I was getting a little annoyed at his cocky attitude.*

"Hey, did you hear what happened to your man, Big Toney?"

"Naw, what happened?" I asked with a lot of concern.

"Big Toney got shot up after some dudes *kidnapped* his ass. They had him in the trunk of the car before taking him home. These cats were cruddy because they robbed him and took everything they could out of his house—and still shot his ass up. After all that, the feds locked him up on his hospital bed while he was still unconscious because of some New York Police conspiracy. You must not read the paper. You haven't heard?"

"Naw, I haven't heard that. Did they have anymore details about anybody else being involved."

"No, they really didn't mention anything about anybody else, but it's the talk of the town. I didn't have a chance to read the whole thing, but what I read sounded serious. I had to tell you that because dat's your man."

I was crushed beyond repair because that could mean a whole lot of things. He was looking out for my best interests while I was looking for the opportunity to run game.

"Now, this what you had to tell me must be important."

"Have you talked to Precious?" I asked looking over my shoulder now.

"Yea, I talked to her ass in passing when I was home, but I try to stay away from her! She is on some crazy stuff now."

"What about Juvenile?"

"He's been on something different here lately, too. We really haven't been doing what we used to—because his ass is changing. He don't even work the strips like he did before or even hang out. He's seeing some new broad that keeps his ass on the run…"

He started pouring out his heart with long explanations of what was unfolding. I had to interrupt and get this game off my chest.

"Has Juvenile talked to you about anything concerning me and him?"

"Whatchu talking about, Fast Money?"

"Man, I caught Juvenile kissing your muthafuckin' girl in your car. He had his tongue down her mouth so long she should've choked!"

"Stop bullshitting me!"

"I never did that before so why would I start now. I'm saying—that's supposed to be your man and he's freakin' your girl. She supposed to be your girl, and she's freakin' your man. I walked down on both of them at Westgate Motel kissing and feeling on each other like they couldn't wait for the bed. The worse part is they were in your car."

"That's what the fuck has been going on!" Tavon said, as if he was trying to work things out in his mind.

"Yo, I wanted to kill his ass right then and there. That's how mad I was! That shit was crazy!"

"Those muthafuckers!" he said.

"It's only so long a fake thug can pretend! That's his career—a fake thug–and he was always that!"

All the while I was talking to him my feet were planted for a fight. I watched my breathing while standing firm in front of him. He was helpless as I kept bashing Juvenile's name since I wanted his place beside Tavon. Nor would I mind hitting Precious again myself.

From the look on his face I could tell that his mind blank was racing a hundred miles a minute. He wasn't letting this go! From man to animal—everything about him changed just that quick!

The last time I saw him like this was when I was in trouble. When things were going good I had a problem with Apple and his crew trying to take over one of my areas. I ran them away, but they came back, and shot one of my workers on Harlem Avenue. I had to get help so I went to Tavon and Juvenile.

All they did was make a long distance telephone call to Virginia, simple as that. We reached the Newport News waterfront in Virginia in no time. When we pulled up at the corner of the pier, Juvenile jumped out of the front into the back seat with me. This unsuspecting looking older white guy walked over to the car and casually got inside. From what I found out this old man Doc was the one to see for guns.

Doc would call Tavon and Juvenile after he unloaded certain international ships at the port. Some ships would secretly be delivering brand new firearms for Doc to sell for American cash.

There was no waiting period nor was anybody interested in conducting background checks. He took us directly to his office trailer where the guns were laid out. The Matrix came to life. I watched as Juvenile pointed to the guns as Doc called out the prices. I purchased three brand new 9 millimeters still in the box and on AK for another thousand.

Rumors travel faster than the speed of light. How the enemy found out how deep we were in arms was beyond me. Somebody told Apple and his crew before things got out of hand. All of us were trying to get paid. Nobody wanted to die. I know I didn't, but we lived with that fear each day we hustled.

After that, Apple did sit down and talk to me. I won the battle and war, so the cost for him trying to hostile takeover and failing was 10G's. From that point on he had to get down with me. He was in no position to say "No." Tavon and Juvenile were both ready to take it to the next level. And that's what I'm thinking about now knowing one of them is going to get killed.

I remember when this happened to my friend lil' David G. He went out of his mind when he caught his wife with another hustler. All he ever told us was, "I'll bang it out with the police before I go to prison. I ain't going down! They'll have to take me dead!"

He was talking about what most did about holding court on the street. His wife having a lover controlled his every thought. She called the police on him because of what he tried to do to both of them. His threats came to pass when police tried to arrest him for a handgun. He was wanted because authorities believed he shot several rounds into his wife's car.

Dave wasn't going out like that when caught up with him! His gun was his attorney. Drawing it on police announced order in the court! Dave's pull of the trigger was his oral argument and defense. Two Baltimore City cops became his judge, jury, and executioner! He not only shot it out with them. He died while trying to do so—because he couldn't let go.

Tavon's banged his fist on the hood of his car before taking his other hand to throw his beer bottle at the glass window in front of us.

"He's dead! Fuckin' my girl—is he crazy!" he screamed. "His ass is dead—that's why she's acting strange and I can't get in contact with either one of them!"

"I'd be mad—trying to kill something, too—but just calm down."

Without too many more words or warning he jumped in his truck. I wanted to tell him that an incident stemming from this could easily have authorities flashing his photo on late-breaking nightly news. I'd seen him in a lot of moods, even when we went to war a couple times. This kid was plotting. Before he even closed the door he was on the phone with Outlaw.

"Yo! Outlaw, get them things for me because I got some snake shit I gotta take care of!" he said on his cell phone before slamming his car door and starting his car.

"Are we gonna hook up and start taking care of shit now?" I tried to ask. *I couldn't see him behind those tinted windows as he pulled off. He raced up Fayette Street back toward Westside. He was probably going where Outlaw and his crews still hustled at one of his shops.*

I jumped into my car to catch up to him. I didn't want him going off the deep end without planning something first. He wasn't thinking. What he had done already was respond. Treating any situation like that meant trouble. And he didn't deserve that. And then I wanted something for my troubles.

I made it through the first light even after it turned red. I ran it because I couldn't concentrate on anything. I was glad that the Light Rail wasn't coming across Howard Street. I stopped at the light on Eutaw Street. I was hoping Big Toney could hold his own weight because of what we were into with Raul. Nobody was looking for me—and they probably won't, unless he says something.

I wanted to work all three ends from the middle and Tavon made it hard. Asking him for a half-a-kilo wasn't too much since I had picked up a quarter kilo from Juvenile already. I had that in the trunk for a sale that I had set up. I could get another quarter from Tavon on consignment and be back on my feet.

I could see him two lights away. I was thinking of what I would say when I catch up with him. I pulled through the light expecting to reach about 70 miles an hour. I noticed two blue siren lights flashing from two dark blue Chevy Impala's with black, tinted windows. One car pulled in front of me to cut me off and another was at my tail. I hit my brakes as fast as I could before reaching Paca Street.

Several white men with blue jackets were running towards me from different directions. They had to be real federal agents because their dark blue jackets had yellow writing on the front spelling FBI. I was frozen in the moment as I watched them point guns at me in the car. I was closed in, but it seemed like I could run and get away—even though I was trapped. My body seemed lifeless after following their orders.

"This is the FBI. Take your hands—slowly—off the steering wheel. Put your hands above your head."

"Alright! Alright! Just don't shoot!" I screamed.

"Now, take your right hand and cut the vehicle off while your left hand stays on your head," he said. "Now, put your hand back on top of your head."

I felt like that was all I could do—listen to his instructions. A black agent crept up from the side and snatched my door open. He pulled me out of my car and took me into custody. Just when shit was getting ready to blow up for me, again--look at what the hell happened. If it wasn't for that Ho', Precious!

POLICE BLOTTER

Baltimore City

The US Marshal's Fugitive Task Force and the Baltimore Regional Apprehension Task Force arrested a man indicted on drug conspiracy charges. Craig "Fast Money" Carter, 25, and Darnel "Big Toney" Carson, 26, of the 2300 block of Eutaw Place were arrested in separate incidents.

Carter, of no fixed address, and Carson were wanted for several state and federal drug trafficking, and conspiracy charges stemming from an undercover investigation in New York resulting in the arrest of New York Police Department Personnel. Raul Rodriguez, 39, of Brooklyn was arrested and charged with stealing millions of dollars worth of heroin, crack, marijuana and cocaine from police evidence lockers. These illegal drugs were distributed in New Jersey, Philadelphia, Delaware, Maryland, D.C., and Virginia.

Mr. Rodriguez testified before a grand jury and his cooperation resulted in more than twenty-three indictments of suspected drug dealers in several states including Carter and Carson. Pretty Jenifer is cooperating with an ongoing investigation and is scheduled to testify before a federal grand jury here in Maryland in connection with this case. In exchange for her testimony, authorities are not opposed to her release.

Maryland and New York authorities are seeking to charge both suspects with more federal and state charges as the investigation continues.

Chapter 34

P-Nut

"[P-Nut] blaming herself /
She wished she could've saved him..."

Jay-Z, "Meet the Parents"
The Blueprint 2

Those kids are crazy out there in the streets. I don't know why that Juvenile has made my son wanna chase him down. He ran in here like a madman trying to take those guns I was holding for him. He was screaming about Juvenile was a snake cause' he was stabbing him in the back fuckin' Precious. Both of them should stick to gettin money and leave that beefing mess alone. Now they're about to fall out with each other--all over that stank-ass girl, Precious. I never liked that girl from the beginning. And now I hate her ass even more 'cause she started sump'n between two men—and that's gonna mess up my rent money and shit! Knowing these two, things could get real ugly. That Juvenile ain't soft either. I heard some stories about him, too.

My child reminds me so much of his father who knew how to hustle and keep dudes on the street in check. He even got his father's violent temper and that ain't good. I wished I could've saved him from that. I sometimes blame myself for some of the stuff he's gonna experience out there. But he's just like his father. That's why I married that man because he was a real hustler and thug from the streets before the terms even became popular.

After all these years, the streets still talk about him like it was yesterday. Leroy was the man when he was involved with this black mob organization in New York. Back in those days the Italians dealt with selected Blacks to get heroin in our towns. Leroy was connected to Frank Mathewson—who, back then, dealt directly with the Italian's himself. Mr. Frank, who they later called the King of New York, was just released from Lewisburg's federal penitentiary. Eventually Mr. Frank locked the whole east coast down, sending large amounts of heroin into Jersey, Philly, Delaware, Maryland and D.C. My husband became Mr. Baltimore because he took over the streets and most of the project buildings.

Child, please! Back then we wore rabbit fur coats with the matching hats, Italian suits with the matching shoes, and would bring fashion from outta town before it hit local stores. Back then you could take some Valium—we called them V's--or drink syrup and alcohol and stay high all day. Those were the days.

I hustled with Leroy and fell in love with the life he was living because he treated me well—and made sure his business associates did, too. We would go up New York sometimes just to attend Broadway shows and other black tie affairs. Eventually, I became a small part of the business.

We separated as soon as he started selling stuff in D.C., but while I was with him I did learn some hustling skills myself. Not long after he left me, his luck changed. Mr. Frank had issues with my husband when he separated from me because his business fell off. He had simply lost control. He had a bunch of women. He started talking business on the phones, dealing with strangers and started losing large amounts of money. All this changed him along with his new love of sniffing cocaine.

Tavon's father beat me when things didn't go his way. And I was no longer his woman. Leroy would beat me until I was black and blue in the face. One time he beat me because he thought I took a hundred thousand from out of his safe. He found out later he'd put it somewhere else.

Nothing lasts for long in that life. The feds rounded them up one-by-one. Mr. Frank was the first in New York to be charged and convicted. He was sentenced to a life sentence for his part in one of the biggest interstate drug conspiracies ever. He was smart enough to run and never be seen or heard from again.

I was already separated from my husband when he was charged as the first federal Kingpin in Baltimore City. Leroy is now doing sixty years with no parole in federal prison. Tavon got his violence from his father. That's one of the reasons why I'm concerned and have to find out what's going on. My son can't hustle in jail. None of us will benefit from him being in there—at least I know I won't!

See, before his father went away I replaced him with another hustler who knew how to treat me right. King treated me with love. That's why I became his partner. And he was good to my son. King became the father my son always wanted, but never had. And he made me a better woman. Money was everything to me until my addiction took over my life. Getting high, putting my hands on some good dope or a rock of cocaine is the only thing that matters, now. My son hate da' shit I've been doing, but I'm gonna get right one day. But for right now, I gotta find out what's going on—after I get high one more time!

Chapter 35

TAVON

"I'm the one who move the stuff /
While you driving around in brand new coupes and stuff /
I swear to God they had me ... hating his guts."

Jay-Z, "Coming of Age"
Hard Knock Life Vol. 2
(feat. Memphis Bleek)

I went straight to my house to deal with Precious after I left my mother's house. I went there to get both of my guns. I always have both of my Glocks attached to my vest underneath my arm for easy access. I never knew it would be Juvenile stabbing me in my back. Fast Money tried to get that through my hard head. I couldn't see it myself, but he did. I made myself a promise. Cause he misused my trust, somebody was going away from this earth—real soon. There was no room for a lot of talk. I was getting to the facts—starting with Precious!

I busted through the front door. The scent of fish being warmed in the microwave greeted me. She had a lime green evening set on with her hair tied up. She was carrying a plate of food in one hand and something to drink in the other as she headed for the dining room table. I was moving so fast we met in the dining room area near the glass display unit. She froze in shock from my fast movements. I snatched her as hard as I could. The anger in my hands forced her whole body to twist against the display unit. Everything came crashing down on the floor! I could feel the sting of the hot food against my legs. She saw the look in my face and started screaming.

"What da' fuck you think you got—a damn dummy?" I screamed. *More glass was breaking as I followed her falling body near the swinging kitchen door. I stood over top of her with my hand ready to slap her ass again.* "I just talked to Fast Money about--" I screamed before she started telling on herself.

"Shit! Tavon, please!" she screamed.

"Tavon, please, my ass—bitch! Now what da' fuck is going on!"

"Nothing happened! I swear, Tavon. People always assuming stuff—when it's not true!"

"What da' fuck you mean nothing happened? First the syphilis, and then the bracelet and now some stupid shit like this!" I screamed before smacking her again.

"Tavon, please! Baby, I ain't lying!" she shouted before she started scratching me.

"I don't wanna hear that baby shit! Don't get shit twisted—because you can die too!"

"Tavon, no! Juvenile did dat' shit—not me!"

"What da' hell is going on, Precious?" I asked as I grabbed one of my guns to scare her.

"You wanna know what's going on Tavon!"

"I don't have this fuckin' pistol for nothing! Somebody gonna tell me something--and it better be you!"

"Tay, you don't need that gun in my face! Put dat' away so I can tell you!"

"You gon' tell me anyway. Now start talking!"

"Juvenile told me—get offa' me Tavon!" she said still fighting to get away. "He told me you wanted me out the motel—and I went! That's what da' hell happened. Now get offa' me!!" she screamed. "He's the one started dis shit! Now go handle him like this—not me!"

"You betta' tell me what happened!"

"Get dat gun outta my face, so I can tell you."

"You gon' tell me any regardless, Trick!"

"Juvenile disrespected both of us," she said still trying to get loose.

"What?"

"He told me you wanted me there at a certain time. And I didn't think nothing of it since the three of us met like that so many times before," she said while holding her face.

"How you end up in my fuckin' car with him!"

"I drove my car our there! He was driving yours so I got inside to wait for you! He didn't say whether you were coming really or we were waiting for somebody else! He is the one who drove me to the bar down the street! We drank some when he told me to come on and that you should be there by now!"

"I ain't tell you or him shit! I ain't call you, did I? Did I tell you to do anything?"

"Tavon you never do. You get him to do everything. How da' hell was I suppose to know—now get offa' me!"

"And—you with dat' aint you?"

"Hell, no—I ain't with dat! I'm suppose to be with you—but you won't let me!"

"What am I, Precious—a damn dummy! That's how you get that shit you gave me! And that's why he was so eager to go with you in the ambulance to the hospital!"

"He said he was the one who moved the stuff while you driving around in brand new coupes and stuff! He was the one who said you were showing off like you're the man—all by your damn self! Not me. He said that shit in New York while we stayed in hotels."

"And you ain't do shit, hah—Ms. Slickass!" I said before slapping her again.

"T-a-v-o-n please! He set everything up! Plus, dat's when he started talking about how you pimpin' him, but you making all the money. I swear to God he said he is practically hating your guts."

"And what was you doing?"

" I wasn't doing shit. He was grabbing on me in the car. That's what Fast Money saw! He was grabbing me—now take that gun outta my face."

"He said he was taking everything—including me—from you! I ain't pay him no mind! Dat's not the first time he was saying that. I was just waiting for you! Now get da' hell offa me, Tavon!"

I pushed her with the gun still in my hand. That's how mad I was. I didn't know whether I was coming or going. I noticed red on her nightgown when I was shoving my gun back in my vest holster. She was bleeding just like my heart was. Instead of hitting her again I just listened.

"I'm not the one who said you changed or you don't know where you came from," she said in tears while holding her face.

"Oh, yea. He said that shit, too—hah?"

"He's the one getting ready to do his own thing and started talking to Dee about it. That's why he said 'fuck you!' Not me!"

She tried to help herself off the floor, but really couldn't get beyond the shock of what just happened. I didn't want to believe what she was saying about Juvenile, but I had no choice. He was trying to take my place because Dee told me how he was trying to start his own thing. He'd been asking him for extra weight—trying to pay with his own money, but I never said anything about it to him. I wanted nothing to come between us. Looking at it now, everything is starting to make sense.

"Juvenile's ass is gonna be dealt with right away!" I said before storming over to the night table. I picked up the phone to make some things happen. One thing for sure, he wouldn't know what hit him. This war was on and there's was nothing he could say.

"Yo, dat snake-ass Juvenile gotta be dealt with. Get da' shit and meet me at the spot!" I said before walking over slamming the door on my way out.

In the News

Baltimore City

Several top law enforcement officials, including the police commissioner, have pleaded guilty to interfering with a federal investigation, falsifying evidence, accepting bribes, and money laundering. Each official cooperated with authorities and provided information implicating previously unknown police officers. They will be sentenced in September.

Chapter 36

PRECIOUS

"Some How /
Some Way /
[You] gotta make it up out the hood..."
Jay-Z, "Some How Some Way"
The Blueprint 2

As soon as Tavon slammed the front door on his way out, I ran upstairs into the bathroom and locked the door. The full-size mirror showed cuts on my body from broken glass, but I was too shook up to get myself together. You could see his handprint on my face. I really didn't need a hospital as much as I needed to call somebody. They were only minor cuts. I had to let somebody know what was going on.

I went inside the bedroom and reached for the charger holding my cell phone. I was shaking so bad I dropped it near the window. I peaked outside to make sure Tavon was gone. I don't know what I would do if I did this and he walked in on me. I picked up one of my cell phones and dialed.

"Hey?" I said in a trembling whisper, "this me!"

"What's up? You cool, gurl? You don't sound right," he said before breaking into a laugh with whoever he was talking to on his end. "What's wrong with you? Was I that good to make you cry?"

"Don't worry about me!" I screamed. "You betta be careful because Tavon knows. He just beat my ass and pulled a gun on me because Fast Money told him what happened. Somehow he found out everything and I couldn't lie!"

"You alright, though?"

"Naw, my face and lips are swollen. Does dat' sound like I'm fuckin' alright!"

"Dat snitching ass Fast Money! After all I did for his broke ass! I'm a deal with him!"

"Juvenile, he got both of those guns on his vest and he's looking for you now! You betta be careful!"

"Whatchu tell him when he asked you?"

"I ain't tell him nothing! Money had to tell him everything!" I screamed through my tears.

"Who did he have with him?"

"Nobody, but he called some guys and told him to meet him somewhere. He said you had to be dealt with!"

"I'm down Westside at one of the spots now," he said with some fear in his voice.

"You betta get all you can and go! He's out there somewhere. Some kinda way you gotta make it out the hood before he gets up there because he may know where you are," I said.

I was scared, and still listening for any noise of Tavon coming back in the house.

"Fuck, Tavon! He ain't the only one with guns! He can bring dat shit if he wants! He betta come correct because I'm shooting first!"

"Just be careful, J!"

"Fuck dat, Precious. He betta be careful because I'm tired of his shit anyway. He's always frontin' on me. I'll take care of that shit—once and for all!"

"Whatchu you gon' do?"

"I'm on my way outta town now. I'm taking all the loot outta here. I'm getting away for a minute, so I can think this thing through. Call me on that cell phone my mother uses. Only my mother, you and my sister know that number. Call me on that one and let me know what's going on. I'm outta here!"

"Juvenile, I love you, here?"

Chapter 37

JUVENILE

"How ironic— /
It would be some fight /
That turned into a homicide /
that would alter [our] life."
Jay-Z, "Meet The Parents"
The Blueprint 2

Tavon put a contract hit out on me! He hasn't been able to touch me because I go down there at night. I told Precious I was going outta town for a reason. I know she'd tell him and he'll believe it. She works for both sides.

He doesn't know it, but I took some of the dope he had and put it out there. I got some people working for me right under his nose. Tavon thinks he's the only one can do this shit. I watched everybody and I caught on to all the moves. Precious is calling every chance she gets to tell me what he's doing. I know how this thing is gonna turn out. This fight is gonna turn into a homicide. This is so big that it's gonna end life as we know it.

I have to watch myself. That's why I have two guns at my reach when I do try to sleep. I haven't been getting much of that lately. I can't believe I'm hiding, moving around like I'm running from the police. I know I can't hide from Tavon and the crews I had been controlling for long. One time I did have to run from the cops. I couldn't come out during the day because the Gun Task Force was flashing a picture of me. They wanted to question me about a shooting that took place. At least that's what they were telling guys when they showed my photo. But that's the life we lived—and anything goes like what I'm going through now. It was hard getting used to, but they want me dead.

Over these weeks I've been thinking about everything. It's like my life is in judgment right before my eyes. Now I'm beginnig to understand what I was up against even more. Now I know this to be true. What you do comes back to you.

It wasn't that serious—not to me anyway. I'd rather cut out of this before it comes to one of us dying. I have a daughter and a woman who loves the ground I walk on. That's where I need to be—not out here wasting all this time.

I called Jameel asking her to talk to him. I'm hoping that the end wouldn't happen this way. I called my daughter and asked her to pray for me. In some ways I'm feeling like death is near and I ain't ready to die. Neither does Tavon deserve this, but I have to protect myself—by any means necessary out here. I just can't make the first move. It had to be a way we could talk this out. That's why I called Jameel in the first place.

"Hello," she said in a mild tone.

"Hey. It's me again. Did you get a chance to call Tavon?"

"Right now we're holding a meeting. Don't think I forgot about you because I haven't. I'm going to do what you asked as soon as I get finished."

"Jameel, this is important! You have to do this right away!"

"So, is what I'm doing, Dorian."

"No Jameel! This is more important! Didn't I tell you he was trying to kill me!"

"I don't mean to sound rude, but our daughter is in another show and we're just meeting to make the final arrangements. I don't know what's wrong with y'all, anyway, Dorian."

I knew what I had to say to get her attention. I needed some help. I will apologize for the lies later, but now I'm trying to save my life.

"I'm tired of living like this Jameel. I'm tired of this and everything else associated with it. I want to come back to what I'm supposed to be doing with you and our daughter. I'm trying to get out of the life."

"You still ain't tell me what happened," she said in a firm whisper so no one would hear her.

"Everything went wrong. We let too many people between us and there was a big misunderstanding, Jameel. Dat's all."

"I've been talking to you more during these last few weeks than I have the rest of the year."

"I told you I wanna get my life together. I really wanna get it right. But, you have to talk to Tavon first. He's the one acting crazy—talking 'bout killing me and stuff."

"Dorian, what have you done to make him like that?"

"Even if I told you—you wouldn't understand. This happened in the street and it's gonna have to stay out there."

I was getting paranoid. I peeped out of the window again. Regardless to who's helping me resolve this, I still have to watch my back.

"Both of y'all need to leave that world alone. I'm going to go to see him, but I still don't understand what's happening—but I do care enough to talk to him. You got to make it up out that no good life of yours, Dorian!"

"I *wanna* get out. *Dat's* why I'm asking you to talk to him because he won't talk to me."

"Well, Dorian. He hangs up on me now. He's not answering my calls either, so I'll go up there in a few minutes. I guess he knows what I'm calling for. But I will chase him down because he's forgetting who we are. We are family because of Tiffany and he better act like he knows!"

"Well, you can say what you want to him! I already know how serious this thing could be. I guess you don't care if I end up dead, do you?"

"That's you talking stupid, not me! 'If I cared.' Is that what you just said? No, if you cared you wouldn't be out there risking your life every day of the week. Anyway, I have to go! I'm not getting involved in this craziness any more—and neither am I going to just wait around for you to get yourself outta the streets. This is the last time. My life and my struggle for our daughter are too important to me. She deserves way more than what you're giving her as a father. So, I'll do it this time, but this is it!"

I didn't want to get her involved. And I know everybody is going to think that is the punk way out. That's not how we do it on the streets. I don't care what people think. I'm doing what I gotta do to save my life because Tavon will take it if I don't take his first. I know him! And with him not taking her calls, my thoughts of his intentions get even worse.

Chapter 38

TAVON

"Y'all fell into the booby trap /
I set the trap-- /
Just to see dude react."
Jay-Z, "The Blueprint 2"
The Blueprint 2

I was thinking about everything that's been happening in my life as I rode in my car down Martin Luther King Boulevard. If MLK could see this world now he'd think his life was in vain. I always knew I'd turn out like this because I wanted to be like my father. Living this way seems the only way out of where I come from. Really, this life doesn't make a lot of sense, but I'm chasing it hoping to be one of the lucky ones. It won't take me long. I can get rich, get out and live on my investments. I really want to get into buying and selling city houses.

I'll take this right on Fayette just to see what's happening in the area. It's slow for us because everybody has been staying away since this war started. Everything was still quiet down there too. It was gloomy, like something was waiting to happen. I watch their heads turn each time I drive my drop top Mercedes on these blocks. I'm like a super star. For a split second, each person staring is in a trance--hoping to one day be in my shoes. They all seem to want to meet me.

I've always had a funny way of looking at things. Tonight I was seeing the city for what is was worth. Daylight had just disappeared about two hours before. The moon was full and the air was free because the streets hadn't become rowdy yet. Tonight, like every night, the street needed a loud gunshot and a scream to set the mood. Sirens had to come and ambulances had to break the crowds from standing around a wounded victim. News cameras appear out of nowhere and disappear like ghosts.

Everybody and their mother gather around to see who it is this time when something like this happens. Gossip becomes our daily dose of medicine. Life seems to be boring without it. We've come to expect evidence from the games cruelty. That's what MLK would find sickening. All that life on these streets could do now is hold its own breath to see when peace would break into violence. This sick ritual wasn't only for this night as I took a left on Monroe Street and saw undercover police search some juveniles on the corner, but every-day-all-night in Baltimore City.

It was dark out because a lot of city lights had been knocked out intentionally. Dimness set the tone for our drug activity. A shadow in the alley could be seen pitching vials to several buyers forming a line. Some addicts would be on their knees waiting to get served. That's how the young kids sell it to the adults who gave them birth. Heroin sales could be bartered and momentary cocaine dreams would come true in the secrecy of these noisy streets. Things were happening.

I looked around and could see empty junk food bags, soda cans, and old trash together in the streets. Potholes were like scatter rugs and broken glass looked like dollar store decorations. I saw school aged children running up and down the block after twelve o'clock on a school night. These kids were no longer innocent. Hands belonging to them could skillfully handle a nine-millimeter. The rules of the game had changed, but, for right now, they enjoyed throwing the forty-ounce beer bottles some of their parents left behind! You could hear street raised kids cursing each other out.

"Bitch, fuck you, bitch!"

"Fuck you cause' you a bitch and yo' motha's a bitch!"

"Well, go get three vials muthafucker?"

"You get it bitch cause' dat's yo' shit! It ain't mine!"

Each night somebody different was getting caught chasing the night. Parents get high and chase drugs in front of their children. Children could be seen selling to adults. Lovers catch their partners cheating with a vial of cocaine. This unpredictable nightlife allowed all types of strange sounds to echo as background noise.

I kept looking around. Alley houses, now vacant, were once places of shelter for families long gone. Old abandominiums now provide shelter to homeless addicts who have gone days and weeks neglecting life's most basic needs. Look at this mess—it's sickening because life has narrowed itself down to drug stash or cash flow.

Fighting for survival is a steady diet for everyone. That war is present in Baltimore. Escaping random gunfire is survival. Injecting a large does of heroin is, too. I remember seeing junkies on a few occasions dragging a body out in the alley because a fellow addict had overdosed. Nobody called the paramedics—that's not survival. Nobody wanted to be a part of a murder charge.

There's no electricity in those abandoned buildings. Extension cords can be seen running to someone else's house. That night light comes from burning newspaper and city streetlights. Torn boxes inside empty rooms become Sealy Posturpedic mattresses. With no running water, the tub becomes a comfortable toilet. Using it another day is nothing new. It has been used as an outhouse inside the old building each time addicts buy a good bag of dope from us. I've seen their sick bodies going through withdrawals. Before injecting our liquid luv into their system, stomachs and bowels give way to nature!

Ass up, pants down, the tub accepts days' old human feces without running water. Nature cares nothing about water just like addicts care nothing about toilet paper. Shit falls down. Pants go up and this life goes on. And now it has come to this. I'm after my old partner's life trying to make street history like my father's generation did before us because he had to kill his partner.

My cell phone's musical ring brought me back into the real world.

"Yo! It's me! Guess, what?" Outlaw said.

"What's up, Kid?"

"He's over here at his stash house."

"Is anybody up there with him?"

"Nobody but him and the girl Butter in the house."

"Oh, yea!"

"Yea. He's up here solo—and dat's crazy!"

"How you figure?" I asked.

"The girl Butter just called me on my pager with the code you told me to give her! The one she used meant he was by his' self,"

"Did she use 8's or 9's? She may have confused it?"

"She used the 9's on my box! He must be there smoking weed."

"Outlaw, make sure, Yo! I ain't trying to make no mistakes."

"Hold on—hold on. I'm riding down through the block now!

"What you see?" I asked him already trying to plot.

"Wait a sec! I'm right here going pass the house now."

"You see his truck, Outlaw?"

"Yea."

"Oh, yea?"

"I see his Range Rover parked around the corner. I got my gun on me now, Tay—what's up? Whatchu want me to do?"

"Don't let anybody see you. Come and pick me up in that hoopty car we got. You call Dead-eye and tell him to meet us up there. Remember this because it's all set. Tell him to park on the corner across the street by the stop sign."

I used my cell phone to make two more important phone calls. This had to go down right.

"Hey, dis me. You still got dat snake's cell phone number I gave you?" I asked excitedly.

"Yea, baby, I still got it. You know I hold all of your stuff near the bed."

"Listen! I want you to call it at exactly 11:00 o'clock. Say what I told you. Say it exactly like I said but get all emotional and shit! I just got a call telling me where he is right now!"

"I got it!"

"Okay. Eleven o'clock sharp, hear? Precious, don't blow this! You gotta put on a different voice."

"I got it Tay, damn! Eleven o'clock!"

"Now, I'm gonna ask you this one more time before I do anything—and your ass better tell me the fuckin' truth! Did he make all that happen for real?"

"Tavon, please! Why would I say it if he didn't do that shit to me. All this is yours! I ain't got no love for him. He did this shit to both of us. He knows how much I love your crazy ass! That's why he did this! So, he deserves everything he's got coming tonight!"

"Well, he'll be getting his reward tonight. You can bet this shit won't come between you and me. If I didn't trust and love your crazy ass—then I wouldn't believe you!"

"Tavon, I luv---"

"Yea whatever, Precious! Just do what the hell I told you—and do it at exactly 11 o'clock!

I dialed another number. The instructions were about the same. It's funny how this thing goes, but I had to do what I had to do. I was setting the trap to see just how this slow dude would react.

"Hey, Homegirl. Dis' is me. You got that snake's pager watch number?"

"Yea, Yo. I got that shit!"

"Well, it's on Alize--and I want you to blow it up exactly 11 o'clock! Put in those numbers I gave to his people's house. That should get his ass crazy enough to see me and your man, tonight!"

"Alright. I got it," she said.

I could hear her new baby son in the background.

"Alright—you sure? Cause' if you can't handle it at exactly eleven then I'll ask somebody else. I know dat was your man and shit, but dis' gotta be done!"

I knew it was hard for Alize since she knew the principles of the game just like we did. She was more of a soldier than most males out there. I did that to make sure nothing would go wrong.

"You got my word. Count dat' as done! What he did was wrong, alright."

"Okay. I need that. I'm gonna take care of that tonight and I'll make sure I put my son in the other room! He can run but he sure can't hide!"

She made sure Outlaw picked me up about twenty minutes later. She knew the game plan better than he did. We circled the block of Greenmount Avenue and 21st Street a couple times giving Dead-eye a chance to get there. Nobody knew our stolen car so it's not like anybody could recognize me. I still ducked low in the passenger seat.

I recognized Dead-eye behind the wheel of that old Buick LeSabre. He was moving slow, almost to a cruise. One flash of our high beams gave him the signal. He knew we saw him. He followed our lead. The next time the lights flashed it would be show time!

I parked right across the street in the car with the music off. Dead-eye parked on the opposite side.

Outlaw was making me nervous smoking those cigarettes. He kept lighting one after another. Smelling that smoke was enough to chase me away.

"Tavon, you should see how big my son is getting. Man, that boy is just like me—and he's gonna be the biggest dealer Baltimore has ever seen. With the money you give me, I'm gonna buy Alize the biggest diamond ring she has ever seen. I wanna make her my better half because that's all she dreams about!"

"Oh, yea," I said only to acknowledge him.

He's willing to start his son in the life just like my mother started me. And then he wants to have a thug wedding. My mind was on something completely different. I wished I could've had Alize by my side instead. Outlaw could've been the one making the phone call at eleven. He went off still talking, but I blocked him out.

In the midst of that I kept thinking. If Juvenile took the bait, the real war could begin and end at the same time. Too many people are getting in it. That coward even had Jameel get involved. This fool had to be dealt with because he crossed blood and now everybody knows.

I had both my guns ready. They were tucked in my vest holsters. One was on the left side positioned backwards underneath my arm since I shoot from my right. The other was positioned on the right. Things were just right for an attack and getaway.

I kept my eyes on that front door because it was nearing the eleven o'clock hour. A black Navigator truck with loud music pulled up and stopped right in front of Butter's house just before the time for the phone calls. The tinted passenger side window rolled down. You could see smoke coming out of the windows. Whoever it was had a problem if they didn't pull off before things went down. They pulled in the right place at the wrong time.

"Yo, who da' fuck is dat?"

"I don't know, but Juvenile must've called them! He may know we're out here, Tavon!" he said, snatching the slide on his nine-millimeter. *His nervous ass grabbed his gun ready to jump out.*

I grabbed my cell phone to call Dead-eye. "Yo, if dat' front door opens up I want you to light that truck up! I still got him coming out dat' door, but I can't get the truck, too. They may be strapped looking out for him!"

"I'm watching dat' truck, too!"

"Don't forget. She will turn the night light on as the first signal that he's coming out. When I flash the lights you start sparking everything in sight!"

"I got it!" he told me before I hung up.

"Put dat' fuckin' cigarette out before they see it!" I screamed smacking it out of his hand with the cell phone.

I gripped my gun, and adjusted my facemask.

"Flash the lights because the night light just came on and the door just opened. That's him—that's him! I'm going!"

"Get dat' bitch, Yo!" Outlaw screamed.

I snatched the door handle and broke straight to the steps. All I kept thinking as I jumped out of the car was how I set the booby trap. This was war and I wanted to see how this dude reacted. Running towards the door I had no intentions on coming back until this was done. Somebody was going away from here. I looked over briefly to see that Dead-eye was jumping out of the other car, too. It was on now!

Chapter 39

JUVENILE

"Oh, Lady don't blow my high— /
especially if you don't know my life."
Jay-Z, "Diamond is Forever"
The Blueprint 2

"Butter, where you get dis' good ass weed from? Dis' shit is the bomb," I said inhaling to no end.

"I got dat' from up on Old York Road. *Dat's* where all the good weed is at right now. They call it *Cheek and Chong*."

"Here. Hit this, Butter," I said trying to hand her the blunt.

"Wait a minute. I got to use the phone."

"Wait. Girl, you betta hit this shit before I kill it by myself!"

"I'll be right there in a minute. All I have to do is make this one phone call."

When I have something on my mind I can always turn to her. She knows what I love and she can roll what I love like a pro. I came up here trying to get that Tavon shit off my mind.

And get some of that fried chicken she cooks. It didn't take her long to finish what she was doing on the phone.

"Boy, give me that smoke so I can catch up with you! Pass me the Hennessy right there," she said grabbing the weed out of my hand and pointing to the fifth with the other. *I watched her slouch down on the couch to get comfortable. I was already on cloud nine. Now she was trying to catch me.*

Her kitchen was set up like a mini-diner. She had bar stools in the dining room and a service area in the kitchen. She'd put on her Aunt Jemima apron and feed everybody in sight. I was relaxing when she called me to eat. I went to sit on the third stool near the corner of the room so I could still see the front door. One time Tavon had keys to her house when we used it as a stash. After eating, I was back where I wanted to be. That couch of hers puts me to rest. I could feel myself nodding off.

"Bring the phone over hear so I can call my man. He loves this shit. I'm a call him so he can come down."

"Yo! I got da' bomb shit! I'm high as shit!" I told him after he answered his cell phone.

"Where you at?" he asked me trying to get what I had.

"I'm up Butter's so park around the block."

"You ain't said nothin' but a word! I'll be right there!" he said.

I remember making the call and putting my cell phone on vibrate before putting it on the glass table in front of me. I don't know how long I was sleep on the couch, but it caught me off guard when my phone made all that noise on the glass and then started ringing loudly.

Butter was up and moving around. She grabbed that noisy toy and handed it to me. Somebody was blowing my high.

"Who is this calling me like this?"

"Oh, my god! Is this Ms. Doris' son Dorian?" the caller asked.

"Yea, who dis'?"

"Oh, my god! You heard what happened to your mother?"

"Oh, lady, don't blow my high with some bullshit!"

"Ms. Doris was shot by a stray bullet through her front window!"

"What—what happened, lady?"

"Oh, my God! Your sister wanted me to call you because they rushed your mother to the hospital. I think she's at University Shock Trauma!"

"Oh, shit," I said in panic. "Butter my mother got shot! I gotta get outta here!"

I dropped the telephone. Then my pager started ringing back to back with my sister's number and 911. Both of them are usually in bed this time of night. She wouldn't call me unless something was wrong. I took the phone and tried to dial her number, but I was too nervous. This was happening too fast. All I kept thinking about was my mother pulling through from a bullet wound—as thin as she is. I had to get to University Hospital.

I heard my buddies pull up in the truck while I was scrambling to get my stuff. That bass in Ty's black Navigator truck can be heard from a block away. His system is crazy.

"Juvenile, shit. You betta get outta here to go make sure your mother is OK. That other shit can wait—just go!" she said turning the outside nightlight on and rushing me toward the door.

I had my bulletproof vest on and my gun. Even though this weed got me going outta my mind, I'm not stupid enough to take it off. I was still going to the hospital and it's going with me.

I reached the door. I snatched it open and rushed down the steps to get to my car parked outside. I didn't care if anybody saw me. I usually go out the back door, but wasn't this time. I had to get to my mother. I made it near the sidewalk when I heard some tennis shoes scraping the black top like some people were playing basketball. The next thing I knew some heavy flashes come in front of my eyes almost blinding me. Loud gunfire sounded off everywhere. I could hear all different size guns going off.

I could feel something hit me in the chest. "What da' fuck!"

My feet became so light they seem to have come out from under me like I was airborne. It was almost as if my body took off flying. Right after that I could feel my body hit the cement. Maybe I was dying. I could hear screams over top of tennis shoes scrambling for cover. Car engines started racing to get away.

I wasn't sure if I was still here or not. I could still hear screams and feel my body being pulled before I went completely out. I think I was hearing Butter cry out.

"Oh, my god, Baby. Oh, my god! Who did this to you, Juvenile?"

Chapter 40

Northern District Police

"Whoever said illegal was the easy way out /
Couldn't understand the mechanics /
And workings of the underworld."

Jay-Z, "D'Evils"
Reasonable Doubt

Things in East Baltimore became routine for my partner and me. We made rounds on the streets where drug dealing was abundant and our fight against them for control was constant. Around 10:55pm we responded to a routine call.

"Dispatch to Baker 131."

"Baker 131—go dispatch."

"Respond to a suspected dealer with a gun on the corner of Homewood Avenue and 21st Street. Over?"

"10-4. Baker 131 responding, dispatch."

"Suspect is wearing a white t-shirt with Yankees logo, white hat, with blue jeans and Timberland boots and is said to have a silver handgun. Please Respond?"

"10-4."

"Baker 132, back up this unit. Respond to a black male with a gun. Copy?"

"10-4 dispatch. Baker 132 in route."

Our jobs are really being drug enforcement officers formally dressed in uniforms. We're trying to uphold an image of truth and justice, but the arrests of top brass downtown goes against what we stand for.

And then there are the streets we patrol. The mechanics and workings of the underworld are tricky. It's our job to give criminals hell. Illegal activities create a do or die situation for us out here and are by no means the easy way out. What they do is hard to understand. That's why we're so hard on them.

Most of the calls we receive on a night like tonight mainly deal with controlled dangerous substance calls from citizens and the suspects who sell them. It's funny when one drug dealer calls us at 911 asking us to arrest another dealer. They call with a full description of the suspect, where the drug stash is and addresses to match.

A call like the one we just received could be a life-threatening one. We approach each one with our holster strap loose and our service weapons ready. This is still Ronald Reagan's war on drugs and it's too dangerous to be taken lightly.

On a call like this, anyone on Homewood Avenue could be armed and dangerous. It only takes a second for one person to pass the same gun in question to someone else before we arrive. First the armed suspect is wearing a red FUBU sweat suit accented with black Timberland boots and a Nike hat. Flash! In a few seconds a fourteen year-old juvenile with black jeans, no hat, and white Jordan tennis shoes is an armed suspect with the same gun.

Nothing is ever routine out here. We want each call to end peacefully. Yet, a peaceful resolution is not always possible. Scenarios in our history have shown the many dangers we face responding to a simple citizen's complaint of a neighbor's loud music. It's too easy for something like this to end in death. Every situation presents a certain amount of danger. That's why we approach suspects with caution because our family and loved ones are expecting us home.

When we approached the area there were three men who fit the profile. We placed each against the wall for a routine spot check. Each check resulted in a negative find. At about 11:10pm, we were just about to let each suspect go when loud gunfire erupted. The shots were so loud we all ducked for cover, even the suspects we searched. They ran to get out of the way of trouble. Under the circumstances, they were free to go.

"Baker 131! Baker 131! Multiple shots fired! Shots fired on and 21st and Greenmount Avenue. Copy dispatch?"

"Shots fired! Shots fired! Greenmount and 21st Street. Dispatch Copy!"

We were both running on the pavement so we could get a visual of what was going on. I jumped in the street. Two cars were speeding in our direction.

"Several vehicles are fleeing the scene," I screamed into my radio.

I could hear him grunting for strength as he pushed me out of the way of the speeding cars.

"Watch out!" my partner screamed. "Dispatch we have two black male suspects in a blue Grand Marquis, 1988 almost hitting us! Tag number LGG 821," my partner said while trying to catch his breath.

We ran back in the direction of our squad car. "Suspects in vehicle are proceeding east on 21st Street! Baker 131 is in pursuit! Copy dispatch?" I screamed out of breath. "A black Navigator truck with tinted windows is going north on Boone—north on Boone Street! No further information! Copy?"

"Dispatch copy. All units--suspects are driving a blue Grand Marquis—proceeding east on 21st--just turned south on Homewood. Copy dispatch?" I screamed.

"Dispatch copy Baker 131."

"We're in pursuit—suspects just turned westbound on North Avenue. We're following the westbound—copy?"

"Copy Unit 131—be careful and proceed with caution! All units copy and respond!"

Police Blotter
Baltimore City

Six-year old shot

Dejuan Young, who lives with his family on 21st Street, was in critical condition after being struck in the face by a stray bullet. He was shot in his home as he walked through the hallway to use the bathroom. He was rushed to Johns Hopkins Hospital where he is listed in critical condition.

Other residents complained of property damage as a result of a barrage of gunfire in the streets. Officials report that there has been an increase in drug-related crimes in this area. Police have no suspects or leads in this case.

Chapter 41

TAVON

"For the love of money.../
You know the demons said it's best to die. /
And even if [somebody] witnesses .../
He'll never testify."

Jay-Z, "D'Evils"
The Reasonable Doubt

"Go! Go! Go! Outlaw--get us outta here!" I screamed.

Everything seemed like a dark dream. I couldn't believe I had to shoot my man! I know this was some demon shit, but he deserved that it because of what he did. His punishment wasn't really for the love of money like people were saying. He violated the code and had to pay.

"Tavon—that fuckin' police is in the middle of the street," Outlaw screamed as he picked up speed to hit 'em outta the way.

"Man, you gotta outrun them, shit! Floor it!" *I yelled looking out the rear window.*

I watched one police push his partner out of the way and saw them running to their squad car. We were the only ones still going in this direction. The truck went the other way, so I knew they would follow us because we used our car as a weapon. I was surprised they didn't shoot into the vehicle like we did the black Navigator truck.

"I'm throwing my guns out the window. Give me your gun—shit! I gotta get this vest off because they're coming right behind us!"

I had lawyers. I knew it was better to have them collect evidence away from the scene. It made a difference whether or not they found that kinda evidence on us or not. I was getting that outta here!

"Here, take it!" he said trying to drive while looking through the back window.

I threw my vest out of my window. "Gimme that mask! C'mon floor this muthafucka!

"Are they still behind us, Tavon?"

"Go through the light—just keep on going! I hear more fuckin' sirens—drive! Drive, Outlaw!"

The first squad car tried to cut us off after we started going up North Avenue. Outlaw handled that challenge by turning left on Greenmount Avenue cutting off the path of a MTA bus. There was another car coming down the other side of North Avenue, but he wasn't close enough for us to stop.

"Keep going—drive! Drive! Drive!" I screamed.

We made it down to Preston Street where he tried to make a sharp right turn because flashing sirens were speeding toward us. He loss control of the steering wheel and crashed into the street pole. I had no other alternative than to run. That was my only chance to get away—and I was going! It took me a quick second to get my bearings together because I was shook up from the crash. I snatched the door latch while trying to figure my escape route. I started hearing shouts from a bullhorn.

"We have the car surrounded. Put your hands up on your head, now! We don't wanna shoot! We're giving you five seconds to get your hands up!"

I kicked kicking the passenger door open and jumping out the front passenger seat.

"Yo, I'm getting da' fuck outta here!"

"Halt! Stop before I shoot!"

I pointed my feet toward that alley. Things were happening too fast. The last thing I remember is trying to get around the car while the shouts came from that loud bullhorn. Loud claps of gunfire sparks lit up that dark street. I could see where a few people in a crowd scrambled in different directions before everything stopped.

Baltimore City
Vehicular assault on police

Two men tried to injure officers with a stolen car after being involved in a suspected shooting, a Baltimore Spokeswoman said. Officers were initially responding to a separate incident.

Vernon "Outlaw" Carey, 20, of the 2500 block of Kinsey Avenue was charged with first degree attempted murder on two polices officers and several traffic violations.

Police said Carey is also charged with carjacking in the possible theft of the stolen vehicle he was driving. The Regional Auto Task Force is still investigating this incident.

Anthony "Tavon" Truston, of no fixed address, was shot several times as he charged responding officers who ordered him several times to surrender. He was taken to University of Maryland Shock Trauma Unit. Carey was questioned and taken to Central Booking. No weapons were found after a thorough search of the area. This police involved shooting is under internal investigation.

Chapter 42

Jameel

"If I die--don't cry..."

Jay-Z, "If I should die"
Hard Knock Life Vol. 2

I wonder who's that banging down my door so early in the morning.

"I'm coming, I'm coming!" I said running down the steps.

I spoke out loud so that whoever was banging on the door would stop and not wake Tiffany up. I opened the door to find a well-dressed Caucasian gentleman standing in the doorway. I was up doing my early morning devotion so I don't think that I looked that bad.

"Are you Jameel Jackson?" he asked very politely.

"Yes I am. How may I help you?"

"Ms Jackson, I am an attorney from Miles and Wheeler law firm. My name is Neil Freedmen. Here is one of my business cards. I have some information here I need to pass on to you—

but first, I need to let know the terms. You are listed here as the contact person for, uhhm. May I come in because this may take a minute?" he asked, looking at me as if I should have invited him in a long time ago.

"I've heard your name being mentioned a few times before, Mr. Freedmen. My child's father and his friend told me if they were in some kind of trouble to contact you at this law firm." I said, as I slowly stepped away from the doorway and opened the door a little wider.

After I heard contact person, I was bracing myself for the worst. I took a quick look at his card and knew this day was coming. Somebody I knew died. I had this funny feeling that it has something to do with what Juvenile called me about. My feet felt like they were beginning to give way under my body. I regained my composure long enough to invite the gentleman in.

"Come on in, sir. Can I get you a cup of coffee or tea?" I asked. If he looked close enough he could see me literally shaking as we walked into the living room.

"Thanks. Coffee would be great," he answered as he looked around in the living room. "But are you sure you are OK? You look a little shaken?"

"I'll be fine--let me get you some coffee. I already have a fresh pot brewing, I'll be right back."

I had to say a quick prayer as I got into the kitchen to ask God to help me through whatever was about to come at me. I've always dreaded this day. But I know I have to stay strong. I'll have my own private time later to figure everything out.

I got back to the living room where he had made himself comfortable. He had a box with other stacks of paper on the coffee table.

"Umm!" he said after taking a sip of the coffee. "This is good – just the way I like it. Now let's get down to business."

"And what's that, Mr. Freedmen?"

"This is the last will and testament of one of my clients who wanted me to read this to you. This was to be done just in case something tragic happened to him because he had no other family he could rely on."

I held my composure, but was sure to hit the ground any second now.

"Uhm-Uhm," he said clearing his throat. "It states the following:

'If I die, don't cry Jameel because I'm entrusting my last requests to you. I know this comes as a surprise to you, but you know I've always trusted you. I've taken out two major insurance policies for more than what you may need to purchase everything for any arrangements that have to be made.

My lawyer, Mr. Freedmen, will also be giving you the sum of $50,000 cash for starters. I have other important papers in the lock box with instructions. Mr. Freedmen is already paid and will help you through. I trust you. Jameel, just remember, you are the only one I can trust with this—and in time I know all things will be understood....'"

Coming soon...

"Business as usual"

The sequel to
"for the love of fast money"

Author's Notes

Nothing we know ''out there'' on the streets is static. That's why our complex lifestyles and stories in the same city streets differ when we tell of our experiences. The players change in our stories, their ages, and so does time. But "The Game" of making a fast dollar still stays the same.

The ***OJay's*** said it first in song. What they sang about in the 70's is still true. We are sadly selling each other out **"For The Love of Money."** Back then, *the life* was much slower and less complicated. Experienced "old heads" controlled certain parts of town. Their distributors were handpicked. Being thorough had its rewards. No need to apply because Street Honor dictated who was involved and for how long. Cardinal rules controlled everybody: No women, no children. Don't do the crime if you can't do the time. Another was don't testify! And – Ooops! – never ever hip a lame to the game!

That was the life in the 70's and early 80's. The phenomenal rapper Jay-Z (of Roc-A-Fella Records) clearly describes what's happening in our streets today. He'll tell you in a minute that money is ***FAST*** and people are cruelly doing whatever it takes to get it! A combination of then and the arrival of the new millennium gave novel life to this book.

"Money $ Money $ Money $ Money $ Mo-ney!/
"Some people got to have it./
Some people really need it!"

Baltimore is well known for that dangerous dollar. People who take risky chances to "get paid" in the drug trade today are being taxed. Most times the costs are more than any hustler is capable of repaying. Once involved, *this life* has its own painful rules: rules that feed from human pain and end in human suffering. Almost anything goes, especially snitching.

This is the one commandment everyone understands on the street: There are no rules! Children in daycare, wifey inside the Lexus truck and grandma resting inside the house are being kidnapped for ransom in the CA$H game. That's the first step of being a money target. Elimination of those uninvolved *is guaranteed* if drug money demands are unpaid. That's the last.

People taking chances are betting their lives, literally. Each time chance-takers step out there, they have no idea whether they will return alive. They still do it anyway.

"People will rob their own brother."

Self-seeking thoughts of "Me, Myself, not my brother and I" create a lethal arena of genocide. Every interest of this all too familiar expression centers on self and the color green. In that vicious world, every player cares about <u>nobody</u> but self and robbery is the thought for the day.

We have learned very well how to prey on each other's weaknesses. We use the wrong means against one another in efforts of improving our individual conditions. Without feelings, people do almost anything for money. In the end, we find our conditions worsening (as we blame sources outside of ourselves for what is going on inside our lives).

Dying is a constant threat and the number one cause is money. Trying to create an unstoppable hustle makes this reality so. That's why our prisons are filled to capacity and graves are being dug en masse. Very few die of old age. This war, a war of us against us, has two desperate sides. Both sides fight hard not to be the victim memorialized in a candlelight vigil, being another homie's R.I.P. tattoo, or remembered on a t-shirt.

In *the game*, one side lives at least another day to conquer another violent challenge while the other life ends in the death of someone we grew up with, someone we once called partner, friend and/or brother.

"The Almighty dollar. Cash Money."

Younger hustlers have created a new arrangement in the streets. It is less reasonable and more fatal. Their *new cash money game* is to "make believe" that there is still a game to be played. It is a setup with multiple traps to fall into. Each chance-taker involved realizes they will go down eventually. It's just a matter of time. What completes each person's story is *how* and *when!* Chances of winning are slim to none–and every *winner* loses.

Each criminal conspiracy reaches "The End" in different ways. Is anybody paying attention to the end of movies like Scarface, King of New York, Menace To Society, and Heat?

Maryland is known nationwide for crabs. Those playing in *the game* are known to promote this "crabs in a basket" mentality. Every time it seems as if someone discovers a way out, others still trapped try to find any way possible to pull them back in. That's why chance-takers are constantly going down either by the hands of criminal cooperators or the police into an overcrowded justice system. Agencies, bureaus and departments hold victory celebrations when the final story is printed on the front pages of newspapers. FBI, DEA, ATF, Maryland State Police, and IRS all win when their part is all said and a criminal conspiracy is undone. Losers end up being named in criminal indictments: "<u>The United States versus Another One Bites The Dust.</u>" Time has given us time to see this over and over again. Nevertheless, new and younger chance-takers emerge daily chasing the almighty dollar.

Baltimore's Charm City is one of the most dangerous cities in the nation. We have a crippling murder rate; but success can be achieved and legitimate tunnels "out" can be created. Dru Hill and Ruff Endz sang their way out. Charles Dutton, Mo'Nique and Jada Pinkett-Smith "acted" their way outta Charm City. Mugsy Bogues, Sam Cassell and Keith Booth "balled" their way through the dangerous courts of East Baltimore into the NBA. Hasim Rahman gained national attention when he "boxed" his way through the streets of Harm City. West Baltimore's own Kevin Liles became the president of Def Jam/Def Soul. It wasn't easy for any of them "making it." But they did! And all still call Baltimore their home.

"People can't even walk the streets./
"People don't care who they hurt or beat."

Sadly, adults are still chasing false reality. They refuse to grow up and take responsibility. Now children are growing up on their own and easily embracing the same false realities and the pain that follows. They all deserve better. Our responsibility is to prepare and provide better opportunities for them.

Many have accepted this crippling way of life because it seems the only choice. Practices from this choice have become a plague – infecting more young recruits who don't care anything about who they hurt or beat. Juveniles following this path think being a *Menace To Society* is the right thing to do. Three facts are loud and clear in their thinking. Fast money promotes life, a Nine (millimeter) protects it, and a bulletproof vest preserves it.

"Give me a nickel [vial]./
[Son] can you spare a dime [bag]?"

Grown men, fathers and sometimes grandfathers of these juveniles, still promoting this life out there are poor examples. Years of being in *the life* have passed. Yet, they can be found still standing right beside young kids on the same drug strips. Generations have evolved and a new millennium has arrived, but old men are doing the same things the same old ways. They have to be reminded of today's proverb: "If you always do what you've always done, you will always get what you have always gotten!"

For those still intent on taking a chance, the end result is foretold. After the fun is death. Following the fame is incarceration. It is there, in prison institutions, where generations of granddad, son, and grandson are gathered.

"A woman will sell her precious body./
For a small piece of paper that carries a lot of weight."

Involved female participants in the ***Ca$h Game*** have taken this sadness to another level. From becoming interstate traffickers, endangering children inside drug houses, corner hustling, setting up murders, robberies, gun-toting, crack-smoking, to eventually serving extensive state and federal sentences.

Too many of our children are in trouble. Men are absent. Too many mothers are unavailable. Who is rightly guiding our children? Young daughters are chasing luv on the outside. Real love can only be found within. Guidance and instructions is a treasure only a mother can provide.

When mothers and fathers value getting high and getting

money more than their children, these choices threaten everything you love. The same facts exist with drug and money highs! What's owed for being in *the life* will be paid on an installment plan.

What we think about ourselves, and the choices we have made, make *us* our own worse enemy: hate-filled thoughts against one another kill us long before anyone dies physically. The strong are continually surviving through violent means—until they themselves change positions from predator to prey. Another one bites the dust.

Almost each corner is a goldmine and urn; and each block is a strip and gravesite. The corner and strip are equal in holding the remains of those we've loss to the streets. The best way to measure the impact of drugs is to look on the streets of cities across the United States. Tomorrow, in Baltimore, more funerals follow. Hopefully, Tupac, there is a heaven for a *G*.

"Money…Do funny things to people."

History's wisdom should have influenced us to pool our human resources in what should have been named "Our Fight For Life." Thank you *Mr. Kurt Schmoke*, former Mayor of Baltimore City. You were right to publicly profess Decriminalization--and later suffer for it. As you predicted, our problem is a public **mental** health crisis. It's not the drugs, but the unhealthy thoughts of the persons choosing it.

Recovery from our drug crises, using and selling, requires more treatment and therapy--not always truth-in-sentencing. Conventional methods of "lock 'em up and throw away the key" are not working. Recovering addicts, ex-offenders on the right track, family, churches, and community organizations need to join forces and take bolder steps to confront these issues of sobriety.

"Don't let money change you."

There are some family and friends who have moved on to "better living." Money will help improve your life, but look back on those left behind. We need you.

Church members and black business leaders, don't make the mistake of thinking it's not your problem. Only when it hits home will nonchalant attitudes change. Then it becomes necessary to cry the "why my?" syndrome in front of television cameras. *Why did my son, daughter, loved one, have to die?* That's when it is too late.

The value adults place on their choices and human life itself is having a "trickle down effect." Those losing this War on Drugs are our children, innocent little children, who are born and grow up in families with unsupportive addicts as parents.

Troubled children grow up. Juvenile delinquents quickly reach the age of 18. They grow from the juvenile justice structure straight into the adult system. Some never will give themselves a winning chance because they foolishly follow in the footsteps and images of family members who played the game before them. Protection and rescue for them has to be timely: Exposing kids to too much too soon is just as fatal as saving them from harm when help comes too little too late. Clearly, they are the losers.

These facts continue: Every year the body counts increase in our cities. Dreams die first and then our people.

******

Each of these forces could have ended any of our lives: the innocent and those involved, but did not. So many deserving souls fell short and did not make it to see this day! From our hearts, especially to the innocent who became victims, we dedicate a moment of silence to each.

I speak for those of us who have taken super-foolish chances with our lives and have lived beyond our own ignorance, and for those of us who have made life-changing errors and later allowed "that which doesn't kill us" to make us stronger... we take this time to thank the Source of our Strength. Still being alive today only happened because we followed in ignorance, through acts of fortune, or luck. It just wasn't our time to depart from this life. We had lives to change and stories to tell. The world wasn't ready to release us yet.

Providing greater clarity of what is happening in our streets is my mission. Juveniles need to know what real life offers a drug dealer and a drug addict: short-lived triumph and certain tragedy. We do have other choices that must be sought out before it's too late.

And now *these pages* are asking forgiveness from those who have innocently and unfairly died by the sword they never swung, and for those having felt the effects of losing a loved one to death, addiction and unforeseen tragedy. *These chapters* speak to those who have loss control of their destinies because of the hell and confusion surrounding them from "Day 1". And *this book* represents all those who wanted to tell their explicit stories but cannot!!

Don't get it twisted! After a city ambulance has hauled another lifeless human body off the federalized streets of Baltimore and crime scene tape is removed and investigating officers have long since departed...blood is still dripping on our city streets! It's sad but true…tomorrow will just be ***Business As Usual—(the sequel to For the Love of Fast Money)***.

In Loving Memory of my nephew:
R.I.P
Tarik Lateef Walker
November 7, 1975 – July 13, 2004

Order Form
Go Daddy Productions, Inc.
P.O. Box 418
Jessup, Maryland 20794

ISBN # 0-9753938-0-4

For the Love of Fast Money	**$15.00**
Sales Tax $0.75 *(Maryland Residents Only)*	
Shipping& Handling	**$3.50**
TOTAL	

Purchaser's Information

Name:______________________________

Info. #______________________________

Address:____________________________

City:__________ **State:**__________

Zip:_____ **Amount requested?** __________

Prison orders shipped directly to institutions and/or facilities will receive an automatic 25% discount of the sale price of the book. Prices are as follows:

For the Love of Fast Money: **$11.25**
Sales Taxes $0.56
(Maryland Residents Only)
Shipping and Handling **$ 3.50**
Total:

***Book club rates are available and autographed copies can be picked up from Words By Wendell**
512 W. Franklin Street, Baltimore, Md. 21201
410-523-7007
Out of state orders call 1-877-523-7007
Order on-line @ go-daddyproductions.com

Manuscripts can be forwarded to the P.O. Box 418, Jessup, Maryland 20794-0418. If return postage is required, please, enclose a self-addressed stamped envelope. Otherwise, all materials received will remain in the possession of Go Daddy Productions, Inc.